The Secret
of
Ophiuchus

Kim Idynne

for Christian

1: Wupatki

Dominic looked again at the clock. Twelve hours remained before his next venture into Wupatki, the place where Hannah Hale had fallen into the underworld. The closer he came to the time of departure, the more unreal it all seemed, until he began to doubt that he would make it back into the strange celestial realm where he had last seen her.

His efforts to sleep late into the morning had failed, and instead he'd spent time reviewing constellation maps and star-related mythology, determined to solve the puzzles of the stars even before he could be challenged with them—but at last he abandoned those pursuits, finding himself unable to absorb anything new. His mind was already racing with memories of his last trip to the underground tunnels of Wupatki, and with the problem of getting back into them. Dominic had been tasked with figuring out how to sneak into the archaeological site. He found that getting into the area would be simple enough, but getting caught was a dire probability. He had already gone out to the site after hours, roaming with a flashlight until he found the blowhole that Hannah had fallen into. The hole now had a grate over it. A crowbar, at the least, would be needed to remove it. Dominic had marked the site with a small flag—a twig with a strip of bright green cotton fabric tied to one end. Though he feared that someone else would notice it, marking the spot seemed wiser than wandering the grounds after hours with flashlights. Removing the grate and setting up the climbing equipment would take time enough.

Dominic resisted calling Surina until noon. He picked up the phone when he could no longer keep his anxieties to himself. As his only confidant in the matter, Surina had already spoken to him several times the previous day to review plans and possibilities, and to answer questions about her own experiences in the celestial dimension. Her stories didn't give Dominic much comfort. Figuring out how to bring Hannah home presented enough of a challenge, but Surina's adventure had provided him with a new worry: that even if he found Hannah, she would refuse to come home.

"When we're removing the grate and setting up the equipment, we'll have to keep an eye out for patrols," Dominic told Surina over the phone. "And we'll need to work as quickly as possible. I can stop by early, and you can teach me how to use the climbing gear, so I won't have to learn on the spot."

Surina paused. "Um…that won't be necessary."

"Why not?"

"Well . . . you know, I'm not a very good liar."

Dominic felt a deep pang of unease. "Meaning what?"

"Meaning . . . I called Greg a little while ago to ask about the climbing anchors, and he was asking me a lot of questions, and I kind of told him what we're doing."

"What do you mean? You told him we're sneaking into Wupatki?"

"Yeah, and he wants to help."

Dominic leaned forward, resting his forehead on his palm and closing his eyes. He'd only met Greg, the grad student who had loaned them his climbing equipment, once. Inviting him to commit an illegal act, on the grounds where he was building his research career, seemed a sure path to disaster. "Help, in what way?" he asked. "He's taking a huge risk even by knowing about it."

2

"He wants to come with us."

"Are you serious? And risk getting caught?"

"Greg has special access to the site," Surina said. "The park closes at sunset, but he's allowed to be there after hours because he's doing accredited research. So—"

"Yes, exactly. And what do you think will happen to his reputation and his career if he gets caught helping us? This isn't just trespassing that we're committing. Once we move that grate, it's vandalism, or breaking and entering."

"I talked to him about that," she replied, "but he knows that the rescue teams have given up on Hannah. I told him that you know exactly where she is, and that the searchers wouldn't let you participate, so you're going down there yourself to get her. It's a life and death thing—not just for Hannah, but for us. Greg can help us get down there, and he can help us get out again. And if something happens and we don't make it out, he can go for help. He offered to drive us. If anyone sees his car in the lot, it's not going to look suspicious."

Dominic let out a slow sigh.

"So, what do you say?"

"Well, there's not much I can say now. Let's just hope he doesn't change his mind and turn us in."

In the afternoon, he took the bus to Surina's apartment. He brought few supplies—just a small flashlight with fresh batteries, some notes, and a gallon of spring water. When Surina opened the door to him, she eyed the jug and smiled. "Afraid there won't be enough water?" she asked.

"I'm afraid of a lot of things at this point," Dominic replied.

They sat in the living room and tried to prepare— mentally, as well as physically. Surina gave a brief lesson on climbing gear, even though they now had an expert to assist them; they counted their supplies, discussed things that could go wrong, and checked numerous times to see if the weather forecast had changed. The reports had promised rain in the Wupatki area, but Flagstaff hadn't yet seen a drop.

Dominic gave his notes a final look-through as the time for departure drew near. He had drawn his own set of star maps on lined paper, with relevant tips based on his previous trip through the zodiac—tips like "Don't be a jerk" at Gemini, "Don't go this way" at Libra, and "Don't kill anything" at Taurus and Leo. Surina leaned over to examine his papers and chuckled softly. "Is that supposed to be a bull?"

"Don't laugh," Dominic replied. "I'm not an artist. I should have commissioned you to draw these maps."

"We might not end up in the zodiac," Surina reminded him. "And besides, those places might change."

"They might, but it sounds like some of them stay the same. I'm going to keep taking my notes; I don't want to forget anything. If we get in there, and come out again, I'm putting you in charge of drawing all of the maps."

"I don't have time," Surina insisted. "I'm broke. I need to work." She stood up. "I'm going to eat something before Greg gets here. Are you hungry?"

"Starving. I'm so afraid of not fitting through the hole that I haven't eaten, but I'm starting to get light-headed."

"Same here. I didn't want to eat or drink too much—not just because we have tight spaces to squeeze through, but because I don't want to have to go to the bathroom while we're down there." She paused. "Although . . . when I went there through Chavín, I didn't have to go the whole time."

"I did," Dominic replied dryly, "numerous times. In Leo."

His gaze lingered on Surina as she headed for the kitchen. He still hadn't adjusted to the sudden intensity of their friendship. Surina had been a stranger to him throughout his first years of college. She was just a year

4

older, and though he saw her frequently, they had rarely exchanged more than a quick hello. And then, this sudden shared goal—this feeling of solidarity and closeness, formed before he even really knew who she was. Dominic found himself studying the details of her face, as though she was a long-time friend who he had never really bothered to look at. Surina's expression was unsmiling and determined as she rummaged through cupboards. Dominic supposed his own face was set in the same expression: grim, but resolute.

Surina offered him the few snacks she had: granola bars, chips and salsa, or stuffed mushrooms. Dominic restricted himself to a few bites of food, still anxiously remembering his trip through the narrow tunnel that led below Wupatki. Surina, too, was fidgety and preoccupied. Her dark hair was pulled into a tight braid at the back of her head, giving Dominic a clear view of her somber face and the faraway expression in her eyes. The two kept up a half-attentive, nervous chatter until Greg arrived. Then they silently carried the water and a duffel bag full of supplies to the parking lot.

Greg, too, was beginning to show doubts. As someone who had studied the site's geology, he knew that navigating the underground tunnels was near impossible, and that the venture might result in nothing more than the ruin of his career. The 45-minute drive to Wupatki gave him plenty of time to second-guess the mission. He repeatedly asked Dominic to explain, in detail, how he would be able to find Hannah Hale. Dominic had a ready stream of reasoning: the particular tunnel through which Hannah had disappeared was too small for the rescue team to navigate, so they simply hadn't entered it.

"But you remember where it is," Greg said uncertainly. "Right?"

"Yeah, I know where it is."

Greg was silent for a while. Then he asked: "If she's

dead, will you be able to handle it?"

Dominic had avoided imagining such a scenario, but a wave of sorrow washed through him now as he thought about finding Hannah's lifeless body in the tunnels—a helpless, bitter grief. He replied quietly: "I'll handle it the best I can."

Greg spent the rest of the drive rambling about his research on Wupatki. His tone betrayed his lingering nervousness; his tall, thin figure leaned tensely forward during the entire drive, and his hands clutched the steering wheel as though it might fly from his hands. Surina, in the passenger seat, turned around numerous times to cast anxious looks at Dominic, but she didn't speak except to give brief answers to Greg's questions.

At the site, no one stood in their way. They parked, and Greg re-packed the duffel bag and carried it behind Dominic, who led the way by flashlight to the little green flag.

As they walked, Dominic lifted his gaze to the stars. He was glad that he couldn't see them. The thick clouds surely meant rain. Water, he had learned, was an important factor in getting back into the celestial realm, though he did not yet know why.

A drop of water smacked his forehead, followed by a few more that splashed into his hair, and he felt a bit of relief.

"There it is." Dominic pointed his flashlight at the marker. "I'm going to start working on the grate. Greg, did you leave the crowbar in the bag?"

"Yeah, it's in there. Are you sure that's what you need?"

"It's our best bet. There are holding mechanisms that have to be pried loose, but they're too flat to be pried themselves. We have to pop them out by lifting the grate."

Surina crouched beside Dominic, helping to pull the grate as he heaved it from the earth, while Greg huddled with a pen light, trying to illuminate the scene without attracting attention. Dominic was struck once again by this sudden, unexpected solidarity—not just with Surina, but with Greg, who he didn't know at all. The grad student's face was barely visible in the shadows, but Dominic could see his eyes, wide and anxious behind his glasses. Greg's banter had finally faded away, and he had become just as silent and grim as his companions.

When the grate had been freed from its bearings, Dominic set the crowbar aside. He wiped raindrops from his face and looked again at the black sky.

"I didn't know what our setup would be like," Greg said in a low voice, "so I need a few more minutes to figure out the anchors. Get your harnesses on. I'll check them when you're done."

The rain was coming heavier now. Dominic wiped water from his face as he helped Surina into her climbing harness. She helped him in return, checking his straps to make sure they were snug. "Does it feel okay?" she asked.

"Yeah, it feels okay," he replied softly. "Doesn't it? In general, I mean. Everything is going well so far. It's even raining—but I'm going to douse myself, just in case."

He tore the seal from the plastic jug and lifted it over his head, letting the spring water splash onto his head and shoulders. When his clothes were mostly saturated, he offered the jug to Surina.

"Might as well," she said.

Greg stared in astonishment. "What are you doing?"

"Getting slippery," Dominic replied. "Trust me, we need it."

Greg continued to stare, shining the flashlight beam on Surina as she poured the rest of the jug over her body.

Dominic moved to stand in front of her. "She doesn't need a spotlight," he told Greg. "Can you check my harness?"

"Uh, yeah." Greg directed the beam at a few different

7

places on the harness. He gave a few hard tugs at the straps. "Yeah, it's good. Good job."

"Are the anchors set?"

"Just about. Let me check Surina, and I'll finish with the last anchor, and then let's get going. The sooner you're underground, the less visible we'll be." He paused, and added: "You're really sure about this?"

"I've never been so sure of anything," Dominic replied. "But to be honest, I'm . . . scared."

"Well, yeah. Lots of things to be nervous about."

"You have no idea."

Dominic took in deep lungfuls of the damp night air while he waited for Greg to make the final checks. The act soothed the pang of anxiety that had risen in him, and once more he assured himself that everyone would make it home. Why all the puzzles, and predictions, if none of them led to anything?

Greg beckoned him, and Dominic knelt at the edge of the blowhole. He felt the night air being gently sucked into the opening—not a strong flow, but Dominic thought he could hear its faint *whoosh* over the raindrops and light breeze.

He experienced a sense of déjà vu as he began to descend. During his last trip down this same hole, the rain had started to saturate his hair, to drip into his eyes and obscure his vision. At the time, it had annoyed him, but now he used it as another assurance. *We're doing it right. This time, I will do everything right. . . .*

The helmet light helped him see the rock walls around him, but the tunnel was too narrow for a glimpse downward. Dominic was glad for the rope, for his tether to the upper world. When he could no longer feel the rock against his feet, he let himself dangle in empty space, waiting until he reached the floor of the underground cave.

He called up to Greg and gave a few tugs of the rope.

Then he aimed his helmet beam around the small cavern, watching the dust particles dance in swirls through the air. Dominic peered at the jagged cracks and ledges, looking for scorpions and other creatures, but all else was still and silent.

And yet he felt some sort of presence there in the stone chamber—something watching him, listening.

"I'm back," he whispered.

Surina joined him a few minutes later. As she was lowered into the cavern, Dominic removed his helmet and used the beam to explore the details of the rock walls. Shadows moved along with the light, showing numerous dark spaces tucked into cracks and holes.

Dominic was afraid of what might emerge from those shadows.

Soft scraping sounds reached him—but those were memories, unpleasant recollections of being dragged along stone corridors by ghastly creatures, human-like things with corpse-blue flesh and terrifyingly blank eyes.

Dominic tried to shake off his sudden fear. He found the small tunnel where he had first found Hannah and began to duck into it. Immediately, he was seized by a feeling of suffocation. Dominic pulled away with a small shiver. He felt himself break into a cold sweat. Memories were rushing to the surface now—memories of helplessness, of fear, of pain and sorrow.

Surina spoke up behind him: "Are we going that way?"

"Uh . . . I don't know. It . . . doesn't feel right, somehow. Or maybe I'm just afraid to go in there again."

"Well, I can't blame you." Surina, too, removed her helmet and scanned the cave with its light. "No rush. Well . . . okay, maybe we do need to move quickly, but let's look around before we decide anything. Maybe there's some other clue we should be looking for."

They wandered the small cavern, examining the cracks

9

and holes in the mottled gray stone, but not finding any other traversable passage.

Then, Surina said: "Look. Isn't this the symbol for Gemini?"

Dominic went to stand beside her. Her beam was pointing at a deep etching in the stone, just above her eye level. It looked like a Roman numeral II, but with a curved base and capital. "So it is," he said. "But . . . ."

He didn't finish the question he was about to ask. Dominic lowered the beam of his flashlight toward the stone floor, where water had pooled below the carving. He crouched and touched the puddle with his fingertips. "Water."

"A lot of it," Surina added. "Not from the rain, right? Where did it come from?"

"Underground?" Dominic suggested. "Maybe there's a crack in the floor."

He pressed his hand into the water, against the flat stone surface. The ground was solid there, but as he drew his hand closer to the wall, he noticed an aberration— something not quite right about the puddle. "The water is crawling up the rock," he said.

"What?"

"Isn't that how it looks? Oh . . . wait. No, this isn't the wall. There's more floor." Dominic extended his hand farther. From Surina's perspective, it looked like his hand was disappearing into the stone wall.

"How are you doing that?" she asked.

"Come stand on the other side of me. Look: This whole section over here isn't one wall. It's two. This one ends right here." Dominic stood up, placing his fingertips on the edge of the wall; it stopped just a few inches to the left of the carving. "There's a gap here, and the other wall is a couple feet farther back." He stepped closer, wedging himself into the narrow gap behind the stone, shining the flashlight into its depths. From where he stood, the passage looked navigable; it cut a path behind the thin sheet of rock, and then it curved out of sight.

Dominic strapped his helmet back on, but he found that he couldn't fit his head through the passageway. He removed the headpiece and set it beside the pool of water. "I'm going to see how far I can get."

"Wait." Surina placed her own helmet beside his. "Don't go by yourself. I'll be right behind you."

"Be careful." Dominic pulled a small flashlight from his pocket and switched it on. "There's water on the floor, so I'm going to test every step to see how deep it is."

He moved slowly through the passage, feeling both hopeful and afraid he'd find a drop-off that would send him hurtling into the underworld. The memories kept coming, and along with them, a gnawing anxiety. Dominic remembered poor decisions he'd made during his last journey through this place, cowardly things he'd done, things he'd said to Hannah that he shouldn't have.

Not this time, he thought.

Rather than dropping off, the floor angled up out of the water—but not for long. Dominic soon found himself at a steep decline. He paused there, aiming his flashlight at the descent, at the still and silent pool at its base. The steep rock looked wet and slippery.

Dominic turned to Surina and was startled by her sudden closeness; she had come up quietly behind him and stood just inches away. Something about the way the light beam played on her face made it seem distorted and terrifying—or perhaps Dominic was just a victim of his nerves, and any specter in the subterranean rocks would have startled him.

Whatever the case, Dominic stumbled backwards in sudden fear. His balance gave out as the ground sloped downward, and his shoes slipped against the sleek, wet rock.

Dominic dropped to his knees, making a panicked

grab for the floor, but in mere seconds he had slid down the ramp and splashed into the dark pool.

This pool was not a mere puddle. Dominic found himself submerged in cold water—not shockingly cold, but enough to make him gasp as he broke the surface. The flashlight was still clutched in his hand; instinctively, he had held it aloft.

He heard Surina calling from above. "Are you okay?"

"Fine," he replied.

"I'm going to come down."

"Wait," Dominic protested. "Let me—"

He had hardly started speaking when Surina began to skid towards the pool. She tried to keep her balance at first, with her arms spread wide at her sides, but she, too, had to drop to the rock floor. Her flashlight clattered away as she tried to catch herself; it disappeared into the water with a soft *plop*, followed closely by Surina, who went in feet first and managed to keep her head above the surface. "Damn," she said. "I lost my light."

"You might have let me look around first," Dominic admonished her. "Are you okay?"

"Fine. What now?"

He shone the beam at the high rock walls opposite them, where the pool disappeared around a curved passage. "Now we swim, I guess."

"All right," Surina breathed. "Dominic, please hang onto that flashlight for dear life."

"I'll do my best."

Dominic swam slowly, struggling to maneuver with only one hand to propel him. Surina quickly overtook him, though her movements were hesitant. Dominic realized she was walking—tentatively, but walking nonetheless. He shone the beam at her. "Can you touch the bottom?"

"Barely."

"Good. That's comforting, actually. Better than a

bottomless abyss." He paused. "I don't want to get yanked underwater and trapped there again. It's . . . painful."

"Well, let's not assume that won't happen."

"Right. Thanks."

"I think I see a place where we can get out of the water. Look ahead of you."

Sure enough, just as they began to round the curve, a ledge appeared ahead. It rose just above the water's surface, and beyond it was a flat platform backed by another high wall. Dominic could already see another tunnel leading through that rock—a tunnel that, by its looks, was more than wide enough to crawl through.

"That looks promising," he said.

Surina reached the ledge first and climbed up, and then she helped Dominic out of the water. They stood at the entrance to the tunnel and stood in silence, the only sound the rhythmic dripping of water from their clothes onto the hard stone.

The tunnel wasn't just wide enough to crawl through; it was large enough for both Dominic and Surina to walk into together. "Let's interpret this as a good sign," Dominic suggested. "We needed sandstone, dolomite, and water to get back into the zodiac, and here we have an abundance of all three—and a tunnel that's practically inviting us in."

"Look," Surina said. "Shine your flashlight up there, above the tunnel."

Dominic angled the beam upward. Over the tunnel, carved deep into the stone, was a single word: *Mabsuthat*.

"Mab-su-that," Dominic pronounced slowly. "It doesn't sound familiar."

"No, but it's a sign," Surina said. "We must be getting closer." She shuddered and wrapped her arms tight across her chest. "I'm cold. Let's keep going."

The passage appeared to curve around to the left. Dominic was about to step into it when he heard a voice calling out somewhere behind him.

He and Surina exchanged glances. "Did you hear that?" she asked.

They heard a strange scuttling, followed by a loud splash—and then a voice again, echoing through the stone chambers.

Surina gave Dominic a look of dread. "No way," she whispered. "Doesn't that sound like Greg? Tell me he didn't come down here."

"He could have. He's skinny enough."

The voice sounded again. It called Surina's name, then Dominic's.

"What the . . . ." Surina let out a sharp breath. "He was supposed to stay *up* there! What is he doing here?"

"So much for getting help if we don't come back," Dominic replied.

Surina went to the edge of the platform and called out: "Greg! We're over here. Keep swimming."

Greg had managed to hang onto his flashlight. Its beam danced crazily on the walls as he hurried through the dark waters. Soon he was slumped on the platform, still coughing from his tumble into the pool. He directed the light beam at the rock walls; the beam shot from left to right, up and down, revealing expanses of rock that curved over his head. The dark stone enclosed the space and left only two ways out: back toward the impossibly slippery incline, or the tunnel that opened just behind him.

"Damn," he said. "I'm an idiot. Are we trapped? I don't think I can get back up that hill."

"We're not trapped," Surina replied.

"But we can't get back up. This is why I should have stayed behind. I'm sorry I didn't; it's just that you were supposed to call up when you both got to the bottom, but I didn't hear anything after Surina went down, and there was no tug on the rope, and I got worried. I figured you came this way after I found your helmets. And now . . . ."

"We're not trapped," Dominic assured him, shining his own beam toward the tunnel. "We have to go that way."

"But . . . we don't know what's in there."

"Looks like it's our only option."

"No, this isn't good," Greg protested. "This place is totally unexplored. It could turn out just like *The Descent*. You know that movie? The group wanders into an unknown cave system, and it turns out there are giant carnivorous things that evolved to—"

"It isn't like that," Surina reassured him. She beckoned Dominic. "Let's see where it goes."

"Wait," Greg said. "What if we fall farther down?"

Surina and Dominic exchanged glances. "We might," Surina replied. "But . . . ." She trailed off, staring into the tunnel. "Dominic, turn off your flashlight." He complied, and she asked: "Do you see anything?"

As his eyes began to adjust to the now-dark tunnel, Dominic caught a glimpse of something—a haze where he shouldn't have been able to see one. "Light," he said.

He felt his anxiety intensifying. *This is it*, he thought. *The portal is probably back there. We're really going in again.*

"That's not light," Greg blurted. "It can't be. It's phosphorescence."

"All right, listen," Dominic said. "I'm going to go in, just a little, to see where it goes. If there's water, I won't step in it. I won't risk falling again." He switched the beam on. "It looks like the tunnel veers off to the left, and that's where the light is coming from."

"It's not light," Greg repeated. "It could be phosphorescent calcite, or glow worms—or something worse." He paused, and then added: "This is exactly what happened in *The Descent*."

Dominic was already moving forward, into the wide tunnel. Surina watched as he began to disappear around the curve; then he stopped.

"What's the matter?" Greg called.

"Come here," Dominic replied.

"Why, what's back there?"

Surina started into the tunnel, with Greg following just behind. "What's back there?" she echoed.

"Come and see."

She walked in the beam of Greg's light, moving to stand beside Dominic. She came to a halt as the source of the light came into view: a crack opened in the wall of rock just ahead of her, and through it she could see a vast, grassy plain, lush and green, illuminated as if by the sun, spreading beneath a bright blue sky. "We're here," she said. "I can already feel it."

Slowly, Dominic stepped closer, getting a better view of the landscape ahead: wide, sloping fields, and a dirt path cutting across the green. "I remember this place," he said. "At least, I think I do. It looks like . . . Gemini." He glanced back, past Surina. "And once again, there are three of us, when there should only be two."

"Well," Surina murmured, "if there are three of us, then I guess there are supposed to be three." She came to stand beside him. She looked through the opening with a strained sigh. "We're in. We made it."

"Yeah, we're in," Dominic replied quietly. "And here's our first challenge: What are we going to tell Greg?"

2: Gemini

Surina stood for a while, gazing through the crack into the bright realm. Short green shafts covered the ground, like thick grass, with a wide dirt path cutting through it. Already she was scanning the rea for clues, but nothing caught her eye except for a simple wooden post beside the trail.

Greg began to nudge past her, but he came to a sudden halt. "What is that?" he asked.

Dominic silently surveyed the landscape. Surina, too, remained quiet.

Greg moved forward again, stopping as the light began to stream onto his face. He squinted as it hit the lenses of his glasses, and even when his sight had adjusted and he had a clear view of what lay beyond the wall, he stood frozen, staring in confusion.

"What is that?" he repeated.

At last, Dominic spoke. "Okay, here's the deal: There's a portal to another dimension underneath Wupatki, and Hannah is in there somewhere. It's why the rescuers couldn't find her."

Greg took a step back. "What . . . what do you mean, another dimension?"

"Just what I said. She's not at Wupatki anymore. She's . . . ." Reluctantly, Dominic gestured to the opening in the stone. "She's in there."

Greg switched off his flashlight. "How is there so much light? How is it daytime?"

"It really is another dimension," Surina said quietly. "I

don't know how else to explain it. It's another place, a place not on Earth, and it doesn't work like Earth does."

"I don't believe in alternate dimensions," Greg replied. "I mean, not *this* type of alternate dimension."

"Well, we're not going to try to convince you," Dominic said. "Regardless of whether it's another dimension or not, we don't have a lot of time to save Hannah—so let's get moving." He looked up at Surina. "Are you ready?"

She took a deep breath. "Does it matter?"

"It doesn't look wide enough to squeeze through, but there might be another . . . wait." Dominic reached out, moving close to the wall and placing his hand into the gap. "It *is* wide enough. It's two walls again, not one. The left-hand wall is farther back."

"I don't think we should go out there," Greg said.

Surina moved to stand behind Dominic. "Then you can stay here and wait for us." She gripped Dominic's shoulder and looked nervously into the bright realm beyond. "Want to go first? I'm right behind you."

"Yes, I can feel that. Are you trying to break my bones?"

"Sorry." She loosened her grasp, but she didn't take her hand away.

Stepping into the light felt surreal—not just because Surina knew that it was night, but because the light of this realm lacked warmth. The air felt less damp and stuffy than that of the cave, but it had an emptiness about it. The grass, too, looked rather like plastic, though it bent beneath Surina's feet as easily as real grass. Not far from where she stood was the head of the path, meandering across the land, where nothing but small green hills were visible in the distance. "I don't think this is Gemini," she said. "When I was in . . . ."

She trailed off as she focused on the post near the trailhead. Dominic gestured to it, noting the large symbol etched into the wood. "Gemini," he said. He gave Surina a pointed look. "Looks like we got the easy version. Wasn't Gemini the place where you had to do all those partner obstacles with Wibben?"

"Yeah. Let's not talk about obstacles." She stepped farther out, making room for Greg to follow. "Remember, this place gets ideas from us."

Dominic glanced back at Greg. He started to speak, but something caught his attention, and he went back toward the wall. Surina, too, turned to look at the massive stone that rose high along the border of the realm, smooth and dark gray, with no other visible openings. There was, however, something unusual at the foot of the wall—a tan-hued object that stood out against the gray and green, obscured by Dominic, who crouched in front of it.

"Did you find something?" Surina asked.

He stood up, stepping out of the way so she could see what he'd been looking at: a pair of boots, with a garment folded neatly across the top, and other objects piled on top of that—items of a similar shade of tan.

She moved closer, stooping beside Dominic and removing the folded material. The boots, of soft brown leather and sturdy laces, were battered but well made. "These look like the boots I wore last time I was here," she said. She began to unfold the material in her hands and found that she was holding two garments: a large sweater and a soft woolen nightgown. "Oh . . . Dominic, put the boots on, quick," she said.

"Why?"

"Because—aren't we supposed to wear these things? They cover up our scent, or something, so Tagua and his . . . his people won't know we're here."

"It's because of the hounds," Dominic replied.

Surina stood up, giving him a puzzled glance as she shook the garments out. A woven belt had also been laid there, along with a soft pouch—a flask, by the look of it.

These, she knew, were all made from the ram of Aries. By wearing them, an intruder such as herself could mask one's scent and blend in with the starry realm. "The what?" she asked.

"I think we have to wear them because of the hounds," Dominic said. "Orion's hounds. They caught my scent and went after me last time. Hannah barely saved me." He turned to Greg, who stood staring at the landscape with pale, glassy-eyed anxiety.

Dominic went to him and nudged his elbow. "Put this on," he said, handing him the sweater.

Greg took the sweater and looked blankly at it. "Why?"

"It will keep you out of trouble. Don't take it off while we're in here."

Several seconds passed, and then Greg began a slow process of stripping off his wet T-shirt. Dominic slipped on the boots and tucked the flask into his pants pocket; he stood with his hands on his hips, waiting for the others to finish.

The fleece dress was too small for Surina to wear; she wrapped it around her waist and secured it with the belt, keeping her eyes on Greg as he struggled to pull the sweater over his chest.

Dominic moved to stand beside her. "Enjoying yourself, are you?"

"What?"

"Never seen a shirtless man?"

Surina lowered her voice. "I'm not checking him out, if that's what you mean. I'm afraid he'll go into shock. Look at his eyes."

"Yeah, I know." Dominic's voice dropped to a whisper. "Stoner eyes. I told you."

She gave him a scathing look. "You're very calm for someone who just walked into another dimension. Now that I'm here, I'm . . . scared. I'm really, really anxious. I can only imagine how he feels."

Dominic shrugged. "He has ways of being chill, even when the situation calls for panic." He brought two fingers to his lips, inhaling loudly, as if smoking an invisible cigarette.

Surina rolled her eyes. "Will you do that the whole time we're here?"

"No. I don't want to overdo it. I'll wait until you forget about it, and then I'll spring it on you again."

She hesitated, studying Dominic's face, looking penetratingly into his eyes. If he was anxious, he didn't show it in the least. "Are you really that confident?" she asked.

"About what?"

"About being here. You told me before that you were scared."

"Honestly, I'm surprised that you're more anxious than I am," Dominic said. "When we went to Peru, you were saying 'We're fine' in response to everything. The car is about to go over a cliff? We're fine! A waterfall is about to hurl us to our deaths? We're fine!"

"I admit," Surina said, "this place rattled me. I think of this as a place where bad things happen."

"And yet, we're fine."

Greg joined them, still tugging the sweater into place. Dominic looked up at him and said: "Looks like we're all going on this trip together. Just bear with it, and don't worry, okay? We'll find Hannah, and then we'll go home."

"How?" Greg asked. "If we can't go back this way . . . ."

"Don't worry, I know a way out." Dominic gestured to the field ahead. "Right now, we're going this way. Just start walking." He started off, leaving the others to trail behind him.

Greg began to follow, but halted and stared. Surina noticed, then, that he was shaking—maybe from a chill, but Surina didn't feel cold, despite being soaked. Her only uneasiness came from the strangeness of this place, the seeming impossibility of it, and from other little anxieties: Hannah, Tagua, and the hounds that Dominic had mentioned. Surina didn't feel good about the small amount of ram's clothes they were wearing. She would probably be okay, but Dominic only had the boots and a flask stuffed in his pocket.

She hurried forward, easily catching up with him. "Here," she said, untying the belt from around her waist. "Wear this, too."

He looked at the nightgown as it began to slip from Surina's hips. "Don't you need it?"

"No. I can just tuck this into my pants." She pulled the fleece gown back into place. "Wear that, please. You've hardly got anything on."

He fastened the belt around himself and frowned at the path ahead. "We'll be walking for a while," he said. "This is what it was like for me in Gemini, last time: just a lot of ground to cover."

"There's no riddle," Surina said, looking again at the wooden marker. They had reached the trailhead, and now that she had a closer look at the post, she found herself scrutinizing it for other markings: symbols, words, anything unusual.

"Hang on," she said. "It looks like there's something on top of it."

Dominic stood on his toes, and then moved back, hoping for a better look. "Is there? I'm too short to see it."

"There's a strip of paper, or something, sticking up." Surina reached up, brushing her fingertips against the top of the marker. She half-turned to Greg. "Greg, come over here; we need someone who's tall. There's some paper nailed into the post." She withdrew her hand. "Can you take a look?"

Reluctantly, Greg began to walk again. He came close

and peered at the post. "It is paper," he said, sounding uncertain. He gave it a light tug. "It's thick. It's . . . not tearing easily."

"Is there writing on it?" Surina asked.

"Yeah." Greg grabbed the paper with both hands, pulling and twisting until it finally ripped free. He gave it to Surina, and she read out loud: "Heal the hero's exploits against twelve celestial beings; thus restore the sacred balance of the cosmic ring. Hero twins must traverse there, in balanced kinship, or despair. Victory comes when contrary qualities unite, and in solidarity work to expel the blight. Labor number one: Advance to Taurus and sleigh the Stymphalian bird."

The three stood in silence for a while. Then Dominic said: "We best not take that literally. I don't think it's a good idea to kill anything in this place."

"It doesn't say anything about killing," Surina replied.

Dominic moved closer. "Doesn't it tell us to slay a bird?"

"It says *sleigh*. S-L-E-I-G-H." Surina handed him the paper.

"What are you doing?" Greg asked. His face was drawn with worry. "Why is this important? Is this a message from Hannah?"

"No," Dominic said. "It's . . . ." He looked at Surina, but she, too, was at a loss for an explanation.

Dominic stuffed the thick into his pocket. "Let's just walk."

They carried on in silence. Dominic led the way, walking briskly just ahead of Surina. Occasionally, he glanced back to ensure that the others were following— and Surina was struck by something in his gaze, some new quality that she had just recently begun to notice. A couple of weeks ago, her only exchanges with Dominic had been at the local record shop where he worked; there was nothing remarkable about him except that he had dwarfism and was much shorter than his peers. He was just a guy, an employee helping a customer, polite and outgoing—until one day the small talk was replaced by a quiet, troubled depth that showed only in his eyes, a look that mutated into a striking, soulful gaze. The superficial chatter ceased; the voice softened; the friendly brown eyes became a contrasting pool of peace and perplexity. Something had happened to him, had changed him, and Surina maintained a nagging curiosity about what it was.

Now, of course, she knew.

Greg had lagged farther behind. Surina slowed down and fell into step beside him. "It's a riddle," she said. "That paper, I mean. This place is full of riddles that need to be solved. They're all related somehow to the stars—to the zodiac, and the other constellations. We're in the Gemini constellation right now. I know it sounds weird, but . . . there are people here. Well, not people, but . . . spirits, I guess. Beings."

"What kind of beings?" Nervousness strained Greg's voice. "You mean like divine beings?"

She hesitated. "Some of them."

"What are they, like, tricksters?"

"Sort of, but not in a bad way." Surina tried to think of a rational way to explain the things she'd seen here: personified constellations, mythical figures, unwitting humans trapped in the starry realm—and Tagua, the wizard desperately trying to get back to the Earth realm. "There are some unpleasant figures. We have to watch out for Tagua. He's the reason Hannah is still here."

"Who's Tagua?"

"He was supposedly a . . . ." Surina was about to say *wizard*, but the idea seemed not to lend credulity to her story. "He's just a jerk. He's stuck here, and he won't let Hannah go unless she helps him get back to our world."

"So . . . we're not just finding Hannah," Greg said. "You're saying there's some weird dude who's holding

24

her hostage." He stopped suddenly, looking back the way they'd come.

"You can't go back that way," Surina said. "Just keep walking, okay? We'll find Hannah and get out. I've gotten in and out before, and so has Dominic."

Greg didn't reply. He followed them quietly.

They walked in silence for some time, and Dominic said in a low voice: "There's nothing here. Shouldn't—"

At that moment, Greg blurted: "There's something on the trail. Do you see that?"

"No," Surina said, but as the top of the slope came into view, she spotted something directly ahead of them. As more of the figure came into view, she came to a halt. "Dominic . . . ."

"Yeah, I see it," he said. He turned around as he realized that Surina and Greg had both stopped behind him. "What's the matter?"

"It's an animal," Surina said.

The figure lay motionless on the trail, a dark golden creature that Surina couldn't quite identify. She could make out the details of a paw at the end of a scrawny limb. At first the thing resembled a scruffy lioness, but after a moment, Surina noticed a wing spread over the torso, its golden feathers flecked with dirt.

"It's a dead animal," Greg said. "There's a dead thing on the path. That's a bad sign."

"No, it's a good sign." Slowly, Dominic moved closer. "Look: It has wings. It could be the . . . ." He paused to re-read the riddle. "The Stymphalian bird. But I'm not sure how we're supposed to 'sleigh' it anywhere."

Surina, too, edged forward. "Are you sure it's dead?"

"Only one way to find out."

Greg hung back as the other two made a slow approach toward the figure. Surina saw no signs of life in the creature. It looked scrawny and starved, and its fur and feathers were matted with mud and dust. As Surina moved closer, she caught sight of its human-like face—no fur there, no feathers, just an expanse of pale, blue-hued flesh, like that of a corpse. Surina could only see one of its eyes from where she stood, but it was closed, its lashes and brow just as dusty as the rest.

Dominic stopped, his expression suddenly grave. "Surina . . . it looks like . . . ."

"It's the demon thing!" Surina stood close behind Dominic, speaking in an agitated whisper. "It's the thing from the Fiery Furnace."

"You mean Fornax?"

"Yeah." Surina gazed down at the creature's strange face, profiled against the path where it lay. That face! Even though its eyes were closed, Surina couldn't forget the bright, outraged eyes that had stared at her from that strange countenance.

Dominic gave her a doubtful glance. "Are you sure it was a demon?"

Surina started to reply in the affirmative, but at that moment the creature's eye opened. It turned its head—a slow turn, as though it was just being roused from sleep. The eyes, red-rimmed and tired, fixed on Dominic.

In a faint voice, the thing said: "You're here."

Surina stepped back, though the thing didn't seem to mean any harm. Its voice had lost its angry edge, and the eyes no longer burned with rage.

"I'm not a demon," the thing said wearily, looking up at Surina. "It's me, Hannah."

It sounded somewhat like Hannah's voice, but Surina shook her head. "That's not Hannah."

Dominic was already kneeling, reaching out to help the creature.

"That's not her," Surina repeated. "It's the thing from Fornax. Hannah was with me when we saw it."

The thing looked up at her again. The whites of its eyes were stained a vague blue, and Surina suddenly remembered the way Hannah's eyes had looked: that same weariness, that same strange tint of blue. The face, too, resembled Hannah. Surina's doubt wavered.

"That was me," the thing said. "It was the future me. In the Fornax constellation, I mean. There were two of me there at the same time. The old me, and . . . the thing that I am now. I was the one who yelled at you and called you idiots, and I'm the one who broke the tree."

Hannah—if that's what the thing really was—began to stand, with Dominic's help. "What happened?" Dominic asked. "I mean, why do you look like *this* again?"

"Virgo did it," Hannah replied. Her gaze was still fixed on Surina. "There really were two of me. Hannah the girl, and Hannah the griffin." She looked past them. "Who's that?"

Surina glanced back at Greg, who watched from a distance with fear-glazed eyes. "That's Greg. He helped us get back into Wupatki."

"Hi," Hannah greeted him. Greg stared back at her with unflinching terror.

"Here." Dominic took the scrap of paper from his pocket. "We have our first riddle. Maybe you can help figure it out." He read aloud: "'Heal the hero's exploits against twelve celestial beings; thus restore the sacred balance of the cosmic ring. Hero twins must traverse there in balanced kinship, or despair. Victory comes when contrary qualities unite, and in solidarity work to expel the blight. Labor number one: Advance to Taurus and sleigh the Stymphalian bird.' Sleigh is S-L-E-I-G-H."

A vague smile touched Hannah's lips. "Hero twins," she murmured. "Remember what happened the last time we were in Gemini? We fought the whole time, and . . . things didn't work out. This time, we have to . . . what does the riddle say?"

"In solidarity work to expel the blight." Dominic gave Hannah a pointed look. "I'm guessing the 'blight' is

Tagua. What about the Stymphalian bird? Is that you?"

She looked lost in thought for a moment. "The Stymphalian bird is something from Greek mythology, but . . . I don't remember what it is." She gestured to the scrap of paper. "There are eleven more of those, one at each realm."

"How do you know?"

"I put them there," she said. Seeing Dominic's surprise, she added: "I didn't write them. Virgo did. She's the one who told me where to put them—and she also told me to put the ram clothes in Gemini, by the rocks. Those were the last things I put down. I was trying to fly back to Ophiuchus, but . . . I got tired. I decided to sit down and try to figure things out." Hannah knelt on the ground. With a clawed fingertip, she traced a series of lines in the dust. "There's a gate at Ophiuchus that I have to open. I was supposed to ride the Orion chariot there, but . . . ."

"You crashed," Dominic finished for her, glancing at Surina. "So I heard."

Surina guessed at the figure that Hannah was etching in the dirt: a standing figure holding two staffs. When Hannah had first shown her the image, she was certain that it was the Raimondi Stele, an intricately carved sculpture that stood in temple ruins in the mountains of Peru; she had traveled to that site, hoping to find passage into the celestial realm. "Are you drawing the Raimondi Stele?" she asked.

"It's Ophiuchus," Hannah said.

Surina crouched beside her. "This is one of the symbols you kept showing me. Before I came here, I mean. It's the reason I went to Chavín in Peru. You were trying to tell me how to get into this place, and I thought you were showing me sculptures from Chavín."

"It's Ophiuchus," Hannah repeated. "We have to solve it before we can open the sun gate."

Surina pointed to the drawing. "Maybe that's not what

you meant to draw, but this is basically what the Raimondi Stele looks like: a figure holding two staffs, one on each side, and—"

"They're snakes."

"Snakes," Surina repeated. "And it's wearing a headdress, and it has a worried look on its face, but if you look at it upside-down, the headdress looks like a smiling panther face with sharp teeth."

"The Ophiuchus riddles are all about looking at things from different perspectives to see their whole meaning," Hannah said. "The last time I went, there was a riddle about how you can't really see Ophiuchus unless you also look at what's around it."

"What about these?" Dominic asked, waving the scrap of paper at her. "The riddles you placed in the zodiac realms—did you read them?"

"Yeah, I read them. They're kind of the same as the one you already have. They're about finding mythical creatures and doing certain tasks. Like . . . the riddle at Taurus is about the Cretan bull, and there's another one that says you have to slay the Nemean lion, and there's one about the Lernaean Hydra."

Dominic looked at the paper in consternation. "Aren't those the labors of Hercules?"

A spark of interest glowed in Hannah's tired eyes. "Are they? If they are, they're related to Ophiuchus."

"How so?"

"I'm supposed to pay attention to the constellations that are around it. Can you guess what's right above Ophiuchus?"

"The Hercules constellation," Surina answered. "So, that's one step closer to figuring it out, right? It has something to do with Hercules."

"Hercules was given twelve labors; that's one for each zodiac constellation," Dominic said, "so I think we're on the right track." He gestured to the path ahead. "Let's keep walking. We should get to Taurus. Hannah, are you okay to walk?"

"Yeah." Hannah stood up and slouched feebly, but an eager glint remained in her eye.

Surina beckoned Greg. "Are you okay?"

"No," he replied, "but I'll follow you. I'll just walk back here."

Greg kept a good distance behind the others. The path led them up a gentle slope, and at the peak of it they could see the border of the next realm: a high wall, and on the other side of it, a vast plain. In the middle of that plain was a strange object. Surina would have mistaken it for a small mountain, but for the curved spire that protruded from one end, and a bulky leg from the other.

"There's something," Dominic said.

"It's a bull," Surina and Hannah replied in unison. Surina added: "It's the bull I rode with Wibben, but it's fallen on its side."

"I crashed the Orion chariot into its horn," Hannah said. "The chariot was out of balance because . . . well, because of me, and the things I did—like leaving you behind." She gave Surina a grave look. "I'm sorry I did that. I won't do it again."

Surina was quiet for a while. She studied Hannah's strange face: the blue-hued skin, the long tufts of feathers on her head that looked like a pair of soft horns. If it wasn't for Hannah's voice, and for those familiar eyes— and for all the other bizarre and impossible things that had happened in this realm—Surina couldn't have believed it was her. "Why did you leave?" she asked.

"Because . . . you probably know why." Hannah's voice again sounded weary and faint. "Before you showed up, I was solving all of the riddles on my own—but things changed. I started to fade, and then you showed up, all fresh and . . . smart, and you were solving everything. I guess I was jealous. But I won't do that anymore," she added quickly. "I'll be part of a team now." Hannah lowered her eyes, looking down at the trail as she walked. "Thank you for coming back."

As they approached the border wall, the land dipped downward, obscuring the giant bull from view. Surina braced herself for a hidden challenge, for some creature or obstacle that couldn't be seen from a distance, but there was nothing to impede the travelers. The wall was a tall brick structure, but at the end of the path, a circle opened in the bricks, large enough to crawl through—and the wall itself was only a couple of bricks deep, so that it could be crossed in mere seconds. Beside the opening stood another wooden post, this one much shorter than the last, and Dominic could easily see the top. He pulled the strip of papyrus from it, and as the group gathered around, he read aloud: "The battle fought, the Pleiades won, advance on the path of the sun, with courage, with strategic arts and seven stars within in your hearts. Labor number two: Catch the fallen Cretan bull whose horn still drives the broken hull; bear it forth to heaven's glen to be reduced and made again."

Surina pondered the riddle. "Whose horn still drives the broken hull," she muttered.

"Let's just go." Hannah gestured to the tunnel. "It's something to do with the bull's horn, so let's go look there."

Greg had been silent throughout the journey, but now he spoke in a strained voice. "Wait, why are we going in there? What are you going to do?"

Dominic tried to reassure him: "We're just following the clues. We probably have to go all the way around the zodiac before we can go home."

"Around the zodiac?"

"We're in the stars," Hannah replied. "This place is modeled after the constellations."

"Just follow us, Greg," Surina said, and started to duck

into the tunnel.

"No, I can't. I'm starting to hyperventilate. I feel like I can't breathe."

Surina restrained a sigh. "All right. Let's sit down for a minute."

Greg leaned forward, resting his hands on his knees. "This seems like . . . a weird hallucination. The creepy bird girl, and—"

"That's Hannah," Dominic interrupted.

"The weird, technicolor landscape," Greg continued, "and the whole 'We're in the stars' thing—it seems like an acid trip, or—"

"Have you had a lot of acid trips?" Dominic asked, giving Surina a sly look.

"I could have inhaled some mold spores, or—"

"Or some cave fumes," Dominic suggested.

"Yes! There are probably cave fumes."

"It isn't a hallucination." Dominic cast an impatient glance at the tunnel. "Are you going to sit, or should we keep going? We don't have a lot of time."

"It's okay," Hannah said. "He can sit."

Greg straightened up. "No, I should keep moving." He started forward again, but suddenly he turned to Hannah. "Can you just stay over there until I'm through?"

"Yes," she replied patiently. "I will stay here."

Dominic waited for Surina to go through the tunnel, and then he ushered Greg ahead of him. "Think it's a hallucination if you want," he said, "but take it seriously, okay? Surina and I have both been here before, and we talked about it afterwards, and we experienced the same things. We weren't hallucinating."

Greg stepped though the passage at a low crouch. "You could have been," he said as he emerged. "If you both inhaled something, or ate something—"

"Like what?" Dominic passed through the tunnel and resumed walking, his gaze fixed on the bulk of the bull ahead. "Moldy food?"

"Mushrooms," Greg suggested.

"We didn't eat mushrooms."

"We did," Surina cut in. "We ate the stuffed mushrooms at my apartment, remember?"

"They were culinary mushrooms," Dominic insisted. "Surina bought them at the grocery store. They wouldn't cause hallucinations."

"I didn't," she said. "I got them from a friend who goes mushroom hunting."

"They were just boletes," Dominic said, "and anyway, Greg didn't eat those, and he's here. This isn't happening because of fungus or fumes. This is a real, actual place, and even if you don't believe that, we still need to get through it and get out quickly, without messing things up. Can everyone at least agree on that?"

"Sure," Greg said.

Hannah and Surina murmured their agreement.

"So, just trust us," Dominic reiterated. "So far, this has been really easy, but it's not going to stay that way. There's going to be—"

"Let's not say that," Surina replied. "Remember, this place gets ideas from us—so let's not make it hard. Let's just assume that this time around, everything will be quick, easy, and painless."

Dominic nodded, perhaps remembering his first difficult journey through the zodiac. "Especially painless," he agreed. "Right. Here's to a quick and easy trip home."

3: Taurus

Taurus was not as Dominic remembered it. Instead, it was as Surina had left it: a flat land containing little more than a giant metal bull. The bright green grass had given way to a mixture of dirt and gravel, and above, the sky remained a featureless blue expanse. No one spoke; the only sound was the crunch of pebbles beneath four pairs of feet. Dominic anxiously searched the sky and the horizon for any signs of danger, for anything unusual, but nothing came.

As Dominic approached the hulking figure of the bull, its details came into focus: the rusted metal body, the still-shining horns curving away from the massive head, an eye that seemed to stare back at him. That eye glowed with a vague orange hue. Dominic could see where the other eye, farther up from the ground, burned a deep red.

"The red one must be Aldebaran," he mused. He walked beside Hannah, going at a hurried pace to keep up with her long-legged gait. "The eye, I mean. You see how the eye up there is bright red?"

"Yeah. I kind of remember something about that star."

"Aldebaran is a red giant, much bigger than our sun. When the Taurus constellation rises above the horizon, Aldebaran rises right behind the Pleiades, so people say that the bull's eye is always fixed on them—even though the bull faces Orion. It's more like an inner eye."

"Yeah . . . because you have to find the stars inside of you," Hannah said softly. "Remember my helmet with seven stars? There's another seven-starred crown at

Ophiuchus: the Corona Borealis. Ophiuchus holds two snakes, and one of them points to the crown. The other one points to Aquila."

"The eagle," Dominic said.

"Aquila is a griffin," Hannah countered quietly. "In Sumerian myth . . . ." She trailed off as something caught her eye. "Look—there's something caught on the bull's horn." Hannah's pace quickened, and Dominic broke into a jog behind her. "I think I know what it is," she called back to him.

The tip of the horn rested about eight feet above the ground. A rough wooden plank was suspended there, its edges jagged and splintered. It bore a partial carving of a bird: the head and part of a folded wing. "It's a piece of the chariot," Hannah said.

Surina came to stand beside her. She put her hands on her hips. "What are we supposed to . . . wait a minute." She reached up and touched the wood. "Isn't this from Aquarius' boat?"

"It is," Hannah replied. "The boat became part of the chariot. Sorry, I keep forgetting—you would already know all of this if I hadn't left you behind."

"Let's take it down." Surina reached up, trying to grasp the bottom edges of the plank. "Greg, can you help? I'm too short to get a good grip."

Greg's face registered unwillingness, but he made a slow move toward Surina. Together, they maneuvered the plank from the pointed horn and lowered it to the ground. Once they were finished, Hannah gazed moodily at the ruined wood—but suddenly her eyes lit with excitement, and she cried out: "My Orion tokens!" She burst into a sprint, but she stopped after a few steps and crouched on the ground. When she stood, she extended her paw-like hands to Dominic and Surina. In them, she held two thin metal plates. The group gathered around to examine them: both were tarnished bronze, one stamped with the word

SAIPH and the image of a foot, the other with the word *ALNITAK* below a crude sword.

"These are the last two stars that I needed to make the Orion chariot," Hannah said. "I looked all over for them. I don't know why I didn't think to look here." She paused. "I suppose it wouldn't have mattered; I wasn't ready to use them yet."

She explained, briefly, how she and Surina had obtained Orion's seven "stars" from Aquarius; how they had ferried the stars to the realm of Orion, whose puzzle was to place the stars in the proper slots to create the celestial chariot. Hannah abandoned Surina on the journey, wanting to solve the puzzle herself—but though her efforts seemed successful at first, the chariot spun out of control and crashed into Taurus. Her failure was memorialized in the night sky, Dominic realized: Auriga, the seven-starred chariot, rested at the tip of Taurus' horn.

Dominic lowered his gaze to the splintered plank, which was, by all appearances, useless. "So, what are we supposed to do with this chunk of wood?" he asked. "I'm guessing it's the broken hull from the riddle, but . . . ."

Surina answered: "I think we can use this to re-make the chariot. When I was here with Wibben, we re-made a boat out of just one fragment. Don't you think that's what's meant by 'sleigh the Stymphalian bird'? Hannah is the bird, and the chariot is the sleigh."

"It *is* a sleigh," Hannah said breathlessly. "It's actually more of a sleigh than a chariot. We're supposed to take the wood and bear it forth to Orion. Then we can make the sleigh, and it should bring us straight to Ophiuchus." She pointed beyond the bull. "The Eridanus River is over there, and Orion is standing in the middle of it." She gave the group an apologetic look. "Can one of you carry the wood? I'm . . . ."

Surina started to lift the plank, but Greg reached out and took it from her. "I'll do it," he said, and he even managed a small nod when Hannah thanked him.

His cordiality mutated back into horror, though, when Hannah lifted her forearm. She tried to move quickly, discreetly, but Greg watched as she tucked the two tokens beneath a flap of skin near her armpit, a fleshy pocket bulging with other small objects. His eyes widened with revulsion.

"I know," Hannah said, unaffected. "It's weird—but I like being a griffin."

As they walked, the note of excitement remained in Hannah's voice. "Dominic, thanks for coming back here," she said. "I thanked Surina, but I forgot to thank you." She called ahead to Greg: "And you, too—Greg."

Greg cast a wary look back at the bird-creature that trailed behind him. "Uh-huh," he mumbled.

Hannah lowered her head. "I'll do better this time," she murmured, as if trying to assure herself. "But I still . . . ." Hannah hesitated. Her strange, blue-hued eyes became troubled. "It's not all gone, but I think I can manage it now."

"What's not all gone?" Surina asked.

"My feelings about how things turned out. There's a part of me that's still disappointed—but it's not as bad as before. I really hated that you had to help me with the puzzles, and that I couldn't do everything myself. I still kind of hate that I'm not as clever as I wanted to be. And I hated that I couldn't persuade Tagua."

"Persuade him to do what?"

"To not be a jerk," Hannah said. "He told me stories about his time on Earth, how he grew up with his grandparents who beat him and treated him like a slave, and how he spent all of his time alone in the barns or in the pasture, thinking about how he would escape. It seemed like no one ever loved him. I thought that if I was kind to him . . . ."

"Then he would learn how to be kind," Surina finished.

"Yeah. But he doesn't listen to me, or care about anyone. I should have stopped pandering to him a long time ago, but I don't like failing at something I worked so hard at for such a long time." Hannah glanced up at the sky, then around the landscape. She lowered her voice and added: "Even after I crashed the chariot, I was angry at you—and at Wibben, too, because I never had a chance to solve the sun gate riddle."

Surina hesitated. "Well . . . we'll keep trying. Together, we—"

"That's not what I mean." Hannah's voice dropped another notch. "I didn't have a chance because Wibben already solved it a long time ago. And now you know how to solve it, too."

This time, shock registered in Surina's face.

"Virgo told me," Hannah continued. "Wibben solved it, but he wouldn't open the gate for Tagua. He always said he would rather fade into nothing than let Tagua into our world. And I know he's right, but I kept hoping that Tagua would come to his senses . . . and then I could open the gate for all of us, and everything would just be good. And I could congratulate myself on saving everyone. Wibben knew I would be tempted, so he told you how to solve it instead of me."

Dominic began to recall the problem of bringing Hannah back to the Earth dimension: Like Tagua, she was locked into the stars by the sun gate, and could only return home if the gate was opened—but it was locked by a complicated puzzle. Tagua yearned for its opening and had imprisoned many hapless wanderers while trying to solve its mystery, eager to return to a world in which his sorcerous powers would be amplified. The other puzzle, then, was how to open the sun gate without letting Tagua through. "Wait a minute," Dominic said. "Are you saying that Surina knows how to get you out of this place?"

Hannah and Surina exchanged glances. "I . . . might

know how," Surina admitted.

"Since when?"

"I couldn't tell you," Surina said in a near whisper. She, too, nervously scanned the empty plain. "We shouldn't talk about it! Someone will overhear us."

"For now, let's just focus on re-making the chariot," Hannah agreed. "We need to get to Ophiuchus as fast as possible."

"Why?" Surina asked. "Is there a time limit?"

A new solemnness filled Hannah's eyes. "There's a time limit for me," she said quietly. "I'm . . . dying. I know I've been In Wupatki for a long time. I feel like a mummy, like . . . the water has been squeezed from my body, and my insides are drying up and slowing down, and they won't last much longer."

"We'll get you out, Hannah," Dominic assured her. "If Surina knows how to open the sun gate, shouldn't we just go there?"

"No," Hannah said. "If I don't solve Ophiuchus first . . . ." She hesitated. "Just trust me: Ophiuchus has to be opened first. Now that you're here, I know what to do."

The group walked in silence for a while, and then they settled into a comfortable chatter. Dominic and Hannah reminisced about the adventures they'd shared, and Surina explained how the realms had been different for her: Leo had been a dangerous court with collapsing floors, while Gemini, rather than a meandering path over gentle hills, had featured narrow walkways over boiling rivers of lava.

Greg began to relax. He still looked pale and anxious, but a glint of interest came into his eye, and he joined the conversation in bursts of eager speech. He even let Hannah walk where he could see her. "So, these places change," he said. "We could come back here later, and it would be different?"

"I'm telling you, these places get ideas from us," Surina said. "I started telling Wibben about the obstacle

39

courses I did back home, and suddenly we were faced with a series of obstacle courses—but that's not going to happen this time," she added quickly. "This time, it's going to be easy. Right, everyone?"

"What kind of obstacle courses?" Greg asked. "Were you training for the Marines?"

"No, I mean like mud runs. They're obstacle courses, but they're supposed to be fun."

"Oh yeah, I've done one of those," he said. "I did the Zombie Run. I actually had a great time. We had to wear a belt with three flags attached to it, and there were zombies lurking all along the route, and they chased us and tried to capture our flags."

"Greg," Surina began.

"The zombies at the beginning act really slow and decrepit, like the *Night of the Living Dead* zombies, but the closer you get to the finish, the more aggressive they are; they're more the *I Am Legend* type. And if they capture all three of your flags, it means—"

"Greg!" Surina cut in. "Don't talk about zombies! I'm saying that your thoughts can come true here. When I started telling Wibben about the obstacle course, suddenly we had to do *those* particular obstacles—and they were not fun. It's like the Stay-Puft Marshmallow Man—have you seen *Ghostbusters*?"

"Yeah, of course."

"It's like when Ray thinks of the Stay-Puft Marshmallow Man, and suddenly it appears, except it's giant and shooting flames from its mouth. That's how this place works. So, let's not manifest any zombies."

"Let's think about things that are easy and nice," Dominic said. "Like, this one time I crossed a flat, boring plain, and it was only a quarter of a mile long. And my feet were tired, but a kind person came along and carried me piggy-back."

"Don't say that, either," Surina replied. "Last time,

Wibben had to carry me piggy-back—blindfolded, across a lava pit."

"Right. Never mind the piggy-back, then."

"So," Greg said, "we have twelve of these places to get through?"

"We can skip some of them if we use the sleigh," Hannah said. "But I *did* put riddles at all of . . . ." She trailed off, coming to a sudden halt. Her lanky griffin body stood tense and still. "Stop," she hissed.

Dominic stopped. "What's the matter?" he asked, but no sooner had he spoken than he saw what had caught Hannah's attention. Ahead, the ground gave way to a gently rushing river—the Eridanus—and on its bank, a child was crouched, a bedraggled figure dressed from the waist down in a tattered white cloth. The child faced the river, so that nothing of its head was visible except for a shock of blue-black hair.

"Let's go a different way," Hannah said, beckoning the group as she retreated. They followed obediently. When the child was out of view, she added: "We can head toward Aries, and try sneaking around the Taurus realm the long way. There's a small land bar over there, between the ocean and the river. Tagua's people rarely ever go there. They're afraid of Cetus, the sea-monster. We can try to cross the river and get to Orion through Lepus."

Greg spoke up: "Who was that kid?"

"It's not really a kid anymore," Hannah replied. "That's one of Tagua's minions. Some of them crossed over with him, and some were captured later, but they all look like that: Blue skin, dressed in rags, blank stares. If you see them, stay hidden."

"Blank stairs?" Greg repeated.

"Yes. Their eyes . . . they just look empty, like they don't have a thought in their heads. They're probably scouting for Tagua."

"Are they looking for us?" Surina asked.

41

"They're probably looking for *anyone*. Tagua needs to feed on other people's energy, and he's becoming weak. Instead of keeping people in his realm at Lupus and draining them, he's been sending them out to catch fresh newcomers—and there aren't as many minions at Lupus now. A lot of those kids are gone."

"Gone where?" Dominic asked.

"I don't know. Just gone, like they faded into nothing. Tagua used them up."

Greg's eyes had that panicked look again. "If he catches us," he said in a strained voice, "could that happen to us?"

"It could," Hannah admitted. "But I don't think that's what will happen." She cast an admiring look at her companions. "We have a good team. We didn't even fight in Gemini. I think we'll make it home."

Greg glanced back toward Gemini, as if he was considering making a run back to the entrance. Dominic was about to make a snarky comment about Greg's commitment to the "team," but instead he said: "Greg, do you know much about the zodiac?"

"We don't really use the zodiac in my culture," Greg replied. "The stars are grouped differently."

"Navajo culture, right?" Dominic asked. "Hannah's dad is Navajo."

"I call us Diné rather than Navajo." Greg glanced at Hannah with reluctant interest and added: "You must know about Diné star cycles."

"No," Hannah admitted. "I used to read a lot of books about Greek mythology, so a lot of the riddles I solved were based on Greek myths."

"I wonder how Greek mythology became so popular," Greg mused. "I mean, Greece isn't huge; it was just some coastal areas and a collection of tiny islands. I suppose it's because they were a literary culture. Their stories spread along with their philosophy and politics." He straightened up suddenly, and his voice became even more enthused. "We have a 'hero twins' star myth, but the stars are in Taurus, not Gemini. And the Pleiades are the 'planting stars,' because their cycle marks the planting season. Most of our constellations are related to planting, hunting, and ceremonial cycles, or they're a reminder of some kind of core value. The hero twins are usually depicted as having complementary values: one is fierce warrior who slays monsters and protects the people, and the other is a gentle one who heals and helps others. The idea is that humans need both qualities, in balance."

"You must be feeling better, Greg," Dominic said. He gave Surina a wily glance. "If you know as much about Navajo star myths as you know about rocks and calcium, you could keep us entertained all the way around the zodiac."

"You're actually doing a much better job than Dominic did on his first time," Hannah assured Greg. "He kept crying because he thought he was dead."

"I didn't cry," Dominic refuted. "At least, not in front of you."

"Well, you whined a lot."

"So did you."

"Fine," Hannah said, "but you're a grown-up."

The banter continued as the foursome approached Aries. Greg relaxed and joined in, and soon he was giving an enthusiastic lecture about his studies at Wupatki, the Painted Desert's geological record that spanned hundreds of millions of years, and the weather processes that created Devil's Bridge. He was still talking when, at the far edge of Taurus, the group came upon another small, round portal in the brick wall. Surina climbed inside first.

"How does it look over there?" Dominic called when she was through.

"Bad," she said.

He paused, having just climbed into the tunnel. "In

what way?"

"We have our first real challenge."

Dominic followed her with heightened anxiety, helping Greg to maneuver the wooden plank between them through the portal. He tried not to look at the landscape until he was finished, but upon exiting, he couldn't help noticing the sudden disappearance of the ground ahead and the two narrow bridges running side by side across the chasm.

"I see what you mean," he said, turning to look at the scene ahead of them. A deep, narrow valley cut through landscape, its sides a mass of red rock. "Not the flat, boring route I hoped for." His gaze fell on a wooden signpost in the foreground. From where he stood, he could see letters scrawled across it.

The group gathered close to Surina as she read aloud:

To Aries, the effulgent one
who serves each cycle like the sun:
born to live a day, and die
to show you stories in the sky,
then rise and grant another turn
to light the world with what you learned.

A Monster Slayer climbed the wall,
and looking down on Yeitso, saw
it's not so giant after all—
while to the blessed other one,
led by the light of Father Sun,
were shown the keys to dominion.

Hero twins may pass this way,
one on each path; all else stay,

or move to avoid collapse:
swimming, flight, or piggy-back.

Surina muttered under her breath. "Piggy-back," she read aloud. "Let this be a lesson on shutting our faces."

"It sounds like it's about the hero twins," Greg said. "Nayenezgáni and Tobadzischini—Monster Slayer and Born for Water. Their father was the sun. They found a way to meet him, and then they climbed back down and slayed the monsters of Earth. The most dangerous one was Yeitso, the giant."

Dominic re-read the poem carefully. "Okay, let's solve it. It sounds like it's just a direction set. Right? Hero twins may pass, one on each path . . . all else stay." He paused. "It sounds like only two of us can cross. The rest have to stay here, or . . . move to avoid collapse?"

"It means the bridges will collapse if there's more than one person walking on them," Surina said with exasperation. "It's the same kind of thing I had to do last time. I shouldn't have mentioned it, or even thought about it."

"I can fly over," Hannah said. "Flight is one of the options. Sorry, but I'm too weak to carry anyone piggy-back."

Dominic moved close to the edge of the drop. As he approached, vague sounds of scraping and popping reached his ears, and he tensed, anticipating that he would look down to see a mass of blank-eyed children scuttling up from below. He let out a burst of dry laughter as the bottom came into view: a red and black mass, a slowly swirling lake of what looked like molten lava. "Well, no one's going to swim in lava," he said, "and we're not leaving anyone behind—so, one of us has to ride piggy-back."

On either side of him, two narrow stone bridges stretched across the chasm, close and not quite parallel. Each was just wide enough for one person to walk comfortably. Something about the hue of the red stone, and the way the underlying rock arched beneath it, seemed familiar.

"They look just like Devil's Bridge," Greg said. "Except . . . look how thin they are in the middle. That rock must only be a couple feet deep."

"Yeah," Dominic replied dryly. "Devil's Bridge. The thing you were just talking about. Imagine that."

"Dominic, I'll carry you," Surina offered. She came to stand beside him, looking with displeasure at the view below.

He gave her a doubtful once-over. "Are you sure? Honestly, you're not that much bigger than I am."

"Greg already has his hands full." Surina crouched and waved her hand, gesturing for Dominic to climb on. "Come on. Let's not waste time."

She tested his weight on her back and found it not too burdensome. Greg held back at first, firing off questions about the bridges: *Will they hold up in the middle? How do you know? Is that really lava? It doesn't feel hot . . . okay, now I can feel the heat. Are you sure we should go this way? Are you sure??*

They lured him onward, Surina with reassurance, Dominic with impatience. They began to cross, Surina carefully treading one bridge with Dominic on her back, and Greg opposite her, a vague heat emanating up from the molten lake and seeping into their skin.

"Do we really need this wood?" Greg asked. "It's hard to see where I'm walking with this thing in the way."

"We want Hannah to live, so yes, we need it," Surina replied.

"I actually used to be really afraid of heights." Greg took a careful step forward, exploring the bridge with his foot before shifting his weight. "It's the reason I started rock climbing; I thought it would help me get over my fear. I've never even crossed Devil's Bridge before; I went there when I was a teenager, but I wouldn't set foot on it because I was terrified that someone would push me off, and there would be no safety rope to catch me. So, this is kind of a big deal. I'm just telling myself that this is a dream, so if I fall, it doesn't matter. Maybe it will help me in real life."

"That's the spirit," Dominic said.

Greg chuckled nervously. He moved another few steps. "Surina, I guess this makes us hero twins."

"Does it?" Surina asked, her eyes locked on the stone path. She, too, was moving slowly, inching forward in micro-steps.

"You know, because we're walking the twin paths." Greg glanced at Dominic. "Sorry, Dominic. If I hadn't tagged along and butted in, then of course, you would be the hero twin."

"I'm fine right here," Dominic replied. "I'm lounging with my arms around a beautiful woman, and you're hugging a piece of wood."

"Guys, stop distracting me," Surina said. "Greg, watch

where you're walking."

"I am," Greg insisted—but at that moment he stumbled, half-dropping to the stone floor as he tried to steady himself.

Surina stood frozen as Greg regained his footing. Dominic heard her take a few ragged breaths, and then she called: "Are you all right?"

"There's a little ridge here, and I stubbed my toe. I couldn't see it because of this damned plank."

"Just go slowly," Surina said.

Greg didn't argue. Nor did he move. While Surina advanced, he stayed behind. Dominic glanced back and saw him staring across the bridge, his eyes glazed with fear.

"You're fine, Greg," Dominic called. "Just focus on taking one step."

"This thing is going to make me fall," Greg said—and then the broken hull slipped from his grasp.

He stared over the ledge as the chunk of wood slapped into the surface of the volcanic stew below; the wood made a hissing, splintering sound, and its edges emitted flame. Surina heard it and came to a halt.

"I dropped the wood," Greg said, a tremor in his voice.

"Greg!" Surina cried. "Why did you do that?"

"It's probably for the best," Greg insisted.

"It's not for the best! Now we'll have to go all the way around the zodiac!"

"Guys," Dominic interjected, but he went silent as a strange jolt went through Surina's body—as though she had somehow been thrown off-balance, even though she hadn't moved. A burst of cracking sounds thundered around them. Dominic watched as the edges of the bridge came loose up ahead, breaking away in chunks, hurtling into the fiery pool in a series of loud splashes.

Surina gasped. Her hands, which had been grasping Dominic's legs, released them and shot out at her sides as she struggled for balance. "The bridge moved!" she cried.

"You two, don't start arguing," Dominic said sharply. "Our first riddle said that hero twins have to move in balanced kinship, or despair."

"I didn't drop the wood on purpose," Greg said. "It just . . . ."

"It's all right," Dominic assured him. "The riddle said the hull would be reduced—and now it's reduced. It didn't actually say that we were going to fly to Ophiuchus. I think we're fine, so let's just focus on getting across."

Surina began to walk again, shakily. Dominic heard her whisper: "I hate this place." He felt her body beginning to tremble; he heard her feet dragging against the bridge.

She stopped. "Damn!"

"What is it?"

"The bridge collapsed!"

"What do you mean?"

"In the middle—there's a gap!"

Dominic took a second to calm his own strain of panic. Over her shoulder, he saw the same sight: a break in the thin rock, a jagged opening that hadn't been there before. "Keep going," he said. "It doesn't look that big. You can probably step over it."

Anxious seconds passed as Surina moved gingerly toward the gap. She inched forward until she stood nearly at the edge.

"It's not that big," Dominic assured her. "Just take a big step, and you'll be over it."

"Okay," she said, but didn't move.

Dominic waited . . . and waited. "Surina," he said, "Just go. We're fine, remember?"

"Hang on tight to me. I need to let go of your legs."

Dominic tightened his legs around Surina's sides. With a grunt of effort, she lunged forward. The bridge held steady as she came down on the other side of the gap.

"You're past the toughest part," Dominic said, trying to encourage her. Surina's whole body trembled, and he could feel the increasing unsteadiness of her gait.

"Dominic," she said, "it's too thin up ahead. Parts of the bridge must have fallen off. It's like . . . a balance beam."

Dominic kept his voice calm. "Well, you're the expert on obstacle courses. How do you solve it?"

"Uh . . . there is a way." Surina looked for Greg, her cheek brushing against Dominic's face as she turned her head. Greg kept pace with her on the other bridge; his path, too, had become warped and narrow, and he walked with his arms spread at his sides.

"Greg," Surina said, "We need to hold hands."

A droplet of sweat fell from his nose. "Why?" he asked, without taking his eyes off the path. "That seems dangerous."

"Look ahead. Both of our bridges are thinning out; they're going to be hard to cross. If we hold hands, it will help us keep our balance."

Greg maintained his doubt. "What if you push me?"

"I won't. Trust me on this, okay? I've done this before." Surina took a deep breath. Slowly, keeping one hand clasped beneath Dominic's thigh, she stretched the other toward Greg.

"Okay," he breathed. "Just a dream. Just a dream." He took her hand, but said: "Don't pull on me."

"I won't pull. That's better, isn't it?"

"Yeah . . . actually, yeah," Greg conceded.

"We have to match our steps," Surina said. "I'll get a rhythm going. When I say 'left,' start with your left foot, and then I'll say 'right.' Like this: 'Left, right, left, right.' Got it?"

Greg agreed, and they started off, matching their steps as Surina counted *left, right, left, right* almost all the way to the opposite side. By supporting each other, they made it past the most dangerous part of the bridge. Dominic felt Surina beginning to relax as the path widened and flattened out. The gap between the bridges also widened, so that Surina and Greg were forced to release each other, unable to reach across the chasm.

As she approached the far side, Surina tensed again. "The bridge is tilted," she said.

"I see that," Dominic replied, "but it's barely tilted. Just keep walking."

"My legs are shaking so much." Surina drew in a short, gasping breath. "Dominic, I'm going to fall."

"No, you're—"

"I'm really going to fall," Surina said. "I need to . . . ."

"Just take another step," Dominic prodded her—but she leaned forward, and Dominic realized she was sinking toward the bridge.

Hannah, waiting on the opposite side, shouted: "Dominic! Keep your feet up! Don't touch the bridge!"

Surina's knees slammed onto the walkway. She stayed like that for some time, on her hands and knees, with Dominic clinging to her back. Over her shoulder, he saw the dark red sludge and black ash moving far below; he felt its heat on his face, and he became hyper-aware of his flimsy grasp on Surina's shoulders and the pull of gravity on his torso. Surina inched forward, and he slid ever so slightly to the right, and then slightly again. Slowly, he moved his feet to grip Surina's sides.

"I'm going to crawl the rest of the way," she said. "Just try to keep your legs away from the bridge."

"Whatever works," he replied. He fixed his attention on Hannah, on the scent of Surina's shampoo—anything but the acrid smell of lava and the dangerous tilt of the bridge.

Again, he waited, but Surina didn't move.

"Surina," he said, "this is a really awkward position we're in. I would really like to not be in this position. Can you just go?"

Slowly, shakily, she made the painstaking trek toward land, while Hannah shouted encouragements and Dominic offered calm reassurances. Soon, the bridge was behind her; soft sands welcomed her knees and hands, but Surina kept crawling.

"That's far enough," Dominic said, releasing her shoulders and sliding off. "You're well onto land now." He rolled onto his back, bringing his hands up to cover his face. "Good lord," he said, his voice muffled behind his palms.

Surina stayed a moment more, arms shaking beneath her; then she collapsed on her side.

"I hate this place," she moaned. She looked at Dominic and added: "Sorry."

He uncovered his face. "That's okay. That actually could have been a lot more awkward, if I hadn't been consumed by terror." He flashed a smile at Surina. "It's like I said: This place is helping us." Dominic got to his feet and found that only Hannah stood beside him. Greg, like Surina, had chosen to finish the crossing on hands and knees—but now, staring down into the lava, he seemed frozen with fear.

"Keep going, Greg," Dominic called. "You're almost across. Just a few more yards."

"The bridge is tilted," Greg said. "I can't keep my balance. When I move my hands . . . ."

"It's because you're panicking. Just take a breath and relax. You're the hero twin, remember? Monster Slayer doesn't fall off bridges. He gets himself together and goes for the goal."

"I'm more like Born for Water," Greg said.

"Okay . . . well . . . Born for Water does stuff, too." Dominic looked to Hannah for help.

"You're supposed to have Monster Slayer and Born for Water in balance," Hannah said. "You're not just one. You're both."

Greg didn't move.

"Look up," Hannah said. "Quit looking at the lava. It looks far away, but if you look forward, you only have a little ways to go."

He lifted his head, and she continued: "See? It's a tiny

distance. Monster Slayer climbed the wall, and looking down on . . . whatever, saw it's not so giant after all. It's just a few more feet. No big deal. You'll be across in a minute."

Greg's hand slid forward.

A minute later he had, indeed, finished the journey; Dominic and Hannah received him with applause as he splayed out on the sand. "That was a lot harder than I thought it would be," he said. "I couldn't watch the ground without seeing the lava on both sides, and the whole time, I felt like I was going to fall."

"You did well," Dominic said. "Both of you."

Greg got to his feet, looking remorsefully at Hannah—only for a moment, though, and then he winced at the sight of her and lowered his eyes. "Sorry about the wood," he said.

Hannah tried to sound cheerful, but her already ashen face seemed haunted by a new exhaustion. "It's all right. We'll still get there."

Dominic placed a reassuring hand on the soft fur of her forearm. "This is actually a good sign," he said. "The riddle told us to bring the wood to a glen, and look: we just crossed over a glen. We did what we were supposed to do. Virgo said we would eventually make it home, and from what I've seen, she's always right."

The anxiety faded from Hannah's eyes, and she smiled.

"We're in Taurus," Surina said suddenly, sitting up. "Right? That seemed very much like a Gemini obstacle. Isn't Taurus supposed to be about facing the bull?"

Dominic shrugged. "Just because we're not in Gemini, it doesn't mean the lesson doesn't apply. Even after we go home, we still need to work together. Maybe that's the reminder we needed; it might keep us out of trouble up ahead."

Greg stopped brushing the sand from his clothes. He looked questioningly at Surina. "What do you mean by 'facing the bull'?"

Surina struggled to explain, and Hannah answered instead: "Taurus usually makes you face your fears, or tests you in some way, so you can get some sort of lesson or courage from it. Sometimes, you don't realize the lesson until later." She patted the fleshy pocket beneath her forearm. "I got what I needed here. In the constellations, Taurus is a bull, and Orion is the one who faces the bull and obtains the seven stars of the Pleiades. I failed last time, but I learned my lesson, and now I have what I needed. When you've gone around the zodiac enough times, you start to see a theme for each place. Gemini is usually about learning to work with someone who's different from you, and achieving balance together—like the hero twins you talked about. Aries is next, and it's usually about . . . self-sacrifice, or taking risks for other people. That sweater you're wearing came from Aries. The Aries ram sacrificed itself to keep us safe; it gave us clothes, and food, and other tools that helped us get through the zodiac."

A surge of emotion showed in Greg's eyes—sentimentality, perhaps, or maybe grief, because he suddenly seemed on the verge of tears. He turned away, gazing out across the bridges. "I'm definitely facing my fears," he said quietly. "I did something really stupid when I was at Devil's Bridge—in real life, I mean. I was there with my family, and . . . I have a younger sister who's like my complete opposite; she's little, she has trouble walking because of a malformed femur, but she's full of energy and not afraid of anything. She wanted me to go out on Devil's Bridge with her, and she offered to hold my hand because she knew I was scared. She's, like, half my size, and much younger, but she was offering to help *me*. I was embarrassed, so I threw a tantrum and complained that she was pestering me; I went back to the car by myself, supposedly because my sister was so annoying." He laughed. "That's, like, a major flaw that I have. I'm a coward, and sometimes I've tried to hide it by pointing my finger at other people. I don't like being up high without a rope and a harness; I was just able to cross the bridge this time because I think this is just a dream. One of those long, detailed dreams that's so long, you tell yourself: 'This can't be a dream; it's gone on for too long,' but then you wake up. This place doesn't feel real; there's no wind, no sun, no life. There's just a blank blue sky, and light coming from who knows where. That's how I know it's a dream. It's just one of those really long ones."

"That's not a bad way to look at it," Dominic said. "Let's get to the Aries part of your dream. We still have a long way to go before you can wake up."

Ahead of them, on the right, was the wall that surrounded the Taurus realm, and on the left was the ocean. Dominic saw its silver-blue hue on the horizon and heard its gentle rushing as he drew closer. He listened to the rhythmic lapping of waves on the beach and remembered, with a slight shudder, his journey through the ocean deep.

"We can cross the river up there," Hannah said, gesturing. "If we keep walking between Taurus and Cetus, we'll get to Eridanus."

"What's that?" Greg asked, pointing straight ahead.

"It's the exit. We're just cutting through a small corner of Aries, so we're already near the end of it. Taurus, Cetus, and Aries intersect right up there."

Dominic didn't know at first what Greg was pointing to, but after a moment he saw it: a low mound in the distance, a tan-hued structure camouflaged against the sandy backdrop. "What kind of exit?" he asked Hannah. "Have you been there before?"

"Yes," she replied. "I put a riddle there. It's where Aries ends, and the other realms begin."

4: Aries

Surina supposed that the group would make a quick journey through Aries, seeing as how they had already reached the border. She was gravely mistaken.

The sandy-colored structure, on closer observance, was made of stone—all a uniform shade, with no cobbling or visible crevices anywhere on its surface. There was, however, a circular entrance in the front; the interior was shadowed and thus remained a mystery. The ocean closed in on the left, and the wall of Taurus on the right, so that the travelers were essentially being funneled into the building.

Some distance in front of it was a wooden post, identical to the one in Gemini, with a scrap of papyrus mailed to its top—identical except that it bore a different message.

Hannah took the scrap in her hand and read aloud.

Labor number three: Be the deer of Artemis who in the stars runs free; from Eurystheus's grasp the hind shall swiftly flee. Also in his grasp will wither seven dwindling flames; preserve or extinguish through auspicious, ancient games.

"These are definitely the labors of Hercules," Dominic said. "In the Greek myth, King Eurystheus commanded Hercules to finish twelve labors, and one of them was something about a magical hind."

"A magical hind?" Surina repeated.

"A deer."

"Okay. So, does anyone see a deer? Or seven flames?"

"I see a lot of water and sand," Greg replied, "and whatever that is." He pointed to the stone structure. "Should we check it out?"

"It looks like we'll have to," Surina said. After a moment, she added: "It doesn't tell us to find a deer. It says we have to *be* the deer."

"Let's hope we don't have to take that literally," Dominic replied. "Becoming other creatures . . . isn't my favorite thing to do."

Hannah deflected from the group. "I'm going to take a look," she said, and before Surina could ask where she was going, her arms shot out at her sides, spreading her wings wide and lifting off from the ground with a great wind.

Surina watched as she circled above, her wings spread straight as she made slow, graceful arcs.

Hannah descended again, landing a few yards away. "It's the same as how I left it," she said breathlessly. Surina could see an excited light in Hannah's eyes. "There's an exit on the other side. When you look at it from the sky, it's shaped like a ram's head." She pointed at the entrance. "This is the tip of its horn."

"Let's go," Surina said, and led the way inside. "Watch out for something that looks like a deer or an ancient game—and for Tagua's spies."

They moved slowly through the tunnel, letting their eyes adjust to the dark, quickening their pace when they saw light ahead. The shelter opened to a wide central court with gold and vermilion pillars—pillars that held up no ceiling, instead pointing to open sky. The walls were likewise painted in shades of gold, vermilion, and aqua, with blooming plants and stylized waves springing along the bottom in sets of three, and spiral and flower designs along the upper cornices. Constellation-themed images adorned the walls: a human jumping over a bull, a dark-haired figure carrying a water vessel, a woman holding a long snake in each hand like a pair of staffs. The floor was painted in the same hues, and along the middle was a series of square blocks, each painted with a particular motif: an eight-petaled rosette, or a group of dots on a patterned background. The blocks comprised a platform that stood about a foot higher than the floor. At its head, on the far wall, an intricate relief sculpture had been carved: that of a ram.

The figure stood upright on its hind legs, and in one hoofed foreleg it held a thin stem with eight branches; two of those blossomed with eight-petaled rosettes, and the rest had young buds at the tips. The figure itself wore a simple tunic, painted in a dull off-white shade, but its body and horns were a sleek, shiny black, and a pair of gold-feathered wings shone at its sides. Its hooves and the area around its eyes, likewise, were a brilliant gold.

Greg was murmuring softly, studying the paintings with intense fascination. As the group gathered near the ram, he leaned close to Surina and whispered: "It's a magical deer."

She turned her face slightly toward him. "It's a ram," she replied. "Why are you whispering?"

"I don't know. I'm afraid of waking it up. Doesn't it look like it's alive?"

Surina studied the figure's face. Its eyes were half-closed, and the eyes themselves were a solid black, but still she could see an expression there—one of peace, of silent meditation.

"It's the closest thing to a deer I can see," Dominic said. He gestured to the platform. "What do you make of this?"

Greg answered without hesitation: "It's the Royal Game of Ur."

"What's that?"

Greg opened his mouth to answer, but another voice

sounded in reply: "A game of strategy and luck—much like the game you've been playing ever since you arrived here."

Hannah tensed. She reached out and grasped Dominic's arm.

A man's voice had spoken. Surina saw no one, but after a moment, someone emerged from the opposite tunnel—not a man, but a child, a slow and scrawny creature dressed in rags. Surina's breath caught at the sight of its face: gaunt and tinged with a dark shade of blue, its eyes expressionless and completely black, like those of a beetle.

Another figure emerged, this one taller—and then another, and another, all disheveled and seemingly starved, all with the same blank face and solid black eyes. One even lacked a tunic, clad instead in a ragged wrap around its pelvis. Seven such figures came from the corridor. Behind this group, Surina supposed, was Tagua—and this time she wasn't mistaken.

Though she had never seen him before, Surina recognized him at once. He was tall—much taller than the scrawny children, and though he was pale, he didn't have the same malnourished frame or emptiness in his gaze. He was dressed in a deep purple robe, and though the whites of his eyes were stained a dark color, Surina could see shrewdness in his gaze, which fell immediately on her as he emerged.

He walked slowly, with a silent step, never taking his eyes from her as he entered the court. No one else moved; the children stayed at the far end of the room, and Surina's companions seemed frozen to the spot. Surina glanced at the other corridor and wondered if the four of them might escape. There were eight in Tagua's party, but his seven minions didn't look particularly strong.

"There's no point in running away," Tagua said, as if reading Surina's mind. "I'm not here to cause any harm.

In fact, I think we might help each other."

He spoke calmly, but his voice seemed to pierce through the chamber. As he came closer, Hannah took a few steps forward, moving between Tagua and her friends.

The pale, purple-robed specter kept coming, until at last he stood face to face with Hannah. In griffin form, she was tall, so that she nearly stood eye to eye with him.

He took the scrap of paper from her hand. He read it quietly, and then he lifted his gaze to Hannah and waved the paper between the two of them. "Are you not tired of petty riddles?" he asked. "Riddles that go in useless circles, and never lead to freedom or power? *I* am tired." He handed the scrap back to Hannah. "I have no interest in capturing a dumb animal that only panics and flees. Instead, I have a fair proposal."

"What is your proposal this time?" Hannah asked softly.

"Someone in this chamber has something that I want. I propose that you share it with me. So many lives are at stake; they are draining away as I speak."

Dominic moved to stand beside Hannah. "And if we don't?" he asked. "Are you going to throw us in a cage, like last time?"

"I realize that was not the best strategy," Tagua replied, looking down at Dominic, "but desperate times call for desperate acts. I hope that I won't need to resort to such an extreme this time around." Tagua gestured to Surina. "This person, it seems, knows the key to free my people from imprisonment. Hannah has given me this simple lead, but it seems she can do no more than that. I want the key that will liberate us."

Surina's gaze flicked to Hannah, who stood tensely between her and Tagua. Had Hannah told him? No—he had spies, and supposedly could see into other realms; he must have found out in some other way.

"I don't know it," Surina said.

"It doesn't surprise me to hear you say that." Tagua half-turned to the scrawny figures behind him. "I must advise you to rethink your reply. You see these people here; their time in the celestial realm is turning them into, for lack of a better term, demons. This place pretends to be full of keys to knowledge, but for everyone who has entered, it has been nothing more than a place of suffering. It eats away at you, gives you hope and crushes that hope. It gives you puzzles that lead to ever more complex puzzles, until at last the seeker goes mad. This place creates bitterness, hopelessness, spitefulness. Like everyone else, I want nothing more than a reprieve from that suffering." His eyes remained locked on Surina's as he gestured again to the blue-tinged children. "They are dying. It isn't just a mortal death. Their souls are dying. When they dissipate, will you congratulate yourself for holding out?"

Surina mulled over a response, but Hannah spoke up: "This place doesn't destroy souls. It renews them." Her voice was resolute, but Surina could hear a vague trembling in it. "Some other force causes their souls to dissipate. It seems to me that the person responsible for their mortal deaths is also the one who would use and kill them in the celestial realm—twice for his own gain."

Surina looked at Hannah in surprise. She seemed, for a moment, not the lost eleven-year-old they had come to rescue, but someone older and wiser. *Someone who has spent an age in the celestial realm.*

Tagua's eyes seemed to become darker. His face remained impassive, though, and his voice was steady when he replied. "Perhaps there is a peaceful way to resolve our dispute."

Dominic asked: "What do you suggest?"

"A game." Tagua smiled—an almost warm smile, as if he was doing his best to feign a friendly air. "There are

63

one or two in your group who seem to have a talent for puzzles and strategy. I'll make you a deal: If your team wins at Aasha, then I will withdraw back to Lupus, and you may pass freely to the next realm. If my team finishes first, your stragglers must join my team."

"Stragglers?" Surina repeated.

Greg, standing beside her, answered. "He means . . . he wants to play this." He pointed to the platform with its decorated squares. "A team wins by getting all their players across the board first. He's saying that he's going to take the players on our team who don't make it across."

"Ah," Dominic said bitterly. "So we might get the cage after all."

"It is my only fair offer," Tagua said crisply. "Note that you only have four players, and you need seven to cross the board. You must choose three people in your party who will cross the board twice. And I have a condition, to make it truly fair. Hannah should be playing for my team, according to the contract she made—but since you would be even more outnumbered, I will make you a deal. Hannah will play for your team, but if I capture her at the end of the game, you will let me trade her for anyone in your company."

"That's a fair offer?" Dominic asked.

"Take it or leave it. My next offer won't grant you the same odds. After all, I have a greater purpose to tend to."

Dominic tugged on Hannah's arm. He gestured for the group to draw back and gathered them near the ram statue, saying: "Give us a minute." When they were huddled some distance from Tagua, he asked in a low voice: "Does anyone know how to play this game?"

"I do," Greg replied. "It's the Royal Game of Ur. I played it in college, when I took a course on ancient Mesopotamia."

"I played it at school, too," Surina said, "but it's been a while. I don't really remember the rules."

"It's a strategy game," Greg continued. "The goal is to get your team across the board first. You have to watch what the other players do, and figure out the best time to put your own players on the board. And you have to figure out when to move them in and out of the safe zones."

Dominic mulled that over. "How good are you at this game? Can you strategize well enough to get Surina and Hannah across the board first?"

"I think so."

Surina was studying the designs on the raised platform, trying to remember the game she had played more than two years ago. "Get the ladies across first, huh?" she murmured. "How gentleman-like."

"I'm not being a gentleman," Dominic said. "It's strategic. He wants you, so we should get you across first. If he gets Hannah, he'll be able to trade her for you." He looked apologetically at Hannah. "Sorry if that sounds cold, but I'm hoping to get us all home safely."

"It doesn't matter," Hannah said softly. "Even if we lose, I think I know what to do."

"If he wants Surina," Greg said, "we should only send her across once. Everyone else can go twice, and I'll prioritize Hannah." He cast a nervous glance at Tagua's solemn group, who stood staring at them from across the court. "I . . . can go last." Greg uttered the words as if he was choking on them.

"So, should we go for it?" Dominic asked. "I think the alternative is getting dragged back to Lupus by those things."

"They're not 'things,'" Hannah countered. "But, yes. Let's play." She lowered her voice again, so that Surina strained to hear her. "Don't worry. Even if he wins, he won't win."

"All right." Dominic gave Greg a light, encouraging slap on the arm. "You seem to know the most, so just tell

65

us what to do."

Greg nodded. He turned to Tagua and started to speak, but suddenly he ducked his head. "Um," he murmured to Hannah, "so . . . just tell him yeah, it's a deal."

Hannah looked in Tagua's direction. "It's a deal," she said impassively.

"Excellent." Again, Tagua's lips flicked into a brief grin. "Let's begin." He went to the end of the platform and placed his foot against the side. Surina heard a small *click*, and then Tagua was reaching down, withdrawing a handful of large black stones, sleek and pyramid-like. She realized that he had opened a compartment inside of the platform. The polyhedrons were placed on top of the platform, and Tagua withdrew another handful and brought them to the other side. "Here are your die," he said. "Take them and make your first throw. Whoever gets the highest number can enter the board first."

Greg picked up the black stones—four of them—and brought them back to the group. On closer view, Surina saw that they weren't a solid black; some of the tips were painted white. "Every white tip means a square," Greg explained quietly. "However many white tips are facing up when you roll, that's how many squares a player can move. If you can, you usually want to land on a rosette." He gestured to a square on the board, one painted with a stylized eight-petaled flower. "This lane, over here, is our side of the board. The middle is a shared lane. If you're in the middle and someone lands on your square, you're out—unless you're on the rosette." He pointed to the one flower in the central lane. "That's a safe zone."

"But," Dominic said, "what about the two rosettes on our side of the board? If the other team can't land there, what's the point of having a safe zone?"

Memories began to click into place. Surina answered: "If you land on a rosette, your team gets to roll again. It gives you a chance to get across the board faster."

66

"Ah. Okay. What about the other symbols?"

"You don't need to know them—not for the game we're playing," Greg replied.

"You're sure?" Dominic asked doubtfully.

Greg nodded. "I'll roll." He held the four die up and "shook" them, though they were too large to tumble in his hands. Rather, Greg's hands trembled, and then he gave the stone die a toss onto the floor. Three of the polyhedrons landed with a white tip facing up.

Tagua's tallest minion rolled for the other team. They scored lower, but Tagua simply smiled and said, "Your move."

Again, his gaze flicked to Surina. She resisted a shudder.

Greg's next roll was a two. Surina climbed onto the platform first, moving to the second square. Its surface was painted with five circles—one in the center, and one in each of the four corners. Though Greg had said she didn't have to know the meaning, she eyed it with the uneasy certainty that in this realm, everything had significance.

Tagua's first player moved onto the third square on the opposite side: a square with what looked like two sets of staring eyes. Greg rolled another two and beckoned Surina to stand on the rosette. Her team got another roll; they scored a one, and Hannah moved onto the board. It didn't seem a bad start.

Tagua moved the next player onto the board at square one, and with the next roll, Greg sent Surina to the middle lane. Everyone else on her team stayed in place while she advanced across the board, first by three squares, then four, then one, then two. This last move brought her to another rosette, and her team rolled again.

A score of three brought Dominic onto the board, ahead of Hannah. The game seemed to hold promise. Surina stepped off the board, and Dominic landed on a center square held by Tagua's team, sending the player back to the beginning. On Greg's next roll, he scored a two and moved Hannah onto the first rosette. He rolled again and moved her to the center lane.

One of the blue-hued children landed on a rosette, and then advanced past Hannah, landing on the central rosette. Tagua rolled a one; the scrawny child moved to Dominic's square. Before he could descend, the figure knocked him violently to the floor.

Surina helped him up. "Are you all right?"

"I should have seen that coming," he whispered, rubbing his knee. He looked anxiously at Greg.

Greg rolled a zero. The next team rolled again and knocked Hannah off the board.

The game, which at first had given Surina a feeling of hope, became a nerve-wracking trial in which fate seemed to favor Tagua one moment, and Surina and her companions the next. Hannah made it across the board on her next round and made ready to start her second. Greg, now a player, had to decide on the team's moves while crossing the board between two corpse-like children with hauntingly empty eyes and sneering, rotting mouths. Surina rolled the die, each time willing them with all of her might to roll a number that would save her friends.

Greg eventually finished crossing the board. For a moment it looked like their team was making the most headway—but Tagua still had pieces perched near at the beginning, and as soon as Hannah entered the game, they were ready to cast her out. She didn't get far. Nor did she land on the other team's players. The tattered children moved freely.

Dominic, once again cast down from the platform, joined Hanah and Surina. "Luck doesn't seem to be on our side all of a sudden," he muttered. "They get every number they need, and we're rolling a lot of zeroes."

Surina felt a sudden tug at her hand. Hannah was

beside her, staring with those strangely dark eyes—blue where they should have been white, and the large irises flecked with dark blue, brown, and gold.

Hannah leaned close and whispered: "We need to forfeit the game."

Surina paused, uncertain if she'd heard correctly. "What?"

Hannah moved closer to Surina's ear. "He's cheating," she whispered, her voice barely audible. "He's a wizard, and he uses other people's energy to manipulate things. He's using those kids. If we don't quit now, they're going to die, and Tagua will win anyway. He'll get me and trade me for you."

Surina looked across the board at Tagua, saw him standing motionless with his arms folded, his gaze fixed on her. She looked again at Hannah. It was hard to read the expression in those strange eyes—eyes that seemed to rest in the face of a lion rather than a human.

Hannah implored her quietly: "Please trust me. I won't mess up this time."

Dominic moved closer. "What's the matter?"

Hannah exchanged whispers with him, and Dominic cast a probing glance at Surina, seeming to ask a silent question. It was likely one of the same questions in Surina's mind: *Can we trust Hannah? And what will happen if I go with Tagua?* Surina didn't know the answer to either, but she nodded at Dominic and mouthed the words: "It's okay."

Reluctantly, Dominic turned to Tagua. "We're going to forfeit."

Greg, still stuck on the last square, looked at him in astonishment. "What? Hang on a second."

"No, we're going to forfeit," Surina said, her gaze locked on Tagua. "Do you accept?"

Tagua smiled, but his dark eyes remained cold and unfeeling. "It seems that fortune is in my favor. You're wise not to waste time; your chances were slim anyway. Better luck next time." He gestured to Hannah with a dismissive wave of his hand. "I will trade Hannah for Surina. The rest of you need not accompany us."

"We'll come with you," Dominic replied. "It's only fair, according to your own conditions."

Tagua replied crisply: "You are not welcome to join us."

Greg leapt down from the board and approached the group, his face drawn. "What's going on?" he whispered, but no one answered. Hannah's eyes were fixed on Tagua, and Dominic and Surina were locked in a silent exchange.

"I'll get going," Surina said.

"Don't worry," Dominic replied softly. "We won't leave without you."

"I know." Surina gave him a quick, reassuring smile and walked away. Tagua may have been sly and deceitful, but he was right about one thing: It was wise not to waste time. Hannah surely didn't have much of it left.

She had hardly rounded the board when two of Tagua's minions grabbed her, their fingers sinking uncomfortably into her forearms.

"Do you need to manhandle her like that?" Dominic asked. "It's not like she's resisting."

"We are merely providing a safe escort," Tagua replied, and commanded the others: "Take the fleece. Bring it to me."

One of the thin creatures yanked the nightgown from around Surina's waist. Tagua took it and held it at his side. "If you wish to return home," he told Dominic, "I suggest you try to make your way to the sun gate at Lupus. Once it's open, no one will have reason to stand in your way." His gaze rested on Hannah, who had followed Surina to the other side of the board.

"I'll go with you," Hannah said. "Like you said, you already captured me."

"I don't believe you'll be needed," Tagua replied. "Your friends, on the other hand, may need a guide."

Hannah was unfazed. "Well, you believe wrongly. You want to open the sun gate, and you need both me and Surina to do it."

"Is that so? How do you figure?"

"Ophiuchus needs to be solved first," Hannah said, "and it's a partner puzzle. One person has to maneuver Lyra, and keep Draco asleep, while the other person maneuvers Ophiuchus. Surina knows music, and I know Ophiuchus, so you need both of us."

Tagua's voice had a sudden, slight edge. "And since when did you know this?"

"I've learned a lot, just lately," Hannah replied. "Flight gives you perspective. You can see connections that you missed from the ground, and you can get close to things that were once too high to reach."

Surina found herself once again trying to study Hannah's face, but the griffin-girl remained unreadable. As much as Surina wanted to trust her, she felt her confidence ebbing, and a cautious urgency rising in its place.

"I'm not sure I follow," Tagua said crisply. "Why does Ophiuchus need to be opened first?"

"It's connected to the sun gate through Scorpius. The queen didn't make the sun gate easy to open; she made it complex. Bring us there, and I'll show you how it works."

Some spasm passed across Tagua's face—something like a grimace. "Very well," he said, and beckoned the group onward.

Surina cast a final anxious glance at Dominic and Greg, saw them watching gravely as she followed Tagua into the far corridor. The tunnel curved gently around and opened to a field of dust on the left, and an expanse of water on the right—likely Pisces, the realm of fish, Surina supposed.

Tagua veered onto the sandy plain. Though Surina tried to see what else marked the landscape ahead, she could only make out clouds of dust being kicked up by a sudden breeze. She raised a hand to shield her eyes, and walked in irritated silence—but then, all at once, the wind and the dust died down, and Surina stopped and gasped.

Ahead of her were three pyramids, one close by and the others at a distance—grand works of polyhedral stone, like the Egyptian pyramids she was familiar with. These structures, however, were of a sleek black stone, and they shifted in a slow defiance of gravity—turning one way, and then another, floating just above the ground as Surina watched in awe. Some of the points, she noted, were stained white, like the white-tipped die that had just fated her into Tagua's hands.

"Welcome to Triangulum," Tagua said with a grin. "The realm of human desperation and power. Do you know how ancient is the urge to know or change one's fate with a toss of bones or a handful of die, or with a message twisted into the bowels of some slaughtered creature? In old times, commoners depended on people of power to roll and interpret the die; knowing the future, they could counsel the lesser on how to stave off starvation, destruction, death. Of course, common people coveted that role." He slowed his pace and turned to Surina, who tried to mask her anxiety. "Can you guess what method they devised to cope with their powerlessness?"

"Cheating?" Surina replied.

Tagua's grin faded. "Games," he corrected her. "If it's just a game, any commoner can role the die and play with luck. It doesn't mean they have power. In fact, rolling the die often leaves them usurped and powerless. It takes a certain level of learning and commitment to achieve the abilities of a true diviner."

Though she didn't want to give him a reaction, Surina

felt herself glaring at him in disgust. She set her gaze on the shifting pyramids, but she was distracted by the movements of the scrawny child just ahead of her—the near-naked one with a cloth around its waist. The ghoulish creature stumbled suddenly, dropping to its knees and drawing in a raspy breath. Its head drew back, and its blue skin suddenly paled to a grayish hue. The arms stretched out at its sides, and as Surina watched, they became dry and leathery—no, not leathery, but grainy, as if the child was turning to a heap of dust.

Seconds later, that heap was blown apart by a sudden gust. Surina watched as the dark hair scattered and swirled away in the wind, the tiny grains scattered, and the tattered cloth tumbled across the ground.

Surina gaped at the now-empty spot where the child had knelt. She looked at Tagua in silent alarm.

"Keep going," Tagua commanded them. "We will follow the Crane's Path." As they resumed walking, he looked at Surina and added: "You probably know it as the Milky Way. If we follow it closely, we can skirt the borders of most of the realms and avoid their riddles. After your last visit here, I imagine that you are tired of the puzzles of this place—and of the deities who create them."

A plethora of snarky comments swirled in Surina's mind, but she kept quiet, looking straight ahead as she approached the field.

"You'll want to take care when we arrive at Lyra," he continued. "There is a particularly nasty dragon there—a dragon with an appetite for souls. I imagine you know the Draco constellation. If it wakes and swallows you, you'll follow its tail all the way to Ursa Minor and Polaris, the portal to human incarnation. Polaris means death," he said, looking pointedly at Surina. "In order to incarnate again as a human, your current life must end."

"It doesn't sound bad," Surina replied, though she had

meant to ignore him. "At least Draco has the decency not to destroy my soul."

Tagua let out a small, sardonic laugh. "You look young," he replied dryly, "but you will find in time that humanity has always been, and will always be, ruled by those who pursue privilege and wealth. There is no noble cause in the world that ever comes fully into power. Justice and equality are lies meant to exploit the masses and keep them powerless. It is true that I never pursued peace, and on Earth I took my throne with careful maneuverings—but I did so to create a strong people. Even in this realm, I pursue power in order to protect others." He looked grimly at Surina. "Does it sit well with you that these six will die if you refuse to open the gate?"

"They're already dead," Surina replied coolly. "Does it sit well with you that you imprisoned their souls for your own gain?"

"You are mistaken. I'm not the one who trapped them here. My only aim is to free them."

"I don't know how to solve your puzzle. That's the truth. The person who knows it is in Virgo. If you want to open the gate, you should go there."

"The realm of Virgo doesn't suit me. Perhaps you can go there in my place." Tagua's mouth pressed into a half-smile, half-grimace as he gestured to the griffin-girl walking in front of him. "Or perhaps Hannah will go to the realm of the dead. She is unlikely to survive much longer. I'm sure you've noticed."

Surina clenched her teeth in silent frustration.

"Your friend Dominic is also feeling the pangs of mortality," Tagua added. "He might have mentioned that he was struck down on his last visit. A sting from Scorpio fills the body with venom that never dissipates."

Not true, Surina assured herself. If anything, Dominic looked healthier after his trip to the stars.

Tagua continued: "All of these riddles, all of this

74

useless striving for answers, have stolen your precious time. Justice, freedom—those things are slippery and fleeting, never a surety . . . but death comes to all, my dear. This place only hastens its arrival."

That was what he said, but Surina didn't hear "my dear." What she heard instead was "my deer." And then she remembered: *Be the deer of Artemis who in the stars runs free; from Eurystheus's grasp the hind shall swiftly flee.*

In myth, Eurystheus was known as a dishonest and cowardly king, one who sent others on quests while he enjoyed the safety of his own kingdom. Surina looked at Tagua and saw the same.

"Be the deer," she whispered.

A look of puzzlement touched Tagua's face.

With a violent jolt, Surina tore her arms away from Tagua's companions. The two creatures were not very strong, but their nails tore her flesh as she broke free. One of them hissed and bit her as she began to run—but she freed herself and ran, fleeing at top speed back the way she had come, her arms flinging tiny droplets of blood.

Hannah called her name. Surina heard something frantic and pleading in that voice, but she didn't look back; she simply did what the riddle told her to do. It had been placed there for a reason. Surely it meant something.

5: Pisces

"I feel guilty," Greg said as the group disappeared through the corridor. He cast an anxious glance at Dominic. "We should follow them . . . right?"

Dominic shook his head.

"Why not?"

Dominic waited until he could no longer hear the retreating footfalls. "Hannah told me not to," he replied quietly. "She left a riddle for us at Pisces. We'll go there next." Dominic saw Greg's uncertain look and added: "I trust Hannah. She said that we can meet up with Surina when we circle back to Lupus."

"Where's that?"

"It's . . . ." Dominic sighed. "We'll get there eventually."

"Why did we forfeit the game? We still had a chance of winning."

"We didn't," Dominic replied. "Hannah said that Tagua was using those kids' vital energy to manipulate the game and cast the numbers in his favor." He paused, overcome with sudden emotion. "She forfeited to try to save those kids."

Greg hesitated. "I don't think those things are kids."

"Well, they're *something*." Dominic motioned Greg to follow him. "Let's go. We need to get through Pisces and ask Aquarius for help."

"Ask Aquarius? Like, Aquarius is a person, or . . . an oracle, or . . . ."

"Honestly, I don't know," Dominic replied.

Outside, they scanned the bland landscape: nothing but dusty land, whose dirt and grime was kicked up by the wind, and a flat sea, whose waters bore a dull gray hue in the meager light—a sharp contrast to the brightness of Gemini. The change suited Dominic's mood. He scanned the plain for Surina and the others, but they were obscured by clouds of dust.

On the coastline, near the water, a wooden structure stood alone. It was only a couple of feet high, and as Dominic moved closer, he could make out its exquisite features; it was a carving of a ram's head, with two horns that curved outward and inward again, two large round eyes, and a thin mouth. On closer observance, he saw that the piece was a musical instrument. Seven strings were fixed on a rod placed between the horns, and the ends of that rod had been left thick and carved to look like a ram's ears. The pupils of the eyes were actually two round holes—to let the sound out, Dominic assumed, as he didn't know much about string instruments—and the thin mouth was actually a bridge that supported the strings. The piece had been carved and painted so carefully that Dominic couldn't see such details until he stood close. He stood admiring it as Greg pulled a strip of papyrus from between the strings.

"Labor number four: Drive the catel of Geryon into Aquarius." Greg raised his eyebrows at Dominic. "Another labor of Hercules?"

Dominic nodded. "Essentially. But . . . that's all it says?" He looked around and saw only dust and saltwater. "I don't think we'll find cattle here."

"No, there's more."

Dominic took the scrap of paper and scrutinized it. "Wait . . . it says 'drive the *catel*.' What's a catel?"

"Not sure. What's Geryon?"

"Geryon is . . . ." Dominic paused. "He's some kind of

three-headed giant in Greek mythology. He somehow fits into the story of Pegasus, Chrysaor, Perseus, and Andromeda. So, we're in the right area. All of those constellations are just beyond Pisces—well, except Chrysaor; he doesn't have one." He read the rest of the riddle slowly: "Like Arion averts attack, play to the winged sea-horse's pack."

Dominic waved the paper gently back and forth as he mused. "The winged sea-horse . . . I think that means Pegasus. It's a winged horse, but it's in the 'sea' area of the constellations. Geryon also lives on an island in the sea. And the pack . . . ." He hesitated. "In the constellations, there are a lot of animals packed around Pegasus. There's Equuleus, Delphinus . . . Lacerta, the lizard . . . Cygnus, the crane . . . and . . . some other constellation that starts with a V, that represents a fox. But I'm not sure how to play to them." He gestured to the wooden ram. "Do you know how to play?"

"I do, actually," Greg said, rather cheerfully. "I mean, I've never played a kithara, but it's close enough to—"

"A what?"

"A kithara. The ancestor of the guitar." Greg knelt and gently plucked the strings one by one, murmuring his surprise as he did so. "It's already tuned. C sharp . . . ." He plucked the strings again, one by one. "E, F sharp, A, B, D, E." He glanced at Dominic, looking almost wistful. "I can play this. Should I just start?"

Dominic walked around the instrument, giving it a careful study. "Go ahead. I don't see any other clues."

Greg began to play, his brow furrowed as he carefully picked out the notes. The tune was simple, but sweet and lilting, almost sappily so. The sight of Greg working so seriously to produce such a simple and innocent sound brought a smile to Dominic's face.

"What was that?" he asked, when Greg had finished.

"The song? Ah . . . ." Greg laughed. "It's from a video

game. *The Legend of Zelda*. It's Epona's Song. In the game, the song is supposed to have a calming effect on animals. And . . . it summons the character's horse, and it makes the cattle produce milk."

"How fitting," Dominic said. "Can you play it again?"

As Greg resumed the song, Dominic's attention was caught by a movement in the calm waters—something emerging through the surface. He watched until he caught sight of a sleek gray form, several feet long, dipping just above and then below again—and then he saw another, and another.

Greg's attention was fixed on the strings, but as the song came to an end, he followed Dominic's gaze. "What is it? Do you see something?"

"Dolphins," Dominic replied.

Greg stood up, straining to see. "Are you sure?" He watched, and then pointed. "Look—do you see that, way out there? Doesn't it look like an island?"

"Where?"

"Right where I'm pointing," Greg said, as Dominic came to stand beside him. "A little island with a forest in the middle."

Through the sea mist, Dominic could make out the dark shape of a land bar far away. It did, as Greg suggested, have some kind of structure rising in the middle—a group of tall trees, perhaps, or some kind of pillar.

"Didn't you say that Goryo lives on an island?" Greg asked.

"Geryon," Dominic corrected him. "Yeah."

"Oh—I saw a dolphin!" Greg's voice conveyed child-like excitement. "There's another one."

"They're coming closer to shore," Dominic said.

"Maybe the 'pack' is a pack of dolphins," Greg suggested. "Although, they're actually called a pod."

Something stirred in Dominic's mind—some memory

of something he'd read. "It *is* dolphins," he replied, and recited: "*Like Arion averts attack.* Arion is a figure in Greek mythology. He was attacked at sea, but he escaped by playing a song that called the dolphins, and he rode away on one of them." He paused, remembering more. "The Delphinus constellation represents the dolphin who carried him."

"So . . . ." The furrow in Greg's brow deepened. "So . . . ."

"Have you ever ridden a dolphin?"

Greg didn't respond. He stared worriedly into the sea.

"I'm going to go for it," Dominic said, shoving the riddle into his pocket.

"Um, okay. I'm right behind you. Just . . . be careful. Don't hurt them."

As they approached the shore, Dominic glanced back with an encouraging smile. "Don't worry; this is normal here. Last time, I rode across the sea on the back of a goat-fish."

"A what?"

"A goat-fish," Dominic enunciated. "Totally normal."

He stepped into the sea and gasped. "Ah," he muttered. "It's cold." A sudden unease overtook him as the scent of salt reached his nostrils, and he remembered his last venture into the sea—the deeply unpleasant experience of becoming a fish. Dominic ignored the feeling and pushed onward. The ground dropped from beneath him, and he swam, slowing a couple of yards away from one of the sleek gray creatures. It lifted its head above the water and faced him with what looked like a cheerful smile. *Just anatomy*, Dominic reminded himself. *Not an actual smile.*

The dolphin came closer, lightly nudging Dominic's shoulder. It made a brief chittering sound and then pulled away to face him again.

"Good," he breathed. "You're friendly . . . so far. How about a ride? I need to get to that island over there." He pointed to the small bulk of land in the distance.

He was startled by a light bump against his back. Another gray figure darted past him and circled back. Now there were two of the creatures seemingly watching him—and then he felt a sudden push against his legs, and another of the creatures rose up beneath him. Dominic reached down and pressed his palms against the dolphin's back, and for a moment he was lifted just above the surface, perfectly perched for a joy ride across the ocean—and then he fell sideways, splashing hard into the water.

He emerged and steadied himself, settling into a slow paddle. Again, he was lifted by an unseen swimmer. This time Dominic expected it, and he braced himself, splaying his hands on the dolphin's smooth, soft skin.

They were moving forward together, slowly leaving Greg behind. Dominic started to call out to him, but gasped and braced himself as the dolphin dipped below the water. Dominic leaned forward, against the push of the sea, putting every effort into staying upright.

"Greg!" he shouted, not daring to turn around.

He heard no response, but just as he was about to politely ask his driver to turn around, he heard Greg's voice calling out behind him—a joyous call, he thought, and a minute later Greg was beside him, riding bareback through the sea with a whoop of delighted laughter. He sat in front of the dorsal fin, his hands well away from the blowhole, as relaxed as if he'd ridden dolphins every day.

The sea became choppy as they moved farther out. The smiles and laughter died down as the two men focused on staying upright, as they scrutinized the island that was taking clearer shape in front of them.

"Look," Dominic called, gesturing to the towering mass ahead. "That's no forest. It's a statue."

Greg stared, his demeanor suddenly serious. "Yeah . . . wow." He paused. "How tall do you suppose that is? A hundred feet?"

"It's hard to tell. Doesn't it look like it has three heads?" Greg didn't reply, so Dominic pressed him: "It does, right? It's probably Geryon."

Dominic could see few details yet, but the statue seemed to be a work of bronze—and the heads looked misshapen, as if they were wearing some kind of headgear.

"He doesn't look friendly," Greg said.

"Well, in the myths, he's not. He's a dangerous giant, but it's not a fair portrayal. He did try to kill Hercules, but that was because Hercules trespassed on his island and tried to steal his cattle."

"But . . . isn't that what we're doing?"

"No," Dominic said, but couldn't think of an alternate explanation of what they *were* doing.

"I have a bad feeling about this." Greg's words quickened; tension strained his voice. "Doesn't this remind you of that scene in *Jason and the Argonauts*, where the Talos statue comes to life and tries to kill everyone?"

"That won't happen," Dominic said, trying to hide his own unease.

"Let's not touch anything when we get there," Greg said. "Including cattle. I'm, like, a hundred percent sure that thing is going to come to life. It's the same as *Jason and the Argonauts*; this statue was guarding something on an island, and Jason's men messed with it." He paused, and added anxiously: "*Hercules* was the one who messed with it! He stole a spear or something, and the statue woke up. Look! Those heads look exactly like Talos. They're even wearing the same helmet."

Dominic didn't know what he was talking about. He did his best to ignore Greg's babbling, until Greg said: "I think I want to stop here. I'm going to swim the rest of the way, so I can make a break for it if I need to."

"A break?" Dominic repeated. "To where?"

"I don't know, but—" Greg gasped. "Something touched my leg!"

"It's a dolphin," Dominic assured him. "They're swimming close together."

"I don't see a dolphin. Something else is here. Don't you feel it? It's like . . . we're being stranded in the middle of the ocean, and we can't see what's under us. Like something is going to come up out of the water and—"

Dominic forced himself to speak in a patient tone. "Nothing is going to come up out of . . . ."

The words caught in Dominic's throat. At that moment, in the distance, something *did* come out of the water: an impossibly large bird, its massive wings spread wide—or so it appeared at first, but as it vanished below the waves, Dominic realized that what he'd seen was no bird. It was a tail.

Greg turned to see what he was staring at, but the water was calm again. "What is it?" he asked.

Before he could answer, another figure thrust from the water. At first it seemed that a large gray hill had emerged from the sea, and then a pair of hills—and Dominic realized that he was looking at a giant, gaping mouth.

Greg's voice was strung with panic. "What is that?"

"It's a whale," Dominic said. "It's—"

The whale made a slow half-turn and slammed back into the water, and the dolphins darted away, so that Dominic was nearly thrown into the sea. He leaned forward, pressing his hands and legs tight against the dolphin's sides. Only once did he dare to look back; he saw only turbulent waves and sprays, and when he called Greg's name, there came no reply.

He raced across the sea, veering to the left of the island and quickly leaving it behind. Straight ahead, through the mists, land appeared: a rock wall of deep gray stone. The

83

dolphin sped onward, so that Dominic feared slamming into the rock—but the creature swerved, so suddenly that Dominic was thrown from its back into the briny waves.

Dominic called out, but the dolphins were nowhere to be seen, and the sea was growing more turbulent. He swam toward the cliff, wiping the sting of salt water from his eyes, scouring the rock surface for any kind of hold. He pulled himself onto a small ledge a foot above the water, but the waves quickly overtook it; he climbed onto another ledge and nestled into a safe spot above the sea.

The water, though, seemed to be rising, and the waves becoming more aggressive, so that Dominic found himself searching for another way up. He found a narrow ledge and pulled himself up, and up again—nervously, as the holds were barely large enough to grasp with his fingers and toes. After climbing a few yards, he found a space wide enough to stand on.

A faint cry reached his ears: "Dominic!"

He turned and looked down into the sea. At first he saw nothing but waves and froth, but then, an unexpected face caught his eye. Surina was below him, her shoulders bobbing in and out of the waves as she tried to stay afloat.

Dominic moved to the lowest part of the ledge. "Surina!" he called. "Climb up here!"

She swam to the rocks, pulling herself onto the first outcrop she could find. Her hands probed the rock; her eyes scanned its surface.

"Over here," Dominic said, pointing. "There are some ledges farther down."

"Give me a second."

"Surina, you need to climb. There's a huge wave coming."

She got to her feet and scuttled up the cliff, not pausing to look back at the approaching waves. Dominic helped her onto the ledge, and they looked out into the sea, at the thick sprays and foaming crests.

"Hey," Dominic said suddenly. He grasped Surina's wrist—gently, but firmly. "What's this?"

"Oh . . . ." She looked down at her forearm as Dominic released her. A pair of long, red scratches marred her flesh. "I had to fight off a couple of those creatures. Look—one of them bit me." She held out her other arm.

"Surina! That looks bad."

"It's fine."

"How did you get away?"

"I just made a run for it," she said. "Tagua was taking us through Triangulum, and I ran back to the ocean and started swimming."

"What about Hannah?"

"I don't know. Sorry."

Dominic tried not to worry. Hannah seemed to have learned how to handle herself, but Tagua was probably furious and taking it out on her. "Here." He undid the belt from around his waist. "Take this."

"Why?"

"Because you don't have your fleece thing anymore. It's just a scrap, but maybe it will help."

As Surina fixed the belt around her waist, Dominic noticed a light etching in the rock behind her. "Surina, lean forward," he said.

She finished tying the belt. "Why?"

"There's something behind you."

She scooted aside and turned, reading the few lines of texts etched into the gray rock:

Andromeda will overturn
Poseidon's flood and Cetus' wrath.
With vanity and legend spurned,
She sings the Nereids to her path.

"Nereids," Surina repeated. "Sea nymphs."

"I'm guessing that the 'vanity' remark is about the

Andromeda myth—that she got into trouble because her mom said she was prettier than the Nereids," Dominic said.

"Okay, but what are we supposed to do with it?"

"Well . . . we're supposed to be at that island over there, but we're stranded on this rock. When I was in Pisces with Greg, we called some dolphins by playing a musical instrument, and they gave us a ride. Maybe there's another . . . ." He trailed off, glancing helplessly around the expanse of bare rock.

"I can try singing the Nereids' Song," Surina replied.

"What's that?"

"It's . . . a song that I heard on YouTube. Just give me a second; I have to think of the lyrics." Surina's brow furrowed. She took a breath and faced the sea. "Tell all the Nereids twinkling," she sang, "I don't know the words, to the whole song. Tell all the sea monsters, something, this sounds like I'm singing it wrong."

Dominic laughed. "What kind of song is that?"

"I don't know the words. I'm doing my best." Surina lifted her chin and sang again: "Sitting here up on the cliff, we're in a plight; carry us on. They'll let this music unite us; we . . . bless the Nereid journey. Ah, ah, ah, ah; oh, oh, oh, oh." Surina paused to cast a sharp look at Dominic, who was doubled over in laughter. "Do you have a better idea?"

He shook his head, and she resumed singing. "Ah, ah, ah, ah . . . . Tell all the billowing dresses, swirling in dance on silken sand. Tell all the waving gold tresses, stroked and caressed by thy hand—look!"

She pointed to the water, where something smooth and gray broke the surface and vanished again. Dominic clapped his hands together in relief. "They're still here!" he said.

"What's here?"

"Dolphins." He gestured toward the waves. "Jump in.

They'll let us ride on their backs."

"Jump back down? Into *those* waves?"

But the waves were settling, and Dominic jumped, plugging his nose and landing with a loud splash. One of the dolphins slipped under him, and he mounted it on the first try. As they broke the surface together, he steadied himself, blinked away salt water, and called to Surina: "Your turn."

She hesitated, looking out at the calming sea, and leapt. Seconds after Surina reached the surface, a dolphin tried to hoist her up, but she fell and came up coughing.

"Are you all right?" Dominic asked.

She nodded and tried again, and soon, they were both safely mounted on sleek gray bodies. The waves smoothed out as the dolphins swam back toward the island.

"What are you smiling at?" Surina asked, once the sound of the sea had died down.

"Isn't this just like a childhood dream come true?" Dominic asked. "Riding a dolphin across the sea?"

She scoffed at the idea. "Um, no. Riding a dolphin across a cold, dark sea full of sharks and stingrays wasn't one of my imaginings." She glanced at him again. "I guess it's nice that you can have fun while we're headed for a thousand-year death."

"We're not," Dominic insisted. "This place is helping us. It might not come in the way we expect, but doesn't it seem like this place always turns our preconceptions on their heads? Medusa is benevolent, Gilgamesh is an anti-hero—"

"Medusa is benevolent?" Surina repeated.

"Didn't you say that Virgo turned into Medusa when you were talking to her, and that the snake-haired sculpture at Chavín is Medusa?"

"Virgo is not benevolent," she replied.

"I don't agree. I . . . I'm a better person after meeting

her." Dominic gazed ahead, at the looming figure of Geryon that became ever more detailed as the dolphins drew close.

"Look!" Surina exclaimed. "There's Greg."

A man stood at the water's edge, facing the three-headed statue. As Surina called out to him, he half-turned; he removed his glasses, trying futilely to wipe them on his wet sweater.

When he looked up again, Dominic saw terror in his eyes.

Their gaze only met for a moment before the dolphin twisted free, sending Dominic into the water. He swam toward Greg until his feet reached the slippery sea bottom and then the wet sand. On the shore, he turned around and shouted: "Thanks for the ride!"

Surina joined him as he stood squeezing water from his clothes. Greg hurried to meet her. "Are you okay?" he asked. "What happened to the guy in the robe?"

"Tagua? I don't know. I ran away."

"You're hurt," Greg said.

"It's fine." Surina turned her arms so that the wounds were hidden. "Have you looked around the island?"

"Not really. I saw Dominic headed that way—" Greg pointed out to sea "—so I came around to look for him."

"There was a riddle earlier, at Pisces," Dominic explained, pulling the papyrus from his pocket. The ink was somewhat smeared, but still legible, and he read aloud: "'Labor number four: Drive the catel of Geryon into Aquarius.' Catel is spelled C-A-T-E-L."

"Drive the catel," Surina repeated. "What's a catel?"

"No idea." Dominic gave a wary look at the metal giant. Its bronze body was weathered with patches of deep orange, brown, and green. One hand brandished a long spear, pointed at the ground, as if ready to slay trespassers; on the opposite arm was a shield. The nearest head seemed to look down at the three visitors, although its eyes lacked detail, staring sightlessly from below the figure's helmet. "Three heads must be handy," Dominic murmured. "It can see the whole island that way."

"And it has six arms," Greg replied. "You can see a couple of the other ones from here. He has three of those spears, and three shields. Doesn't it seem like security? He's sitting on top of a closed room, protecting whatever's inside."

The base of the statue, Dominic could see now, was several feet high; a metal door stood ajar in its center. Surina noticed it at the same time and started to hurry ahead, saying: "Here's something."

"Don't go in there!" Greg shrieked, so loudly that Surina jumped.

"Why not?" Dominic asked.

"Because . . . *Jason and the Argonauts*!"

"Oh, that." Dominic looked at Surina. "Have you seen this movie, *Jason and the Argonauts*? Greg thinks this statue is going to come to life, like the one in the movie."

"Oh, yeah," Surina said. "The giant metal guy." She looked up. "He does look similar, except . . . three heads."

"It's the same," Greg insisted. "Talos sat on a crypt-looking thing like this one, and the door was open, and it turned out that the treasure of the gods was in there, and Hercules went in and stole something."

"Hercules? Was he in that movie?"

"Just don't touch anything," Greg said. "This is definitely a bad sign."

"It's a good sign," Dominic countered. "The riddle mentioned Geryon, so we know we're in the right place."

"I won't touch anything," Surina assured Greg. "But let's just peek inside. There might be another riddle."

Dominic started away. "You two have fun. I'm going to check out the other side of the island."

He'd seen a flash of red on the beach, and as he moved closer, Dominic slowed in surprise. A speedboat sat near the shoreline, a shiny red vessel with the word "GERYON" painted in black along the side. Dominic quickened his pace, jogging to the boat and peering inside. It was a simple model with an outboard motor, but it looked new and fully functional—and clean, as if someone had just finished washing it. The padded seats, the windshield, and even the hull were spotless except for a few drops of sea spray.

"Guys," he called.

He headed back to find Greg tugging Surina away from the metal giant. They had come around to the side of the statue, so that a different head seemed to look down at them. Dominic had to admit to himself that it did seem "like security."

"Ow!" Surina exclaimed, prying Greg's fingers from her arm.

"Sorry," he said. "I forgot you're hurt."

"Did you find anything?" Dominic asked.

"There's a room full of stuff," Surina said, "but it's too dark to see anything."

Dominic jabbed his thumb in the direction of the boat. "There's a speedboat back there. I say we drive it to Aquarius."

"We shouldn't take anything," Greg said.

Dominic held up a hand. "Hear me out. The boat says 'Geryon' on the side, and the riddle told us to drive Geryon's catel. No one knows what that word means. There's no cattle, as in cows; we've established that. There's a lot of sand, and a statue with a dark room under it, and a lot of salt water—and there's a boat. Which of these can we drive to Aquarius? For all we know, 'catel' means 'boat.'"

"Let's go," Surina said, starting away. Greg hesitated, and she waved him on impatiently. "Come on. We can't waste time."

He followed, but he kept his head mostly turned toward

the statue, stumbling every now and then as his feet dragged in the sand. Surina reached the boat first, whistling softly as she peeked inside. "Can I drive it?" she asked. "My dad used to let me drive his boat when I was a kid."

"Sure," Dominic replied. "How do we get it into the water?"

They three of them pushed the boat easily and soon had it afloat. Surina clambered inside and sat near the motor. Dominic started to follow her, but he saw Greg still on the shore, standing stock-still and staring at the giant. Dominic trudged back to him, his shoes and pants heavy with seawater. "Greg," he said, "this really is our only option." He gestured to the statue. "If that thing does come to life, what are you going to do—just stand here?"

"I'll run that way," Greg replied, pointing down the shore.

"Ah." Dominic paused. "Well . . . I don't know what to say to that."

"Guys, let's go," Surina called.

Greg stubbornly refused. Dominic tried to think of some idea that would coax him into the boat, such as "You know, if you stay here, you'll starve," and "If Hannah dies, it will be your fault."

"There must be some other way," Greg insisted. "You guys are rushing it. I know I said I'm a coward, but this isn't cowardice talking; it's logic. I'm *one hundred percent* sure that thing is going to come to life."

"You really shouldn't say that," Dominic replied wearily—and then an idea came to him. "One hundred percent," he muttered, and began walking. "Fine."

"Where are you going?" Greg asked.

Dominic didn't answer, but began to jog—and then, as he thought of Hannah, to run. He ran in spite of his water-saturated feet, all the way back to the metal door that stood open like a sinister temptation. Inside, the room was

91

dark, as Surina had said. Dominic could make out very little detail aside from a shiny sliver of gold just inside the room. He reached out, felt a column of smooth metal beneath his fingertips. A pole—no, more likely a spear. He lifted it, hefted it in his hand, and carried it outside.

Dominic retreated several yards from the statue. He waved the heavy length of gold in the air. "Look!" he shouted. "I stole something!"

He kept jogging, back toward the boat, back toward Greg who was screaming something that Dominic couldn't quite make out.

Suddenly, the shouting stopped. In its place Dominic heard a loud, groaning creak; it came from behind him, behind and high above, and he instinctively dropped the spear into the sand.

Dominic dared glance back.

Two of the heads were staring at him now. Not just one, but two.

He ran, no longer because of Hannah, but in a mortal panic. He heard more creaking behind him, felt a small quake in the earth that he imagined was caused by a massive footfall. Greg, too, began to run—not along the shore, as he'd said, but in a mad dash for the boat.

The sand, the wet pants, the soaked shoes kept Dominic at a nightmarishly slow pace. He felt another thud, and he knew that the next step could crush him dead. He whispered pleas and prayers under his breath, leapt into the water and pushed toward the boat, then hurled himself over the side.

"What the hell did you do that for?" Greg shouted.

Dominic sat up and looked back. The creaking had stopped; the giant stood still, no longer atop the chamber, but at the place where Dominic had dropped the spear. It slouched slightly forward, two heads still staring in the trespassers' direction, one of its own spears poised in mid-air.

"Surina," Dominic said, "start the engine."

"I'm trying," she said shakily. "Fuel, choke . . . um . . . neutral . . . throttle." She pulled and turned levers as she spoke, and then she sat with her hands raised helplessly in the air. "Where's the cord?"

Dominic reached past her and pressed a button beneath the throttle. The engine hummed to life, and the boat slowly moved away from the island.

"Can we go faster?" Dominic asked.

"No," Surina snapped. "Dominic, why did you *do* that?"

Dominic's heart raced; he struggled to keep his voice steady. "I did it," he said, "because of the story you told me about Piscis. You thought he was trying to stop you, but after a while, you realized he was forcing you to go faster, so you could make it back home." He paused. "Hannah is running out of time. I made us go faster."

6: Aquarius

Dominic didn't remember Aquarius being so beautiful. He struggled to remember it at all; he supposed that his own experience of Aquarius had been a small shelter full of broken vessels—the place where he'd been snatched by a terrifying bird. Now, he was in the grand realm that Surina had described: a pillared temple of pale stone, deep in a cave, surrounded by blue waters that shone ethereally where sunlight beamed through open skylights. The temple itself glowed with such beauty and peaceful energy that the initial sight of it brought tears to Dominic's eyes.

Surina had navigated across the sea, determining that she simply had to steer in the opposite direction of Triangulum. Soon, some cavernous rock formations had appeared on the right; Surina drove inside, and the sky was replaced by a high rock ceiling—plain at first, then hung with stalactites of varying hues of tan. Surina turned the motor off as the temple came into sight, and the boat drifted on the quiet waters, bringing the travelers ever closer to the softly shining sanctuary.

Surina leaned over and whispered to Dominic: "This is Aquarius' temple. I came in on the opposite side last time, but it's the same place."

Dominic, too, leaned closer. "Why are you whispering?"

"I don't know," she said.

Surina and Greg reached out as the boat approached a stone platform. Greg held the vessel in place while the others climbed out; they returned the favor, and as Dominic crouched there, his gaze fell on the small post that rose from the platform. Surina had intended to tether the boat there but couldn't find anything to tie it.

"What should we do about the boat?" Greg whispered.

"Nothing we *can* do," Dominic said with a shrug. "Let's leave it. We have this to attend to." He picked up the strip of papyrus that rested atop the post. "Labor number five: Inasmuch as you are able, help to flush the Augean stable." He shoved the paper into his pants pocket. "Should we go in?"

A narrow walkway led toward the temple. The travelers passed beneath an elaborately carved entablature, mostly embellished with sea creatures and wave forms. Dominic was surprised to find that the central area was surrounded by a large moat. The central platform held three long tables, all of which were bare except for a stone pitcher and a few empty glasses. At the end of one table was a silver staff, standing upright in its base; it was crossed with three silver rods, each hung with what looked like small bells—or seashells, perhaps—and at the top there perched a small silver bird.

"This is different," Surina said in a low voice. She followed a narrow walkway to the center, stopping at the smaller table and pulling out a chair. As she sat, she turned to look into the clear waters of the moat. "It wasn't this quiet last time . . . or this empty."

"Maybe it *is* empty," Dominic suggested, trailing behind Greg on the walkway. "We might have to solve this one on our own. Should we look around?"

He had barely finished the question when he saw a sudden, quick movement in the water—a dark shape flitting toward him. *Piscis*, he thought, remembering Surina's description of the fish-faced creature that had emerged unexpectedly from the moat. He braced himself as the figure burst from the water with a loud splash.

Dominic had just enough time to see what looked like a large merman rising up beside the platform; its tail split grotesquely into two lengths, as though someone had drawn a sharp sword through it. Before he could comprehend the scene, he was jarred by a sudden shove; Greg had panicked and fled past him down the walkway. Dominic found his balance again, barely avoiding a plunge into the clear water.

Aquarius stood in the temple, a man of no remarkable feature aside from his glowing eyes. He was modest in stature; his aged, weathered flesh was a deep brown, almost black, contrasting sharply with the white tunic that hung to his knees. The fish tail was gone, and in its place were two very human-looking legs. His eyes were obscured by a layer of fringe that hung from the turban on his head, and as Dominic looked on with a sense of wonder and dread, the two glowing orbs became less intense, until at length the eyes glowed no more. Aquarius reached up and removed the turban.

"Your friend startles easily," he said, his voice calm and strong. His gaze flicked to Dominic, full of gentle warmth—yet the eyes seemed to be comprised of cold colors, slate-gray and black and flecks of a crystalline hue that looked like shards of ice.

Aquarius set the turban on the table. He sat down across from Surina.

"You're not going to offer us a beer, like last time?" she asked.

"No. Nor will I make you read from my book of riddles," he replied.

She couldn't restrain a smile. "I expected to see Piscis. Actually, I kind of looked forward to it."

"Piscis is needed elsewhere," Aquarius replied. "There has been much commotion in the realms lately. Tagua, in particular, has been . . . disruptive." He turned to Dominic. "Come and sit."

Dominic moved quietly to the seat beside Surina, keeping his gaze fixed on Aquarius, intrigued by the humanness of his form. The close-cut hair on the water-bearer's head and face was a mottled black and gray, as if with age, and his flesh was creased and worn.

"Do you know much about Tagua?" Surina asked.

"I know his past," Aquarius replied. "On Earth he was a simple shepherd, but he enticed a princess to marry him, and through murder he maneuvered to become a wizard and king—a greedy and duplicitous king. But when a shepherd becomes a wolf, his own hounds will hunt him. His subjects turned on him, so that in his desperation he escaped to the stars. Now he sits in Lupus, the constellation of the wolf. It isn't an auspicious seat. The fate of Lupus is to be slain by Centaurus.

"Yet, to be bound in Lupus isn't a curse," Aquarius continued. "In it you will see not only the predator, but the devoted family. When a wolf cub is born, the pack helps to take care of the new offspring. If the cub is orphaned, the adults adopt it as their own."

Surina looked aghast. "Tagua isn't devoted to anyone."

Aquarius regarded her gently. "Hannah is also bound to Lupus, and Dominic was also imprisoned there. And you, Surina, readily accepted the call back to this place. Why?"

She didn't answer at first, but looked back at him in somber silence. "Please help us rescue Hannah," she said at last. "I know this place has a trail of riddles for us, but . . . what are we supposed to *do*? I don't know how to solve the sun gate riddle. Hannah doesn't have much time, and—"

"Have you seen the sun gate riddle?" Aquarius asked.

Again, she hesitated. "No."

"It is true that this place has a path already made for you. If you entered at Gemini, you're nearly halfway around the arc. Here, there is no linear time unless the masters make it so."

"But you *have* made it so," Surina said. "Time is passing here, and Hannah is fading. I can see it in her eyes."

"There is something else about Hannah that has changed. When you found her here, in Gemini, she reminded you of someone—or some*thing*. What was it?"

Surina hesitated. "The . . . demon thing from Fornax."

"That 'demon thing' was Hannah, wasn't it?" Aquarius asked. "But you were there with Hannah in her human form. How is it possible that the future and past Hannah were there at the same time?"

"Because you made linear time happen here," Surina answered uncertainly. "And . . . you ran those timelines together, in the same place."

"So we did. Here, your future self can meet your past self. If you could meet *your* past self—the one who came here through a temple in the mountains, and who joined yourself to a broken man—would you warn yourself, or would you allow things to progress as they have? It *is* possible to alter your past. What is not possible is to know every consequence of that alteration."

Surina's lips pressed together. Dominic knew her thoughts perfectly. Whenever she'd spoken of her first encounter with the starry realm, of the beginnings of her relationship with her ex-husband Victor, her voice seethed with anger and regret.

Aquarius' gaze shifted to a point behind Dominic. "Greg Yazzie, come and sit down. You are in no danger here, and your presence is just as important as that of your companions." He returned his attention to Surina and added: "You will have a chance to maintain this timeline, or to change your past and alter these events for yourself and your companions."

Surina sat in troubled silence as Greg moved toward

the table; he didn't sit, but lingered nearby.

"Just me?" Surina asked at last.

Aquarius gestured to Dominic and Greg. "For these two, it wouldn't be a challenge. Their challenges lie elsewhere. Your new companion has been tested thrice and will be challenged thrice again. In Aries, the realm of self-sacrifice, Hannah chose to put herself at risk rather than sacrifice a powerless few. In Taurus, she learned that even if she crashes while pursuing balance, she has the means to try again." The water-god flashed a tiny smile. "I can't resist just one riddle: The Stymphalian bird is a winged creature known for its aggressive attacks on those who try to feast on it. Its claws are like swords; when it flies, its feathers pierce like arrows. In Greek myth, it's associated with Ares, the god of war. Who is the Stymphalian bird?"

Surina frowned, supposing that she and her companions had made a mistake. "Hannah doesn't fit that description."

"She will," Aquarius replied quietly.

Dominic spoke up: "What about this labor: Inasmuch as you are able, help to flush the Augean stable?"

The old man's gaze seemed suddenly introspective. He leaned back in his chair. "Ah, yes. The Augean stable. Do you know much about the Greek myth?"

"As much as I know about Geryon's cattle," Dominic replied. "Just the basics."

"You will find reflections of those myths here. In the Greek myth, Geryon tends a herd of 'cattle' whose coats are stained red from following the path of the sun."

"The zodiac," Dominic said.

"Perhaps. In the myth, the hard part isn't stealing Geryon's cattle; it's keeping them together and herding them to the next place. When cattle are frightened, they scatter and flee." The water-god's gaze flicked briefly to Greg. "Covetous individuals try to add them to their own flocks and keep them divided. In the Greek myth, when Hera saw Hercules herding the cattle, she sent a gadfly to bite and scatter them. These realms, you'll find, are full of such gadflies. You have already been bitten by one or two." Aquarius paused, his strange, icy eyes seeming to spark and glimmer with some unseen light. "We have an interest in reuniting these so-called 'cattle' and compelling them to work in harmony. Whenever they are scattered, we will create lines that lead them together again. We would set them once again on the path of the sun, and teach them the balance between humility and strength, so they can advance the cause of harmony on Earth."

"Do you mean people like us?" Dominic asked. "If you do, you might choose a better word than 'cattle.'"

"One of your own kind chose that symbol," the water-god replied wryly. "As for the other labor: In your world, in your time, to 'flush the Augean stable' is to rid oneself and one's community of corruption. That process always starts with oneself, and it isn't something you accomplish at once. It's a life-long process, and a deeply unpleasant and challenging one—and people are easily misled on its course. Consider Wibben, for example, who thought he was cleansing himself of corruption while becoming ever more corrupt, and who sought the rites of the underworld not to empower himself, but to disempower others. He sought the symbols of the underworld without understanding their significance."

Dominic recalled what Surina had told him about Wibben: that he'd come to this realm by accident while seeking ancient, magical tools, hoping that they could be used for power and domination. Instead, his quest resulted in countless cycles of futility and punishment in the stars.

"You, Dominic, studied the Sumerian legends before coming here," Aquarius said, "especially those related to your journey through Leo. According to those legends, when I helped Uta-napishtim escape the great flood, what did I tell him to do first?"

Dominic hesitated. "Design a boat?"

"Give up his worldly possessions," Aquarius corrected him. "*I* designed the boat—a vessel of seven tiers, each tier divided into nine sections, a vessel to preserve all life." A brief smile accentuated the lines around Aquarius' eyes. "Tagua also came to the starry realm seeking eternal life, but he clings to worldly possessions. Like a hoarder, he also stole sacraments of the underworld—but his greed and fear make him incapable of solving their mysteries. Things in the zodiac are often not what they seem. Geryon, for example, guards a valuable treasure. What is that treasure?"

"Um . . . ." Dominic hesitated.

"I thought we weren't going to do riddles," Surina said. "That's, like, five riddles so far. I would say that the treasure is that room full of gold spears or whatever, but you're going to say I'm wrong."

"That room is full of junk. Geryon is tasked with ensuring the survival of something more vital than chunks of metal." Aquarius paused, again resting his gaze on Greg. "Greg Yazzie, these two have answered my riddles, but I have not yet posed one to you. You need not answer it now, but only consider it: What is the true preserver of life?"

Greg stood like a statue, his only movement that of his eyes as they widened in anxiety.

"The underworld, Virgo, is the most powerful of all the realms," the old man continued. "It looks like death, but it holds the most sublime power of life. One can only approach by releasing one's grasp on one's former self, and by giving up one's worldly possessions. Yet, Wibben's society tried to mimic Virgo's rites of transformation by hoarding symbols. Other societies also seek to partake in her rituals, in pursuit of wisdom; Plato did it, and so did many other humble philosophers, as well as power-mongers. Be careful, because the rites of sacred respect, and those of depraved intentions, can look similar; one can easily slide into depravity without realizing it." Aquarius' gaze shifted to Surina. "Virgo's rites terrify the one who lacks wisdom, but they strengthen one who has courage."

Dominic interrupted. "So, if this labor isn't something we need to finish now, then . . . can we go?"

"Indeed, you must," Aquarius said. "You have a long journey ahead of you." He lifted a hand and beckoned Dominic. "Give me your flask."

Dominic handed him the leather flask, and Aquarius poured into it the last bit of water from the stone pitcher. "Take this to refresh Hannah. She has had the longest journey of all, and this may bring her just enough strength to finish it. Tagua has drained her; she has spent too much time in his presence, has sympathized with him, has been misled by him. That is why Hannah must be the one to flush Tagua from the bright stables. It is easy to cast out a villain when he is a stranger, but in your own world, how easy will it be to confront and cast down someone who is close to you? What if, next time, the one you must hold accountable is your friend, your sister, your brother—your own child? Will you set things right, or will you perpetuate injustice with lies and excuses?" Aquarius extended the flask to Dominic. "Take this, and remember as you travel: Whatever is in your heart—your regard for others, your yearning for justice, your ability to be honest with yourself and to learn from your mistakes—is more important than any rite or sigil."

"I'll remember it," Dominic said. "How do we get to Capricornus?"

"By boat." Aquarius gestured to the temple entrance. "Look behind you. The water is rising."

All three travelers turned at once to see that the calm

102

waters were now flowing rapidly, and that they had risen nearly to the level of the platform.

"Tagua is growing bold," Aquarius said. "He has agitated Cetus and caused a landslide into the Eridanus. The river has flooded Phoenix and Sculptor, and a great wave is coming from the Cetus realm." The water-god smiled wryly. "Tagua has an aversion to this temple. He's trying to flush you out because he can't enter; he has no power here, just as he has no power in Virgo's realm. Virgo is a realm of transformation, and Tagua abhors that more than anything. Change can make one more powerful, wiser and more attuned, but there are many who fear it as a kind of death; they cling to imbalanced impressions of themselves. Tagua does have some ability in the stars, in general; he can levitate, see over great distances, and use the life force of others—but he cannot transform. That is his greatest weakness." Aquarius pushed his chair back and began to stand. "Go now, and take the boat to Capricornus. You're right; we have created linear time here, and established action and consequence. If you don't act quickly, you won't like the result."

"Noted," Dominic said, standing. "Let's go. Quickly."

The boat still floated where they had left it. As they approached, Dominic asked: "Which way to Capricornus? It's the opposite of where we came in, right?"

"Sort of, but we can't just drive the boat around the temple," Surina said. "There's a barrier in the . . . ." She trailed off, looking out across the flooded arena. "Never mind. We can go around, but we'll need to go slowly. There are barriers that we might bump up against." She slipped into the boat and reclaimed her place beside the motor.

"We can't go *too* slowly," Dominic said. "This place has a ceiling; we need to get out from under it."

"Noted."

The waters had risen over the walkway; Greg splashed into the boat, struggling to keep his footing on the now-submerged stone path. The boat surged upward as a thunderous noise seemed to shake the arena. Water gushed through skylights; stalactites broke loose and plummeted around the boat, and Greg let out a startled cry as a large spike split the water beside him. The obscured skylights dimmed the chamber, and the trio frantically looked for a way out.

"It doesn't matter which direction," Surina called, raising her voice over the sounds of the motor and the turbulent waters. "Just look for an opening. I can't see one."

Dominic looked up, saw the stalactites coming ever closer. "What about the way we came in? There should be an opening to our left."

"It's underwater now," Surina said. We need to find another way."

She picked up speed, no longer concerned about underwater obstacles. The ceiling continued to close down on them, until they found themselves maneuvering around the longest of the stalactites and seeking the highest point in the chamber.

"We're screwed," Dominic said. "Can we come up with a plan B?"

"Wait, wait, look!" Surina cried. "There's a message."

She pointed to the chamber wall, where three figures were carved in relief in the smooth amber stone: a horse, an eagle, and an insect, each with a pair of wings spread at its sides.

The boat brought Dominic closest to the carving. He leaned toward the words scrawled beneath it, straining to see in the darkening chamber, and read aloud:

I plow through worlds a sacred circle
to enter first, my triumph gained.

From silent dark, my songs are carried
to herald here the blooms and rains.
With cryptic flight and colors dazzling
I transform without fear or pain.
First pairs of the last in three odd lines spell my name.
A push is all I need to bore into the next domain.
Another choice may put your noble efforts all in vain.
What am I?

Dominic swore under his breath. "Okay . . . any ideas? We are . . . *really* short on time. Like, the boat is about to flood, and we will have to solve this underwater, and even if we make it, we'll—"

"I don't get it," Greg said. "What do we need to do?"

"This riddle refers to one of these symbols: the eagle, winged horse, or fly."

"It's a cicada," Greg corrected him. "You can tell by its eyes."

"Fine. A cicada. It looks like we have to choose a symbol and push it, and it will make an opening for us. The riddle spells out the answer—in the first pairs of the last three . . . whatever. I don't think I can solve it that way."

"It's the cicada," Greg said.

"You mean, that's the answer? How do you know?"

"In folklore, the cicada is the one who escaped a flood by digging a portal into the fifth world," Greg said. "It won a challenge there. It spends a long time underground, in the dark, and then it emerges and transforms. It's wingless, and then it has wings. When it sheds its old skin, it comes out shining and multi-colored. It's cryptic, it sings, it's associated with—"

Surina leaned across Dominic and pushed hard against the cicada figure.

Stone slid against stone, grinding and groaning as a

portal opened above the boat, sending grains of sand into the travelers' eyes—but the opening was slow, and the boat rocked and turned, inching away from freedom. Dominic blinked the dust from his eyes and stood up, grabbing the edge of the opening and pushing his feet against the boat, trying to guide it into place. "Stand up," he commanded the others. "Grab the edges. Push the boat into the middle."

The others hurried to help him, and moments later the boat had risen high enough that it was no longer in danger of drifting beneath the ceiling. The travelers let go and sat down, watching as the ground around the portal disappeared beneath the rising sea.

The floor of the boat had taken on a few inches of water; Greg and Surina made a futile effort to bail it with their hands, and Dominic tore off his shirt, soaking up the water and wringing it back into the sea.

"Good enough," he said, shaking out his shirt and struggling to put it back on. "Thank you, Greg. Where to next?"

Surina looked around and sighed. "Well . . . we're in the middle of the sea, and now I have no sense of direction. I can't even begin to guess which way to go."

Dominic gestured to a mountain that rose in the distance, a dark and ominous-looking peak. "That's the only visible land mass. Should we head there? Even if it's not Capricornus, it might give us an indication of where we are."

Surina steered in that direction, her jaw clenched, her brow furrowed. Dominic rode in silence for a while, and then he called to her: "What's wrong?"

"I hate this place," Surina replied.

Dominic chuckled. "I can relate. I used to say the same thing. I don't hate it anymore, though. I'm grateful for it."

She raised her eyebrows, perplexed and perhaps offended. "Well, it's easy for you. Aquarius complimented you, but he took jabs at me."

"Did he? How so?"

"Oh, you know. I'm the only one who isn't okay with my past. And that thing about Virgo—the reason I have a grudge against her is because I lack wisdom."

"He didn't say that."

"It was implied," Surina said. "He looked at me when he said it."

"Well, he had to look at *someone*."

"Don't patronize me."

"All right." Dominic turned around to face Greg, who sat at the front. "Good call on the cicada," he said.

Greg replied: "A cicada is usually a good sign."

"What folklore is that—the one about the cicada escaping the flood?"

"In Diné legend, the cicada helped humans escape the floods of the fourth world by burrowing into this world," Greg said. "There are variations of the story, but a common one is that the cicada was challenged by a creature who could pierce itself with arrows and survive. The creature said that the cicada could only stay if it proved itself as indestructible. So, the cicada pierced itself and shed its old skin. Not only was it uninjured, it came out more colorful and beautiful than before, and it even grew wings and played music. The challenger was so impressed that it invited the cicada and the others to come and live in the fifth world."

Dominic leaned over to give him a fist bump.

"Remember, this isn't a leisure ride," Surina called. "We need to keep an eye out for Tagua."

Dominic nodded his agreement. For some time the trio rode in silence, keeping a solemn watch on their surroundings. The only notable movement came from Greg; he kept ducking his head and holding his face, sniffling and clearing his throat.

Dominic leaned forward and tapped him on the shoulder. "You all right?" he asked.

Greg half-turned and nodded. He didn't fully face Dominic, but Dominic caught a good enough glimpse to realize that Greg was crying. He paused in befuddlement, and then he asked: "What's the matter?"

Reluctantly, Greg turned around. "Ah . . . ." He scoffed at himself, lowered his head and wiped at his cheeks. "I'm just being sentimental. It's the cicada thing."

Dominic raised his eyebrows questioningly.

Greg flashed a sheepish smile. "Like I said, I'm a big scaredy-cat. It's been on my mind a lot lately. It's caused a lot of problems for me, and it's, like, the biggest thing I'm trying to work on."

He paused, and Dominic was about to ask what that had to do with a cicada, but Greg went on: "Some of it is just embarrassing, like . . . I get startled easily, I actually scream during scary movies—but some of it is really shameful. Like the Devil's Bridge thing, and like . . . a few years ago, my sister was getting bullied by a group of boys in our old neighborhood. She's little, she's nice, she has a limp, and she was an easy target. These boys would sometimes come up to me and start insulting her, and I would laugh and agree with them— not because she deserved it, but because I was afraid of them. They were much smaller than me. They were just little kids, but I was afraid."

Greg laughed again, an anguished laugh that contrasted with the fresh tears forming in his eyes. "I have all of these causes I want to support, but when the time comes to stand up, I get scared and back out," he said. "I'm trying really hard, though, especially since . . . well, my grandfather, my *shicheii*, was always the one who told me to be brave, but now he's gone. He knew I was a big chicken, and he would tell me folk tales about the cicada and how brave it was, thinking it would inspire me to become brave. He said that before it transforms, the cicada is just a worm with feet. It crawls low to the ground. Its head has been stuck in the ground for so long that it comes out weak and bumbling. Before it molts, it's just a drab gray or brown, but when it finally sheds its former self, it has wings and a strong voice, and it shines with all kinds of colors: green, aqua blue, yellow, orange, gold, pink. It plows through dimensions and does all kinds of amazing things. All the cicada needs is to listen to the cycles of life, and to follow them, so it can find the right place to shine.

"My *shicheii* had a stroke last summer," he continued. "I went to see him in the hospital, and he was asleep most of the time, and the nurses said he was having trouble speaking . . . but he woke up when I was there, and after a while he looked at me and smiled like he wanted to say something. So I held his hand, and I waited, and finally he just said, 'Be the cicada.' He ended up having a second stroke a few minutes later, and he died." Greg wiped at his face again. "It's corny, I know. But . . . ."

"It's really not," Dominic replied. "If it hadn't been for his cicada stories, we all would have drowned back there."

"You think so?" Greg laughed again, tears still spilling onto his cheeks. He took off his glasses and set them in his lap. Though his eyes were red, and his eyelids beginning to swell, his gaze was calm and clear. "That's what my grandfather always said: That if it hadn't been for the cicada, and its ability to transform, humanity would have drowned." He wiped his eyes with the collar of his shirt. "I felt his presence back there. I feel like the cicada was a sign, put there especially for me. A good sign." He lowered his face into his hands and wept.

"I'm sorry," Greg said when he lifted his head. "I'm just crying because I miss my *shicheii*. It was really hard on my family when he died. And I . . . wish I could have become stronger when he was alive."

Dominic was quiet, still trying to overcome his surprise, but at last he said: "Honestly, *I'm* a little ashamed. I've been sitting here thinking, 'What was the point of that stupid cicada riddle?' I forget that it might have a meaning for someone else."

"The Geryon thing, and Devil's Bridge—those all had meaning for me," Greg said. "I feel like they're reflections of things that have happened in my life— things that gave me anxiety, or . . . situations when I acted like a jerk." He paused. "I've been trying really hard to change. It's the reason I agreed to help you find Hannah; I thought that by taking a risk to save someone, I was being brave and selfless. It's the reason I went down the blowhole after you—although, in retrospect, that wasn't brave. It was really dumb. I'm a coward, but I'm usually not stupid. I'm still not sure why I did that."

"You needed to be here," Dominic said.

"Maybe. Yeah, I think so. That guy, Aquarius, was talking about flushing out corruption—and there's so much corruption, so much oppression in our community that needs to be dealt with. I joined a group that focuses on land rights, because it's something I care about and I thought it would be a good starting point, but sometimes I'm still a coward. It's embarrassing."

"Your grandfather would be proud," Dominic replied. "People can't change all at once. Making the effort, and sticking to it, is what counts."

Greg nodded. He sniffled and turned back to the

front of the boat.

Dominic glanced back at Surina, but she seemed oblivious to the exchange that had just transpired. Her eyes were stern and focused on the sea; the motor droned loudly beside her, and she sat directly behind Dominic, so that he blocked her view of Greg. Her perspective assured that she had missed the moving speech, and Dominic vowed that he would share it with her later—perhaps when they were safe at home.

He resumed his watchful stance and rode on quietly toward the dark mountain.

7: Capricornus

The mountain proved to be an unwelcoming mound of gray and black rock with wisps of greenery scattered around its base. As the boat approached, Greg called out: "It's a sign!"

"What's a sign?" Dominic asked.

Greg pointed to a diamond-shaped metal signpost rising from the water. It read: *Capricornus. Rough road ahead.*

"This is it," Dominic said. "Where should we dock?"

"It looks like there's a good spot ahead of us," Surina replied. "There's a trail leading up the mountain. You've been here before, right?"

"No," Dominic said. "When I was in Capricornus, there was just a lot of water and a goat-fish lady. Nothing really happened. We rode from Scorpius to Aquarius on her back, and she told stories."

They pulled the boat up onto shore, an expanse of hard pebbles that crunched noisily under their feet. Another signpost awaited them; Surina examined it while Dominic and Greg secured the boat on land.

"It's a map," Surina said as the men joined her. "We're right here." She pointed to a spot labeled *Algedi (Alpha Capricorni).*

Dominic moved closer. "How do you know?"

She lowered her finger, exposing a red arrow and the words "YOU ARE HERE."

"Ah," Dominic said.

"It looks like we can get to Sagittarius if we follow this

trail—but it goes up into this peak." She pointed at the nearest mass of rising rock. "It's labeled on the map as Beta Capricorni. We can enter Sagittarius over here, at Omega."

Dominic studied the map. It did, indeed, show a dotted trail leading toward an area marked "Sagittarius," while a separate trail led to the peaks marked *Nashira (Gamma Capricorni)* and *Deneb Algedi (Delta Capricorni)*. The path to Sagittarius was the shorter, with one peak to navigate: the smallest peak, labeled *Dabih (Beta Capricorni)*.

Dominic lifted his gaze to the mountain ahead. It was small on the map, but he felt his heart sinking as he looked across its breadth and height.

"I think I found the labor," Surina said. She reached behind the signpost and struggled for a moment before freeing the strip of paper. "Labor number six," she read aloud. "Capture the Erymanthian bore; a mighty bluff sustains its roar, so to this nearest summit climb. You'll bear it forth all in good time." She paused. "'Bore' is spelled B-O-R-E."

Dominic let out a small sigh. "The nearest summit is . . . high. Let's go."

They followed the path toward the rising peak. Dominic tried to shake off a sudden sense of doom as they walked; the area close to shore was green with small shrubs and tall cacti, and the path had become soft and sandy, but as they drew closer to the mountain, the green hues faded to stark gray. Sharp stones poked from the dirt path, the brush looked half-dead, and the skeletons of barren bushes reached toward the travelers like grasping claws. The trail wound up into the base of the mountain, and to Dominic's right there was only rock, mud, and deep crevices leading into darkness.

"This place reminds me of White Tank Mountain," Surina said. "I did a run there last year."

"A mud run?" Greg asked.

"No. Well, sort of. It wasn't supposed to be a mud run, but it rained, and I slipped at—"

"That's unfortunate," Dominic cut in. "Let's change the subject."

Surina walked in silence for a while, focusing on the stone-riddled path. "Actually, the map reminded me a little bit of a White Tank map I saw. This trail we're on would be along Goat Canyon. The Capricorn is a goat, isn't it?"

"Sort of," Dominic said.

"And doesn't 'Algedi' come from the Arabic word for 'goat'?"

"I don't remember."

"I just think it's interesting." Surina held out her hand. "Is it raining?"

"I really hope not. I'm sick of being cold and wet."

"Surina, what's the run at White Tank like?" Greg asked. "Do you go up into the mountains?"

"*I* didn't. I just did the 5k, but there are longer runs that go up into the mountains. The people who did those came back even muddier than me."

"I did the Zombie Run at a ski hill," Greg said. "It was pretty intense at first, but only the first kilometer was on the hill."

"I've done a mud run at a ski area," Surina replied. "Our first obstacle was a knotted rope on a steep hill. There was a creek right beforehand, and everyone had to cross it, so we were all soaked when we got to the ropes—and the ropes got saturated with water. They were so slick that people's hands kept slipping, and people were sliding down the mountain and crashing into each other."

"Guys," Dominic said. "Remember, this place takes your ideas and makes them real. That already happened with the piggyback bridge thing, and it happened with the

Geryon statue coming to life. You guys talked about those things, and they happened."

"Geryon didn't come to life because I talked about it," Greg insisted. "That was an informed prediction."

"The bridge thing wasn't an informed prediction," Dominic said. "Right? Surina, you know what I'm talking about."

Surina looked apologetically at Greg. "He's not wrong."

The trail curved outward, and Dominic had a glimpse of flat land beyond. A narrow trail led across the realm, and at its border was a large stone archway with the word "SAGITTARIUS" across the top. Beyond that, Dominic saw nothing of note except for a small square structure. "Look," he said. "You can see Sagittarius from here. It's not that far away—and it looks like this trail just goes around the base of the mountain. I don't think we'll have to do any climbing."

"The paper said we have to climb," Greg replied.

"Well, let's not talk about it."

The trail curved back inward. It curved in at such a severe degree that it ran into the mountain, coming to an abrupt end. The travelers suddenly found themselves on a narrowing path that disappeared into a flat wall of rock. Though they were still at the mountain's base, they were several yards above the ground; a steep cliff rose both above and below, and only route remained: a single knotted rope that trailed up the cliff, leading to a ledge some thirty feet above.

Surina winced as she looked at Dominic. "Sorry," she said.

"I'll go first," he offered. "I don't . . . ." He trailed off as a sudden gust of wind sounded nearby. No—not wind, but rain. It fell in a sudden rush, dousing the travelers and the rope alike.

Dominic stared at Surina, blinking away the water that

dripped from his hair onto his face. "I'll go first," he repeated.

The knots on the rope were spaced so far apart that Dominic couldn't quite reach the next. After just a few knots, he felt his skin beginning to blister as he tried to tighten his grip around the sleek length and pull himself to the next knot. His shoes slipped uselessly against rock; the rope became ever wetter, sliding through his grasp. Surina and Greg tried to support him with directions and encouragement from below, and Dominic tried to refrain from telling them to shut up.

"Hey," said a voice just below him. Dominic looked down to see Greg just inches from his feet. "I'm going to go up one more notch, and you can stand on my shoulder. I'll hoist you up to the next knot."

"Thanks," Dominic said, and felt truly grateful.

They made a slow, awkward climb toward the ledge. After several slips and heart-pounding moments of panic, Dominic heaved himself up and scooted toward the mountain with a deep sense of relief. Greg followed a moment later. He turned to cheer Surina on as she finished the last few feet to safety.

"Just like a mud run," Greg said, grinning as he helped Surina onto the ledge. "That was fun, actually."

"It wasn't bad," Surina said, wiping water from her face. She held out her forearms and examined the scabs forming there, and Greg's expression changed to one of concern.

"I forgot about your arms," he said.

"They're fine," Surina said. "They're a little chafed where the rope brushed against me, but it looks like they're healing." She let out a nervous chuckle. "I'm glad. I was worried that it would be like a zombie bite—that it would fester and get worse, or that it would start to turn me into . . . I don't know."

The trail curved inward again. While the next section

remained obscured from view, Dominic tried to think of anything but ropes and mud runs. Instead, he envisioned dry deserts and wide mountain paths descending toward flat ground.

The rain stopped. The tension in Dominic's shoulders eased.

"So," Greg said to Surina, "do you plan on doing more of those runs?" His voice hummed with enthusiasm. "There's one that I might do this fall, and a few next summer. If you're going, we could meet up."

"Maybe," Surina said. "I'm a little wary of mud runs now. I got hepatitis after the last one, and my doctor thought I might have gotten it during the run."

"Oh. Wait . . . you got hepatitis?"

"Yeah. My liver was seriously inflamed. The doctors didn't know what was wrong at first, so I had to go back three times. The third time, I was so weak I could barely walk; one of my friends had to roll me into the hospital in a wheelchair, and I ended up needing a hospital bed. I was out over a thousand dollars, even with insurance, and I was sick for months."

"Oh." Greg pondered that for a moment. "Yeah, now that I think about it, I'm surprised I didn't catch anything from the Zombie Run. I found out later that people were drunk and peeing in the mud baths. There were these deep pits—"

"Guys," Dominic said. "Please stop."

Surina came to a sudden halt. "Damn," she said.

Another wall of rock blocked the way. Another rope led upward—a ladder, rather than a single length. The trail on which the travelers stood was much higher now, several stories above ground and nearly halfway up the mountain, and the rope was much longer.

"Damn," Dominic echoed softly. He glanced again toward the steep drop below, and then decided it was better not to look.

He found the ladder easier than the rope, its rungs damp but well within his reach, and slicker in some spots than others, so that he had to feel across each rung's breadth to find a secure grip. His already-blistered palms burned with the effort, and when he reached the top and pulled his quaking body onto the ledge, he found himself pleased at the sight of snow. Dominic crawled to the nearest snowdrift and thrust his burning hands into it.

"Brrr," Surina said as she reached the top. "I'm freezing! Oh, my god, Dominic—are you insane? Why are you in the snow?"

He withdrew his hands and stood up. "I'm not a fan of this version of Capricorn. Let's leave."

The path cut across the mountain, following a low groove that ran between glistening formations of black stone. Columns and boulders rose on either side, patterned by cold winds, dotted here and there with hardy shrubs.

This trail was wider than the other, so that at least two of the party could walk side by side. Greg and Dominic took the front, while Surina lagged behind, trying to warm her hands by blowing into them.

"This is getting a little ridiculous, don't you think?" she asked. "It's like this place is giving us challenges just for the sake of being annoying. Making us swim in the ocean, cross a dangerous bridge, climb mountains—for what? There's no lesson, or . . . ."

"Would you prefer a lesson?" Dominic asked.

" . . . No. Well, I suppose the bridge had a lesson, but not the ocean."

"There might not be a lesson for *you*," Dominic said, "but that doesn't mean there's no lesson. Anyway, there might be some great purpose behind our adventure in the ocean. You got to sing the glorious Nereids song. Who knows what might come of all your *ooh-ooh*ing and *ah-ah*ing." He glanced back, smiling in response to Surina's sour look. "Also, I gave you the belt. Who knows; you might save the world with that belt."

They walked on in silence for a while, and then Greg looked down at Dominic with a twinge of remorse. "Hey. I know I kind of said this already, but I'm sorry I knocked you down back there."

"What? Back where?"

"At the temple."

"Oh, that," Dominic said. "Well, I can't blame you. Frankly, I thought Aquarius' entrance was more terrifying than the Geryon statue."

They slowed as they came to an obstacle: a bush that blocked most of the path, growing thick and greenish-gray between two boulders. Greg began to push past it, carefully bending the branches as he went. "Yeah, you seemed underwhelmed by the statue," he said. "I know I was being a jerk—you know, when I said I was going to run off and leave the two of you. But like I said, I'm working on it. We're cool, right?"

"We're cool," Surina answered, joining them.

Dominic started to agree, but stood gaping as a dark figure filled the space opposite the boulders. He caught sight of two dark eyes filled with spite, a face ghastly and angry as a hellion, and thin lips that spit the words: "I wouldn't come this way if I were you."

Greg looked at the specter—and a second later he fled, knocking Surina into a snowdrift as he went.

Dominic recognized the purple robe and hateful, mocking face. Tagua had been waiting for them. He held out a hand, and a moment later the bush uprooted and burst from between the boulders, its branches scraping Dominic's arms and face.

"That's better," Tagua said crisply. He stepped through the rock-walled portal, followed closely by four ghoulish children, and lastly by Hannah. He gestured with one long, thin hand toward Surina. "Let's see your latest command," he said, and one of the ghouls immediately

119

went to Surina and thrust a hand into her jeans pocked. Surina gasped and shoved the creature, but it came away with the strip of papyrus clutched in its fingers.

Tagua took it and read aloud: "Labor number six: Capture the Erymanthian *bore*." He let out a dry chuckle. "Here we have three bores, but I only need one—and just as easily captured as in the myth. I have gleaned some knowledge about Greek tales; I confess I don't know much about the Erymanthian boar, but here is what I do know. Hercules hunted it and discovered it quickly. Just as simply, he startled it out of a thicket and chased it into deep snow. I didn't even need to do that; one of the other *bores* did it for me."

Dominic tried his best to look unimpressed. He let out a loud yawn. "Oh, I'm sorry—who's the bore? Rambling narcissists are the most tedious of all. You probably haven't stopped praising yourself long enough to consider that."

From the snowdrift, Surina gave him a look of fearful amazement. She mouthed the words: *Shut up.*

Tagua's smile vanished; his face settled into a slight sneer. "Here is what else I know. The boar was a beast who ravaged the lands. It caused starvation and disease . . . much like the devastation you caused in Leo." Tagua's eyes shifted from Dominic to Surina. "Did you know that your friend killed the king of that land, and devastated its inhabitants, all for his own gain?"

"Yes, she knows," Dominic replied. "What happened to the other kids who were with you? Did you use them up? What was it—the flood? Did that take a life or two?"

"Those creatures," Tagua sneered, "are not alive. But they do have *substance* that is both tangible and—"

He let out a sudden *oof* as Dominic punched him. Dominic meant to aim for the stomach, but at the last moment he decided that the ghoulish man deserved a low blow. He slammed his fist into Tagua's crotch instead.

"Let's go," Dominic said, beckoning his companions. "I'm sick of listening to this moron."

"Dominic!" Hannah cried. She ran to him, placing herself between him and Tagua. "Don't," she whispered pleadingly. She leaned forward, close to Dominic's ear. "Trust me; you need to let him take me and Surina."

He looked probingly into Hannah's eyes. She looked sincere—but perhaps he just saw what he hoped to see.

And then Hannah's eyes were gone, replaced by a sudden blackness, by breathlessness and pain. Someone—something—had knocked Dominic back several paces, several yards even, hard onto the unyielding rock. He bounced into a sitting position and tried to gasp for air, but found himself sinking back onto the rock, still breathless.

"Tie her," Tagua snapped.

Dominic heard a ripping sound. He craned his neck, struggling to see. One of Tagua's minions had torn a strip of fabric from his tunic. The other yanked Surina to her feet. Dominic watched helplessly as her wrists were tied behind her back.

"As I was saying," Tagua continued. He was trying to sound unruffled, but Dominic heard a high, unsteady rasp in his voice. "He chased the *bore* into deep snow. He then bound it—" He yanked on the tie that bound Surina's wrists— "much more securely than before, and he brought the creature back to Mycenae, a place of culture and sophistication, far away from its fellow beasts."

Dominic took a shallow, pained breath. He couldn't resist asking: "What culture? You're running out of prisoners."

Tagua's lips spread into a mocking grin. "Prisoners? You mean, people like Hannah? She is bound to Lupus because she placed my crown on her head. She willingly became part of my kingdom and vowed to serve me—so *you* could go home, back to the mundanity of your own life. Would you take the same risk to save your friends? It is a gamble, but the weak must always decide which deal to take, and simply wish for luck, while the powerful determine the stakes." He beckoned his remaining companions, who latched onto Surina's arms and led her forcefully away. As they departed, Tagua cast a final smirk at Dominic and called: "Better luck next time."

8: Sagittarius

Dominic became conscious of someone watching him—of a pair of brown eyes peeking over the top of a nearby rock, eyes framed by spectacles and wide with alarm.

"Are you okay?" Greg asked. He stepped down from behind the rocks and crept toward Dominic, glancing nervously down the path Tagua had taken.

"I'm really not," Dominic said. "My back . . . ."

"Can you stand up?"

"Give me a minute." Dominic closed his eyes. He tried to draw a deep breath. "I have a weak back. He might have really messed it up."

"Good thing it's not real," Greg replied.

Dominic shifted slightly, felt a stab of pain. "What?"

"Your back getting slammed against the ground. It's not real. Right? This place is a hallucination. We're probably sitting back in the cave in Wupatki. Or . . . ."

"Let's hope so," Dominic said.

"I was going to say, 'Or we're dead.'"

"In which case, I still didn't hurt my back. Right now I'll take either option."

After a few minutes, Dominic managed to stand upright. He declined Greg's offer of help, and together they made their way across the mountain path—a simple but tedious path that zigzagged down the mountain and across a flat plain. There, the earth was studded with the same cacti and scrawny shrubs, the landscape mostly a wash of browns and grays with little green to be found.

The few bushes on the mountain path were dry and brittle; no breeze blew through them, no birds and insects chirped there, and the only movement Dominic could see was the dropping of dead twigs. He walked in numb silence, staring down at the stone-studded trail and wishing it would end.

He found the next riddle wedged between two stones on the archway into Sagittarius. "Labor number seven," he read. "Steel the mare of Diomedes, driven to a final choice. The fire that she has held within must find release through her own voice, the captor thus consumed by death; the weary captives then rejoice." He showed the scrap to Greg. "'Steel' is spelled S-T-E-E-L."

Greg looked up at the arch. It was comprised of deep brown and russet stones and mortar, unlike the rock that comprised the mountain. One side bore a carving of a centaur-like man, with a panther's body instead of a horse, two wings spread wide behind him, his tail sectioned and barbed at the end like a scorpion's tail. His hands clutched a bow loaded with an arrow; snakes stood on either side of him, balancing upright on the tips of their tails.

The opposite side featured a similar figure: a man holding a panther on a leash, the other hand grasping a bow and a single arrow. The same pair of snakes bordered him, and above his head was a small scorpion. The rest of the arch was patternless except for the word "SAGITTARIUS" spelled in beige stone cuttings across the top.

"Sagittarius is a horse, right?" Greg asked.

Dominic drew a finger against the outline of the half-panther. "It's a centaur. Well . . . it's an archer, usually depicted as a centaur. This shows a half wildcat, though, rather than a horse." He stepped back, looking from one figure to the other. "These are both depictions of Nergal, the Sumerian deity. The Sagittarius constellation is supposed to represent him."

"Nergal?"

"Yeah. He's . . . the god of war and death." Dominic paused, and added: "Inflicted death. Not natural death."

"Is that a bad sign?"

Dominic sighed and didn't answer. He stood looking at the landscape beyond the arch: small, flat, unremarkable except for a small ziggurat in the center.

"Not much happening outside," Dominic said. "Let's go inside."

The ziggurat was built completely of bricks, varying in length and shades of brown, red, and tan. Greg took a deep breath as they approached and let out a wistful sigh. "It's like we're at Wupatki," he said.

"Wouldn't that be nice," Dominic replied.

"This looks like the tall house—the way it supposedly looked back when people lived there. *That's* a good sign, right? It might mean we're getting closer to home."

They paused at the only visible entrance, an open rectangle that led into darkness. A few angular pillars were visible in the space ahead, and the rest was obscured by the lack of light.

"There's a ladder to the upper levels," Greg said. "Should we climb it?"

"Sure. My hands could use more blisters."

The wooden ladder leaned against the exterior, sturdy and well-constructed—far preferable to Capricornus' rope ladder, Dominic thought. He climbed and walked the promenade on the second story, peeking into the entrances of the central court and finding more darkness.

"Well," Greg said, "it's just as creepy as the ground floor."

"I don't see any carvings, or symbols," Dominic mused. "Just plain brick."

"Is that important?"

"The riddle told us to look for a mare. I'm looking for

a carving—or a statue, or something."

"Do you still have your flashlight?" Greg asked.

"Nope. I lost it somewhere in Pisces. It probably fell into the sea."

"Maybe it isn't an animal," Greg said. "These riddles seem to use a lot of plays on words. 'Mare' also means nightmare—well, except it's more like a demon that tries to attack you at night. It sits on your chest and tries to steal your life force."

"I don't think that's what we're looking for," Dominic replied, withdrawing from the dark space. "Let's go up another level. There must be another ladder somewhere, or stairs."

Greg followed, but continued his theory: "Didn't the riddle describe something sort of demonic, though? Like, a mare who's full of fire, and who holds people captive, and she's going to unleash her fire and inflict death?"

"I didn't interpret it that way."

"Can I see it?"

Dominic handed him the scrap. Greg read it silently and said, "We should be on our guard."

"I already am," Dominic replied.

"It sounds like we need to free people from the night witch." Greg paused. "In folklore, the night witch rode a horse. Maybe that's the symbolism: instead of a centaur, it's a night witch on horseback."

Dominic stopped. He turned and looked up at Greg. After a moment, he held out his hand; Greg gave him the papyrus, and Dominic stood staring at him until Greg finally said: "Sorry. I'll stop talking about demons and night witches."

"Thankyou." Dominic continued around the corner. Another ladder led up to the top level; the brick promenade there took up more than half the area, so that it was more like a rooftop with a small enclosure erected at one end. Dominic crossed the roof toward the shelter,

gazing across the landscape toward the next realm—
Scorpius, he recalled.

Inside the shelter was a single window, and on its
frame rested a wooden archery bow; it stood upright on a
rotating pedestal, loaded and ready to fire. Dominic went
to it and found that it was placed to his own height; the
scope above the arrow rest stood at his eye level.

"What is it?" Greg asked.

"I'm not sure yet," Dominic replied. He peered through
the sight, and then he withdrew. "I think I can see all the
way into Scorpius." He leaned close again. In the
distance, a low hedge was arranged in the outline of a
scorpion. Dominic could see a few figures gathered near
the end of the tail, black-haired and dressed in pale
garments. "Someone's down there," he said. "It looks like
. . . ."

He was about to say *Tagua's minions*, but as he shifted
the pedestal, he caught sight of a familiar face.

"It's Surina," he said.

He quickly diverted the bow's aim. He pulled the arrow
from its rest and set it aside.

"Is she all right?" Greg asked.

"They seem fine." Dominic peered into the scope
again. "Tagua is there, too. Actually . . . the way he's
standing right now, he's an easy target."

"So . . . what are you going to do?"

"I'm only going to do what the riddle told me to do. It
didn't tell me to shoot Tagua."

"Are you sure? It said to inflict death."

"I learned my lesson about shooting things in this
place," Dominic said. "Tagua is already dead, and I don't
think an arrow will do much to him. It will just piss him
off. And the riddle specifically said *she* will inflict death.
We're just supposed to 'steel' her." He moved the scope,
looking out across the landscape. A carved slab, which
looked much like the Raimondi Stele, stood just beyond

the scorpion's left claw; it surely marked Ophiuchus. The tall, enclosed structure beyond the right claw, a pale building that resembled a large concrete block, was probably Lupus; its size and shape matched what Dominic remembered of its interior. "They're headed for Ophiuchus. We might catch up to them if we head through Scorpius."

"Can I see?"

Dominic stood back, and Greg stooped low to peer through the glass. "I see a nightmare," he murmured.

"What?"

"Hannah. In this light . . . wow. She really looks frightening." Greg stood upright and gestured to the arrow that now rested on the windowsill. "I know this will make me sound like a jerk, but . . . are you sure that thing is Hannah? Because we have a steel arrow, and over there we have something that looks like a nightmare. It has claws, it has a terrifying face, it has a tail . . . ."

"We're not shooting Hannah," Dominic said flatly.

"Can I see the riddle again?"

Dominic handed him the paper. "You can—but one of us will get stabbed by that arrow before Hannah does. Understand?"

He watched through the scope as Hannah led the way into Ophiuchus. She paused at the threshold and let the others enter first, and as she stood facing him, Dominic could not deny that she looked like a nightmare. Her hands were thin and clawed, and the little tufts of feathers on her head looked like a pair of horns.

At that moment, Hannah looked up. Her gaze seemed to meet with Dominic's; she looked with such intensity that he was almost convinced she could see him.

Slowly, she raised her hand. She held it open, palm aside, and then waved it back and forth. Her fingers wriggled; she made a fist and jabbed it outward, and then she jerked her hand up and made a "peace" sign.

Dominic stared in confusion, and then it hit him. "It's our secret handshake," he murmured.

"What?" Greg asked.

Dominic didn't reply, but watched with quiet amazement as Hannah lowered her hand. *Does she know?* he wondered—and then he remembered that Hannah had read all of the labors, had been the one who placed them. She probably guessed that he and Greg had reached Sagittarius, that they now stood looking down at her and wondering what to do next. Perhaps she understood even more than that.

Though in some ways, Hannah was still the person he remembered, she had changed—and not just in physical form. Surina had described her behavior on the Eridanus as impatient, despairing, tired, and defensive of Tagua. Dominic had yet to see such traits. Even now, as he looked through the scope at Hannah's lion-like form and fading eyes, he saw only a quiet wisdom and weary determination.

Slowly, he drew back. "Let's wait and see what happens," he said.

"For how long?"

Dominic hesitated. "I don't think we should wait here. Let's try to catch up with them."

Greg stared at him in confusion. "But . . . ."

"I think that our task here is to do nothing." Dominic said. "We need to trust Hannah to make her final decision—to end things with Tagua through her own power."

Greg looked unconvinced, so Dominic continued: "Remember how you were so sure that the Geryon statue would come to life? I'm just as certain that Hannah is handling things over there. She needs my support . . . and I need her to do whatever it is she's destined to do."

9: Scorpius

Surina stood at the tip of Scorpius' tail, its point marked by a sleek reddish-brown stone raised up in the shape of a giant scorpion stinger. Its slender tip narrowed and curved into a sharp needle—and on that needle was impaled a strip of paper. Hannah picked it up and read aloud:

"Labor number eight: Obtain the girdle of Serket; she'll teach the song which heals your stings. Advance to Lyra; play the cosmos on the girdle's uncoiled strings." Hannah turned to Surina and stood looking at her, as if waiting for something.

Surina shook her head, mouthing the word: *What?*

"Surina is a music teacher," Hannah explained. "There's a lyre in Lyra, but it doesn't have any strings." Hannah didn't break her gaze from Surina as she spoke. Seeing that Surina still didn't understand, she added: "We need your belt."

Surina felt a small sting of resentment. The words felt like a betrayal; Tagua hadn't noticed the belt yet, as it remained hidden beneath Surina's T-shirt. She saw his eyes dart to her waist, and she instinctively tied to place a hand over the belt, as if to protect it—but her hands were still tied snugly behind her back.

"What about it?" she asked Hannah.

"Take it to Lyra," Hannah replied softly, "and uncoil it."

Surina hesitated. "Do you think we can use the yarns as lyre strings? That won't work."

"It's the only thing that makes sense," Hannah said, "so we need to try it." She reached for Surina's arm with her furred paw. "Come with me."

Surina shrunk away from her, but she said, "All right. I'll go."

The realm of Scorpius was marked by little more than a low, thorny hedge with tiny purple flowers and bulbous leaves—a row of shrubs arranged in the outline of a scorpion. Hannah led the group through the left-hand claw, which opened into Ophiuchus: a small, circular, domed chamber with a large stone slab standing upright in the center.

The gray slab was carved from top to bottom, the lower section with the image of a feline figure in an elaborate headdress—almost identical to the Raimondi Stele that stood at Chavín, but with a less cartoonish and more detailed face. The figure stood facing the viewer, gripping two staffs, one on either side; one staff blossomed at the top, emitting a small bud and two curving leaves, while the other remained bare. The feet and hands bore protracted claws, sharp canines protruded from the open mouth, and stylized snakes comprised its hair—and yet, the figure didn't look ferocious. Its upward gaze was full of worry, its mouth open in astonishment.

The upper section bore the image of a man, suspended upside-down just above the staff-bearing figure. He wore a simple loincloth around his waist, and in one hand he wielded a club, ready to bring it down on the staff bearer's head.

"That's Hercules," Hannah said, pointing at the top figure, "trying to conquer the beings of the underworld." She pointed to the lower figure and added: "And that's Ophiuchus."

"Yeah, I remember," Surina said, thinking of all the time she'd spent studying the constellations—mostly in books, less often under the light-polluted night sky.

131

She looked again at the feline face of Ophiuchus, at the eyes that stared upward—and as Hannah also looked up, Surina realized with a sudden sense of awe that aside from the snakes, the figure looked remarkably like her.

Surina followed Hannah's gaze, and across the curved ceiling she saw an arrangement of golden stars. She immediately recognized it as the Draco constellation. Superimposed around it was the image of a dragon, outlined in varying shades of sparkling gold against the deep blue stone, its tail long and meandering, its wide mouth exposing the dark tunnel of its throat.

As they walked past the stone, Surina saw that it was not a single slab; it had an identical carved surface angling toward the back of the chamber. Hannah noted Surina's surprise. "It's a triangle," she said. "A triangular prism. It has three carvings, one facing each portal." She gestured to the other two exits: to the left, an archway labeled *Lyra*, and to the right, another that read *Corona Borealis*.

"Are all three sides the same?" Surina asked.

"Exactly the same," Hannah replied.

"I beg pardon," Tagua interrupted crisply. "Are you giving a tour or solving the puzzle?"

Hannah didn't respond, but entered the left-hand realm: a miniature, domed arena with a circular stone floor, in which the sole object of focus was a small lyre in the shape of a bull's head.

The instrument was made of polished wood. Its horns comprised the soundbox, with two sound holes in the shape of nostrils, and the horns served as the arms. A lighter grain of wood had been used for the center of the face, so that a vertical stripe descended between the eyes, while the sides were a darker chestnut. The central stripe ended in the flared nostrils, between which was attached a stylized wooden ridge—and below the head, a plaque announced the next riddle.

Hannah turned to Tagua. "Surina has to play the lyre to keep Draco asleep. You'll have to untie her hands."

Tagua muttered his approval. One of the silent youths went to Surina's side and tugged the ties loose. She looked down at the red marks on her wrists and the scratches along her arms, and she tried to flex the stiffness out of her fingers.

Surina loosened the belt from her waist and fumbled with one end. "I can't pull it apart," she said.

Hannah smiled—a weary smile, but a smile nonetheless. The blue tint in her eyes seemed to have deepened, and the pupils dilated, so that only a sliver of the brown iris remained. Her face was a sickly gray-blue, but that brief smile gave her a sense of vibrancy.

She reached out and, with a few quick maneuvers of one claw, she sliced through the ends of the belt. "I'm meant to use my claws in this realm," she said quietly.

Surina began to unravel the yarns, but she slowed her pace as she noticed another kind of fiber mixed in with the wool. She paused to count the threads.

"What's wrong?" Hannah asked.

Surina shook her head. "Nothing. It's . . . catgut."

"What's that?"

"It's a cord made from animal intestine. It's used to string musical instruments." Surina continued to unravel the threads, adding: "I guess we'll have strings after all." She cast an anxious glance at Tagua; he stood in silence a few feet away, his face grim and watchful.

Surina finished dissembling the belt. She knelt before the lyre and laid twelve catgut strings in front of it. Her gaze fell on the bull's eyes—two large ovals set with deep brown stones—and she was overcome with a strange sensation: a sense of peace and calm, but one so powerful that it made her hands tremble. She took a deep breath and looked down at the plaque, reviewing the task at hand.

AN ENIGMA AND RIDDLE:

Clever Chronos cleaves away his antiquated being;
Ring within a ring will sound a portal's opening.

Offal reigns will free the tunes of which the bovine
dreams.
If the player yokes his horns, he'll undergird your
schemes.
So you must attune him, a quintuple plus two halves.
Three starts empower griffin, viper, calm the
frightened calves.

"Ah . . . it's an enigma," Surina muttered. "Those are hard. Don't you have to take the first letters of a word and think of a word that ends with the same letters?"

"I think the answer to the enigma is *circle*," Hannah replied. "I figured it out before."

"Where do you see that?"

Hannah pointed to the word *Clever*. "'First three' means the first three letters of the enigma: C-L-E. They're the last three letters in 'circle,' and the second line describes a circle. Well, actually, it describes two circles."

"Okay. So that's the enigma, and then there's a riddle after it?" Surina scanned the next lines. "Three starts. That means the beginnings of three lines, right? Offal, off, offi . . . ." She was silent for some time, and then looked up at Hannah for help. "I don't see it."

"What about 'a quintuplet plus two halves'?" Hannah asked. "It must be a clue."

Surina looked again. "It's probably talking about music, but I still don't see the three starts. Offi, offit, offifth . . . ." Suddenly she inhaled sharply. "Oh. . . ." She glanced back at Tagua, saw him watching with his arms folded, his remaining three spirit-deprived ghouls close by his side. "I wonder if it's 'circle of fifths,'" she said softly. She pointed at the lines, drawing her fingertip along the letters as she spelled them aloud. "O-F-F, I-F-T-H—"

"And the *s* in 'So' makes the last letter," Hannah finished. "It's 'circle of fifths.'"

Surina frowned. "There's a problem. First of all, we're missing part of the lyre. There's no yoke."

"It's back here," Hannah said. She reached behind the lyre and picked up a broad wooden stick studded with tuning pegs—two rows of seven pegs. She held it out to Surina.

Surina turned the yoke over in her hand. "This is made for a double-stringed lyre," she said. She stood up and moved to the opposite side of the lyre, and found it exactly the same as the front. "It's a double lyre," she said. "I can play both sides at the same time. I think this might actually work."

She took the yoke and fit the spools onto the tips of the horns. The yoke slid easily into place. "The catgut is the *offal reins*; it's made from intestines," she explained.

Hannah winced. "Lovely."

Surina knotted the ends of the strings and threaded them through the first tailpiece, and then across the notches in the nose chain, which served as a bridge. As she worked, Hannah said quietly: "I've tried to solve this puzzle for a long time. Virgo kept encouraging me, even though she knew I didn't have the strings or the knowledge to solve it. I needed you." She smiled again and added: "That was the real lesson."

Surina tried not to think of Tagua, who listened silently to their muted conversation. "What do you think will happen when we play the lyre?" she asked.

"I think we'll empower a griffin and a viper, and calm some frightened calves. There's a griffin constellation right beside us, in Cygnus; a lot of people see it as a swan, but in Sumerian mythology, it was a griffin . . . or a winged panther, or something. And the viper is Draco."

Surina finished threading the strings through the yoke. "This is played open-string, so there will only be twelve notes," she said. "A 'quintuple and two halves' probably means a diatonic scale—five whole steps and two half-steps. But we're also supposed to use the circle of fifths, so . . . I'll try the diatonic circle of fifths."

"Do you know how to do that?"

"Yeah. I'll do an easy one—C major—and just play the chord progressions. I'll, um, I'll do triads and single notes. Does that sound okay? Or should I just—"

"I don't know anything about music," Hannah replied. "It sounds great."

"Okay." Surina worked slowly, humming every now and then as she turned the tuning pegs with shaking hands. "The circle of fifths is a progressive wheel," she said, trying to calm herself by focusing on something other than Tagua. "It's like a map; you can use it to create a song that includes all twelve notes on the Western scale, but instead of being dissonant, it has beautiful harmonies and chord progressions." Surina paused to check the pitches and added: "These strings don't stay in tune very well. I'll have to adjust them a few times to get the right pitches." A tremor sounded in her voice. She was overcome, still, by a conflicting sense of peace and doom—of something significant about to happen, something benevolent but frightening.

"Okay," she said at last, lowering her quaking arms. "I'm going to play."

"Not yet," Hannah said. "Wait until I bring the keys to Ophiuchus. I'll tell you when to start."

"What keys?"

"The stars from Orion. I thought I had to use them to rebuild the chariot, but I got to Ophiuchus another way. I think the only reason I rode the chariot in the first place was so that I could crash. I learned more from that than from anything else." She gave Surina a peculiar look—an expression that Surina couldn't quite interpret.

Hannah reached beneath her arm, into the fleshy pocket, and withdrew the topmost objects: a pair of metal discs. The surface of one disc was exposed in Hannah's palm, the one marked *Alnitak* and stamped with the image of a sword. "There's a reason it took me so long to find these two," Hannah said. "Saiph represents the supporting foot—the willingness to stand upright. Alnitak represents . . . ." Hannah didn't finish the thought. She tucked the discs back into her pocket and turned to Tagua. "I'm ready to open the gate."

Tagua's eyes lit with greedy interest. "Guard her," he snapped at the blank-eyed children, but Hannah stopped them. "We need to keep Lyra clear," she said. "If there are other people in the chamber, it will mess up the acoustics, and Draco might wake up when I open the gate—and there's nowhere else Surina can run, anyway. If she leaves, she'll have to pass through Ophiuchus."

Tagua frowned, but he complied. He and the others followed Hannah back into the Ophiuchus chamber. The wide entryway, and the close proximity of the stone slab, allowed a close view of the happenings there—and when Hannah spoke, the chamber's acoustics carried her voice clearly.

"These staffs represent balance," Hannah told Tagua. She reached out, lightly touching the gray slab with one long claw. "One side is flowering, blooming, giving. The other side is bare, withholding. In the constellations, the blooming staff points to Corona Borealis, the crown. The other side points to Aquila . . . the griffin."

"That's fascinating," Tagua said dryly. "What does it have to do with opening the sun gate?"

"Ophiuchus gives clues to the sun gate. Everything I've learned here, even what I learned from the libraries outside, has led me closer to unlocking the gate."

"I confess," Tagua said irritably, "I am starting to doubt that you have the slightest clue how to open the sun gate."

"I do have a clue," Hannah said, "but I've had to come at it in a roundabout way. Things that seem irrelevant, or coincidental, sometimes give us the most important hints. Here's an example: My grandmother, my mom's mom, was a writer. She died a few days before my sixth birthday. I never read any of her books, but when you let me go outside to the Apple Valley library, I happened to see a book that she wrote. I only had enough time to read a few pages, and to see that the book was dedicated to me.

On those pages, one of the characters is telling a story about a *pligi*."

"And how is that relevant?"

"My grandmother was Greek," Hannah said. "*Plege* is a Greek word for 'wound,' and *pligi* comes from that word; it means a wounded, broken soul. The story goes like this:

"Once there was a little creature called a pligi who couldn't satisfy its appetite. It floated near a lake, looking for things to eat, and sometimes it would find animals and feed off the animals. But one day a man came to the lake to think about his troubles. The man had been arguing with his wife, and his daily work was wearing on him, and his body was full of aches, and his friends were disloyal. He said to himself, 'Why do I struggle so hard to do the right things, when it gets me few benefits? Ah, I'm just having a hard day; I'll work it out, and things will get better.'"

Surina watched in anxious confusion, her trembling hands poised near the strings. She didn't move, didn't make a sound, but thought: *What the hell is she doing?*

"The pligi heard him talking," Hannah continued, "and it whispered in his ear. It said, 'You work hard all day for your wife, and then you come home and she argues about trifles. Why should you work hard to support your wife?' And the man thought, 'It's true—but my wife works just as hard and takes care of me as well.' The pligi said, 'Your wife pretends to work hard all day, but how much can she really work? You toil all day, but she throws a few potatoes in a pot, wipes the floor, and calls it a day's work—and then you come home tired, and she complains.' The man was quiet, thinking about this, and the pligi continued: 'Without your wife you would have fewer expenses, and then you could work less and have fewer aches. Your wife is causing your misery. Who does she think she is?' The man kept quiet, and the pligi said, 'Your friends don't care about you. They look for ways to manipulate and use you. They stand by your side when you're doing well, but they avoid you when you're downcast; they cast you down even further. Why would you maintain friendships with people? People are worthless. Their hearts are impure.' The man said, 'It's true; the hearts of humans are impure.'"

Tagua's voice dripped sarcasm. "Unless the pligi can open the gate, I do not care."

"The pligi was pleased by the man's words," Hannah continued, "and it said, 'Your own heart betrays you and makes you weak. People take advantage of it and use it to trick you. Why would you need your heart?' The man said, 'You're right; my heart is a weakness. I'm going to throw it away.' So the pligi ate the man's heart, closing its mouth around the organ inside the man's chest, and the man was glad that he wasn't responsible for his heart anymore."

Tagua's face had soured. He bared his teeth, blue-white teeth streaked with black, and seethed: "I am not interested in tedious morality tales!"

"It is relevant," Hannah said calmly, and continued: "The man went home to his wife. She had made a supper, so they sat down to eat—but the woman didn't know that there was a third guest at the table, one that can't be sated by the food of mortals. The pligi had doubled in size, but it was still hungry, so it tricked the woman, telling her 'Your husband is distant from you. See, he's ignoring you and withholding his love. Give him your love so that he remembers what it tastes like.' So the woman gave her love, and the pligi ate it."

With disdain, Tagua said: "You have ten seconds to come to the point."

"The pligi saw the woman's patience, and it said, 'Woman, your husband is frazzled by his work and quick to lose his temper. Give him your patience and your understanding, or he will never remember the value of those things.' The woman gave everything the pligi asked for. Soon there was nothing left of the woman, but the pligi was still hungry, so it said to the husband, 'Look at this ill, depraved woman. This is not the woman you married. You should leave her now. Misery loves company, and if you stay, it will eat you up.' The husband looked at his wife and believed the pligi, so he went to find another woman—and the pligi ate the next woman, too."

Hannah watched Tagua in the dim light of the chamber, as if waiting for a reaction, but he merely glared back at her.

Hannah said: "My grandmother wrote that story because it was the story of her and my grandfather—and of her parents, and my parents too. With my parents, it was my mom who cut down my dad every chance she got. My dad used to take me aside and explain that she couldn't help it because she'd been abused. He didn't know that my mom hurt me with the same abuse, because she would only do it when other people weren't listening.

141

My grandmother was worried that I would carry on the cycle—that I would become angry like my mother, or passive like my father. He put up with her abuse quietly, because he was afraid of hurting her even more. My mom never had any reason to change."

Tagua approached her, his slow steps echoing in the chamber.

"A few weeks after my grandma died, my mom moved to another country—and I was glad. I thought I would finally live in a peaceful home with my father. But then I lost him, too. And now I'm here . . . with you."

Tagua stood close and leaned forward, close enough that Hannah surely felt his cold breath on her face.

"Of . . . what . . . *relevance* . . . is that?" he hissed.

"I will open the gate," Hannah replied, "but I want something in return."

Tagua seemed to freeze. Seconds passed, and then his dark eyes narrowed. "What do you mean?"

"I want your robe," she said softly.

He stared, uncomprehending.

"And I want your wizard's helm," Hannah continued in the same quiet voice, "and your precious stones, and the gold ring that you keep hidden away. And I want your shawl made of blue and silver threads, and your staff made of blue stone. If you give me those things, I will open the gate for you."

Tagua straightened up. His breath escaped in a whispered, mocking laugh. "I see. You're starting to make demands, are you? I can't give those things to a mere girl."

"Do I look like a mere girl?" she mused. "Why can't

142

you give those things up? Do you think you can use them to rule when you get back to Earth?" Hannah added with emphasis: "Those things don't belong to you. They have always belonged to the underworld."

Tagua stared. He was trying, Surina realized, to mask his surprise—both at Hannah's audacity, and at her understanding.

"I already know where you keep those things," Hannah added. "I'll take your robe now, and I'll get the rest myself—right after I open this gate."

"Did the presence of your friends make you brave?" Tagua hissed. His voice, though venomous, betrayed his uncertainty. "You talk about opening gates, but you haven't solved a single section of the puzzle."

"The presence of my friends made me grateful," Hannah replied, "and I told you before: I solved the riddles. Ophiuchus kept telling me to change my perspective, and I started with you. When you insulted me, I tried to put myself in your shoes; I asked myself, 'What would I have to be thinking in order to say those things?' When you sucked the life from people on a whim, and destroyed them without the slightest care, I asked myself the same thing. I kept finding ways to change my perspective—and I finally see how everything is connected, and how it all works."

"Just like that? You suddenly figured it out, all by yourself?"

"Not suddenly," she replied, "and not by myself. The sun gate is a reflection of the Ophiuchus gate; the solution to both gates is a balanced pair of circles."

Tagua's eyes burned with a mix of emotions—

desperation, suspicion, excitement. "One gate unlocks the other?" he asked.

"The gates have to be opened in order," Hannah said. "Before now, I had no order; I let you abuse the heavens because I felt sorry for you. But now I'm here with the seven stars of Orion, the warrior who faced the Bull of Heaven. I'm here with my hero twin, the one who has been my constant support." Hannah looked toward Surina and called: "Play the lyre."

Surina felt a sudden terror wash through her. Her hands shook so that she could hardly place her fingertips against the strings, but she managed to pluck the first few notes. *CEG, C, C, E, G, GBD, G, G, B, D . . . .*

She played through a full cycle and started again, but she faltered as a strange groan resounded through the Ophiuchus chamber. Surina glanced up, and for a moment her fingers froze. Hannah was changing. Her eyes seemed to burn with a hot fire; the furry tufts around her face elongated into sleek, meandering masses, slithering things that resembled snakes, so that Hannah looked even more like the image on the stone slab. A memory struck Surina: Virgo, the queen of the underworld, with snakes forming around her countenance. *To humans, serpents often represent the underworld: challenges, fears, and death. . . . When humans seek the center of the labyrinth, they often look only for birds and the heavens, but the underworld is inevitably there as well. When the figure on the Lanzón looks up at the cosmos, it must also look past the serpent.*

Surina blinked, and Hannah looked herself again—her griffin self, at least. Surina forced her gaze away and plucked at the strings, whispering the names of the notes to help herself focus.

She stopped whispering as Hannah began to speak again. "The anzu, the griffin, has to be the one to open Ophiuchus," Hannah said, "because the griffin has flight. It has painstakingly learned knowledge, and it has claws."

The rumbling grew louder, and Surina heard a sudden, frantic cry from Tagua: "*What are you doing?*"

She looked up. The Ophiuchus chamber was turning, the top of the chamber rotating rapidly toward the bottom. Draco descended toward the floor, becoming more detailed as it moved, so that it was no longer a mere outline dotted with stars. Its face was detailed with greenish-gold scales. Its eyes burned fiery orange, but they receded into the background as the mouth widened and the pink folds of its throat were exposed—and all around its face was a glowing, golden orb, deep and three-dimensional, as if the dragon was centered within a tunnel of light.

Tagua and his minions tumbled to the floor. The scrawny children slid across the stone toward Draco—and then Draco hit bottom, and Surina watched as Tagua's minions were swallowed up into the dragon's mouth.

Hannah didn't fall. She flew. Her wings kept her suspended in mid-air—and with one tawny, long-toed foot, Hannah caught the shoulder of Tagua's purple robe. He hung there by the grace of her talons.

The stone prism, also flipped on its head, now depicted a different scene. Instead of lunging toward the staff bearer, Hercules was now falling helplessly toward Draco—and Ophiuchus, rather than succumbing to Hercules' club, was pushing the hero into the dragon's

145

open mouth. Its face, too, had changed. The two little dots on Ophiuchus' chin now served as narrow, cat-like eyes, and instead of staring upward with a surprised and fearful frown, the feline figure grinned.

"What have you done?" Tagua demanded, clasping his hands around her foot.

"Look below you," she said.

He didn't look. In a panic he thrashed, but he stopped at the sudden tearing of the robe.

"These chambers tell stories," Hannah said. "The Lupus chamber tells of a lowly shepherd who married a princess and sacrificed her to the underworld. He wanted to gain the favor of underworld demons and become a sorcerer."

Tagua's hands slipped on the downy feathers around Hanah's foot. He secured his grasp on the robe and clung to it in desperation. "Hannah!" he begged.

"But the princess rose from the underworld and used his sorcery against him," Hannah continued. "She trapped him in another dimension, and he forced his entire village to become trapped with him, so he could feed on their life force while he tried to find a way out."

"I'll give you the damned ring," Tagua hissed. "I'll show you where it's hidden."

"If we know how to look, the stars tell us all we need to know. They show us the balance between leadership and humility, and the importance of labors and joy. And they teach us the importance of giving . . . and of cutting off."

Hannah looked down at Tagua a moment more. In a choked voice he said something that Surina couldn't quite hear—something about understanding. And Hannah did understand.

"Better luck next time," she told him softly. "I mean it." Hannah clenched her strong toes, so that the razor-sharp talons sliced through the fabric of the purple robe. Tagua fumbled and lost his grip, and he tumbled into the bright pink mass that was Draco's throat.

Surina gasped. Her hands froze once more; the music stopped, and the dragon slid back toward the ceiling—and for a moment, Hannah remained suspended in the center of the Ophiuchus chamber, with the Draco tunnel passing just behind her. She seemed to bask in its golden light.

Dominic and Greg's stroll through Scorpius was rather mundane. It was only when they passed through its left-hand claw that Dominic heard a strange and terrible roar, and he stopped in sudden fear as he glimpsed the interior of Ophiuchus. Hannah was suspended in its center, eyes glowing, wings spread wide, with a blazing golden light at her back that made her look like a fierce archangel—and then the light faded, and she collapsed to the stone floor in an exhausted heap.

Dominic rushed to kneel beside Hannah, gently grasping one of her furred arms. "Hannah?" He paused, suddenly uncertain. "It's you, right?"

"It's me," she murmured. "I'm alive. I just . . . ." She rolled onto her back, onto a thick purple cloth that Dominic recognized as Tagua's robe. She closed her eyes, and her chest rose and fell with deep breaths.

Dominic looked up as Surina hurried into the chamber. "Where's Tagua?" he asked.

"He's gone," Hannah said.

"Gone where?"

Hannah pointed to the ceiling. "Really gone. Swallowed by Draco." She opened her eyes, turning her head to look at Surina. "I needed you and Tagua to be here at the same time when I opened the Ophiuchus gate," she said. "When we were in Taurus, I said out loud that you knew how to open the sun gate, even though I knew that Tagua was listening. I had to convince him that Ophiuchus needed to be opened first, and that you had to come with us. You're a music teacher, so I figured you were the one who could solve Lyra. It was the only way I could think of."

"Good thinking," Surina replied softly.

"Remember how in Hydrus, music kept the dragon asleep for a cycle? Hydrus is at the south celestial pole, but Draco is at the north pole. Things are flipped here; music wakes things up." Hannah drew her arms beneath her, trying to hoist herself up. "We need to keep going."

"It's okay to rest," Dominic said.

"It's not. I can rest later." Hannah pushed herself up from the floor, but fell back as she tried to stand.

"Here." Dominic pulled the flask from his pocket and opened it. "Aquarius told me to give this to you. Drink it."

Hannah complied, tilting her head back and swallowing the contents of the flask. She let out a wet cough and sat for a minute with her eyes closed.

She slowly rose on unsteady legs, and Dominic reached out, letting her use his shoulder as support.

"I have some things I need to do," Hannah said, picking up the tattered robe. "There are things that need to be put right, and then we can open the sun gate." Weakly, she beckoned the group onward. "This way."

She led them through the portal marked *Corona Borealis*. Greg hurried to walk beside Surina, murmuring concern and inquiries, but Dominic's attention was consumed by a familiar sight. The *Corona Borealis* realm was just a small chamber. At its center was a small wooden pedestal. A winged headpiece rested there, a silver helmet with a delicate metalwork over the forehead: an eight-petaled flower bordered by curving foliage, set with seven tiny, glowing stars.

"Isn't this your helmet?" he asked.

Hannah picked it up. "It is," she said, "but I don't need it."

"Are you sure? It has the stars and everything. You might need those at Virgo."

She handed the helmet to Dominic. "I'm not going into Virgo the usual way. You take it."

"No thanks. I had a bad experience with that helmet."

Hannah smiled. "The helmet didn't do that. Virgo did it." She placed the helmet on Dominic's head. "You wear it well. Just trust me, and keep it on."

"It's too tight."

"It's supposed to be uncomfortable."

They bickered about the helmet as they passed through the miniature realm, but Dominic didn't remove it. The opposite end of the chamber opened to an outdoor area, and the travelers suddenly found themselves on a bleak landscape of black rock, with a few scrawny pines twisting their way up from the ground.

"I have to fly ahead of you," Hannah said. "If you go

this way, through Boötes, you'll end up in Virgo. If you can, try to go around it to Leo or Cancer. I'll meet you when I'm done."

"Done doing what?" Dominic asked.

"Tagua stole some things that belong in the underworld." Hannah lifted the torn robe. "This, and . . . other things. They're just symbols; Virgo doesn't need them to have power, but I'm returning them so other people don't abuse them."

Dominic studied Hannah's face with a growing sense of urgency. "Can't someone else do that?"

"No," Hannah said. "It's not just that. I have to . . . help the dead."

"What dead?"

"The ones in Lupus, to begin with. They're wandering . . . ." Hannah glanced back across the jagged landscape. "I have to go."

She hesitated, though, and stared at Dominic. After a moment she reached out, and with one long claw, she gently pulled on the leather cord around Dominic's neck. A stone pendant hung at the bottom—an oval stone etched with the image of a deer. "You're still wearing this?" she asked.

"Of course." Dominic tucked the pendant safely beneath his T-shirt. "Remember, I promised to take you home and help you find your clan. I've already found some of them. We just need to get you back. Okay? Forget everything else."

"I can't," Hannah replied. "I've only done the first thing." She gestured toward the *Corona* chamber. "Ophiuchus is just the beginning. I had to send Tagua back to Earth through Draco. It's—"

"Wait, you sent him to Earth?"

"To be reincarnated as a new person," Hannah said. "That's what Draco is; it leads to Ursa Minor, the portal to incarnation. Tagua will be born as a human, but he won't remember his past existence, and he won't have any power. Draco's tail is the real river Lethe. People have their memories erased as they make their way toward the celestial pole at Ursa Minor. It's the doorway back to Earth." She looked away again, anxiously. "I have to hurry. When you get to Cancer, wait for me there. I might still be in the underworld."

Before Dominic could protest, she flew off with a rush of her wings.

"Great," Surina breathed, looking around helplessly. "There's no trail, and no sign. Which way do we go?"

"There's kind of a trail." Greg pointed to a divot in the rock. "Should we just follow that?"

The trail was easy enough to follow, though it was interrupted here and there with chunks of loose stone, and sometimes with foreboding cracks that seemed to have no bottom. Greenery occasionally peeked through the smaller cracks—slender stalks with indigo and violet flowers, bell-like blossoms with pistils and stamens instead of clappers. "This actually reminds me of Lava Flow Trail," Greg said. "You guys have been to Sunset Crater, right? Doesn't this remind you of the trails with all the volcanic debris, and all the cracks leading to who knows where?"

"I don't remember Lava Flow Trail being this hard," Surina replied.

"Well, it isn't, but the scenery is kind of the same." Greg held his arms out, balancing himself as he stepped onto a loose rock. "I've spent a lot of time camping out at Bonito. The energy around Wupatki and Sunset Crater is pretty intense. I would always have these dreams about the volcanic activity there—like, I'd be walking along, and the ground would just start quaking underneath me, and there would be this deafening roar. And the earth would just split open, into a crack about a mile deep, and lava would just shoot up and incinerate everything in sight. I felt like I was dreaming its history."

"Let's not talk about lava shooting up and incinerating everything," Dominic suggested.

"Sorry." Greg made a short leap over another pile of rocks. "Surina, have you ever hiked The Wave?"

"No."

"It's about three hours north of Flagstaff—and it's, like, amazingly beautiful, and kind of trippy."

Dominic grinned. He cast a sly glance at Surina. "I bet a lot of your nature hikes are trippy."

"Not like *this* one has turned out to be," Greg muttered. "This . . . I don't know what I've gotten myself into here. I knew there would be some risks involved in coming down here, but I don't even know what the risks are now. I mean . . . instead of 'Greg Yazzie broke into Wupatki and got kicked out of his doctoral program,' it might be 'Greg Yazzie had to abandon his studies because he's in a straitjacket.'"

"Oh, that's right," Dominic mused. "Your family name is Yazzie. It's Navajo, right? What does it mean?"

"Yazzie? It means 'little.'"

Dominic frowned. "Are you sure? It doesn't mean 'warrior,' or 'star,' or something like that?"

"I'm sure. Why?"

"It's just . . . I had this friend—he's actually the one who came here with me, initially. He said that one of his friends gave him an honorary Navajo name: Chąą' Yázhí. He said that it means 'Star Warrior.'"

Greg chuckled. "Chąą' Yázhí doesn't mean 'Star Warrior.' Someone was playing a prank on him."

"Why, what does it mean?"

"Um . . . ." Greg half-smiled, half-grimaced. "It's an insult. It's like calling someone a little turd."

"Ah," Dominic said. "That's fitting, actually."

"My uncles used to give that name to white people who showed up at our ceremonies and asked for Diné names," Greg added. "They would pretend it was a really flattering name, like Great Eagle or Amazing Thunder Warrior. After a while, they decided it wasn't very kind, or educational, so they stopped."

"That was decent of them," Dominic said.

"I can't wait to tell them about this place. I mean, assuming that we can really get out of it."

"They'll think you're nuts." A smile played in Dominic's eyes as he glanced at Surina. "They'll think you smoked one to many."

"No, people have to *know* about this," Greg insisted. "I could write a book about it. I admit, I think that maybe I died, but if I make it home . . . wow. I won't even know where to begin."

"You really shouldn't begin something like that," Dominic replied—and then he came to a halt, swearing under his breath.

"What's wrong?" Surina asked.

"Lava," Dominic replied in a sour tone, "at the bottom of a deep crack."

The three leaned over, looking into the deep crevice, staring at the stream of white-hot light below.

"Well," Greg said, "at least it's not shooting up and incinerating everything."

"Wait a minute," Surina said. "That isn't lava. I think it's part of . . . ." The words trailed off as three pale shapes came shuttling down the glowing stream—blue-tinged shapes wrapped in white tunics. As they passed just below, Dominic saw the shocks of black hair above three serene faces, their eyes closed as if in sleep.

"Um, doesn't it look like there are people in there?" he asked.

"I think those were the kids who were with Tagua," Surina replied uncertainly. "They're on their way to . . . Earth. We must be in Draco. This is its tail."

"Are you sure?"

"Yeah, I'm sure. Watch."

Dominic knelt beside her. "How can we be in Draco? I thought we were going the way of the shepherd."

Greg, too, moved closer to the ledge. "Wasn't Tagua a shepherd?"

"We *are* going the way of the shepherd," Surina said. "The bad one, not the good one." She drew in a sharp breath and pointed to the golden stream. "There he is!"

Dominic almost didn't recognize Tagua without his robe. As his lanky figure passed through the stream below, tangled in white cloth, he looked scrawny, harmless, and peaceful.

"We should have gone to the right instead of just going straight ahead," Surina said, looking downstream. "We just went back to Draco. See how the stream curves over there? That's probably the curve that's right next to the Boötes constellation. If we keep going that way, we'll make it to Boötes, and then to Virgo and Leo."

"Sounds good." Dominic stepped back. "Let's go, before the ground starts quaking under our feet."

He had hardly finished speaking when the ground began to tremble, its movement accented by a few deep groans and cracklings. It quaked for a few seconds and then rested.

Dominic exchanged an uneasy glance with Surina. "My fault," he said. "I'll just shut up now."

The rock floor shook again. It fractured beneath Dominic's feet, and as he struggled to steady himself, the section of rock on which he stood began to slope downward toward the precipice. Greg flung his arms out, knocking Surina off balance; her knees slammed against the hard stone.

The ground continued to shift. The slab of rock beneath Dominic gave way, and he quickly leapt from its surface, landing on the nearest ledge. He found himself no longer at the top of the cliff, but somewhere beneath it, grasping for footing as the rock settled into place.

Surina peered down at him from a higher ledge. "Dominic, hurry—climb up here."

"I don't know if I can," he said, scanning the rock surface for another hold.

"This way," she said. "I'll climb down and pull you

up."

She started down, but the black rock fragmented beneath her feet, sending her hurtling a few feet down the cliff.

"Surina, don't do that," Dominic said. Another deep groan came from within the ground. Dominic held his breath and braced himself, but only a tiny avalanche of pebbles rained past him—and then he released his breath, and the ledge broke away, leaving him hanging by one hand.

"Dominic!" Surina cried. She slid down the cliff again, moving in a hurried panic.

"Surina," he said, hearing the fear in his own voice.

She looked down at him, and he saw that fear reflected in her eyes.

"Don't," he said.

"Just wait," she said. "I can go down a little further."

"You'll fall," he said. "It isn't stable down here. Surina, don't do that!" he snapped, as she stretched her leg toward a heap of loose rock.

"If you come any closer," he said, "I'm going to let go."

She froze. "No!"

"You can't fall," he enunciated carefully. "You're the only one who knows how to open the sun gate."

"I don't!" she insisted. "Wibben is the one who knows!"

"Don't come down here," Dominic repeated. "I swear that if you come any closer, I will let go. Go back up."

"Dominic, no. Let us help you." Surina looked around frantically, as if for a sudden solution, but found none.

"Dominic, you can't fall either. You'll die. You'll forget everything, and—"

"I know," Dominic said. "But like I said, I trust this place." He paused, feeling the sudden push of tears behind his eyes, and added: "I don't want to die, either. I really wanted to go to the Snowbowl, and all that other stuff we talked about. I'll—" He felt his grip slipping as he spoke. The rock vanished from beneath his fingers, and he grabbed for another hold, but he felt only a flat, unforgiving wall of stone—and then there was nothing but air and the sound of Surina screaming his name.

10: Libra

Entry into Lupus was simpler than Hannah anticipated. She was accustomed to waiting outside the foreboding walls, either for Tagua's greedy and hopeful tidings or his disdainful criticisms, but in his absence those walls had crumbled. Lupus looked like a realm of broken concrete, wide open to the sky, and Tagua's subjects wandered the ruins aimlessly.

A short wall of rock still stood on one side, and the tunnel to Libra remained open, accessible beneath a thin layer of rubble. Hannah didn't need to see the riddle she'd placed there. She had read it enough that she still remembered its simple command: *Labor #9: Steal back the fruits of the Hesperides, the children of the great night sky. Steal back the tools within their midst that in the underworld should lie.*

Tattered garments, the clothes of children who had suddenly evaporated or crumbled to dust, lay strewn among the rubble. Hannah collected them and sat for some time, tearing fabric, tying knots, until at last her first project was complete.

The rising and falling platforms of Lupus were now in fragments on the floor. Hannah flew to the upper level, where Tagua had spent most of his time hidden away in the back rooms, trying to view and control the rest of the starry realms. She tied one end of the knotted tunics to a sturdy column, and then she retreated past broken partitions and jagged holes to the chamber where Tagua had fawned over his prized treasures. There she rested a moment, sitting on the purple robe with her eyes closed, trying to catch her breath.

"Almost done," she whispered.

A rectangular depression had been made in the wall, lined with white and tan bricks. From a column of those same bricks, a human figure in a tiered gown had been carved. On its head was a golden helmet, decorated with stylized waves of hair at the top and a braid pattern around its circumference; two stylized eyes looked out from the forehead, and an ear was stamped into each side. A string of beads hung around the statue's neck, deep blue beads swept with gold; another necklace hung with two heavy teardrop-shaped beads, deep brown and decorated with circular forms, and beneath those was the blue and silver shawl that Hannah had demanded from Tagua.

These garments, she had learned over time, had been stolen—though she couldn't be certain if Tagua had stolen them on the Earthly plane or in the stars. She'd learned only enough to know that they belonged not in Lupus, but in Virgo.

During her time in the stars, though she had been tasked with learning about the sun gate, Hannah had discovered much more about Tagua. He considered Virgo his arch enemy. He obsessed over her powers and spoke of her with hatred and veiled envy. In front of others, he insulted Virgo's underworld rites, but in secret he devoted himself to learning and mastering those same rites—a goal which he was unequipped to achieve.

Hannah removed the necklaces and laid them aside. She arranged the silver and blue shawl around her shoulders, pausing for only a moment before adding the heavy beads around her neck, and then the lighter beads. Hannah quickened her pace, pulling Tagua's purple robe around her shoulders, and then lifting the helm from the statue and placing it on her own head. She hurried not because she wanted to wear such things, but because she wanted to take them off again.

A staff of deep blue stone leaned just inside the brick compartment. Hannah studied its designs as she tested its weight in one paw. Gold streaks washed across its surface. A dragon's head comprised the handle, and along its length were carved scales and claws and spiral forms.

Lastly, she took Tagua's gold ring, a coiled ring decorated with two opposing dog faces, their eyes wide and fangs bared. Tagua had kept it hidden behind a loose brick, but he looked at it so often, and caressed it so much, that Hannah had long known its hiding place. She slid it onto her thumb and trudged back through the rubble.

The staff hung heavy in her hand as she descended to the lowest floor. These instruments, she knew, supposedly had power, but she didn't know how to use them, and didn't particularly want to.

So she stood in the midst of the ruins, looking around at the zombie-like figures. There were only a couple dozen now, much fewer than when she'd arrived. Hannah shouted at them: "Tagua is gone! You're free!"

A few drifters looked up at her with dark, vacant eyes. They stopped wandering; they stopped picking uselessly at debris.

"Come with me to Libra," Hannah shouted, gesturing toward the tunnel with the staff.

The zombie-like figures stared. Their tunics hung from their shoulders like soiled rags. Nobody moved, so Hannah went to the nearest one: a small, skinny child with long black hair. She started to take the creature's hand, but recoiled when it bared its teeth and hissed.

"Never mind," Hannah muttered. As she contemplated what to do about the wanderers, a flash caught her eye—a gleam of gold somewhere in the wreckage. Hannah looked again and saw jagged shards of metal protruding from the floor. *The holding crown,* she thought—the crown that Tagua had made from shards of the sun gate, the thing that had trapped Hannah and so many others in this realm. Her first impulse was to destroy it before it trapped anyone else.

She went to the crown and found it only slightly bent. She smashed it with the bottom of the staff, over and over again, until it looked like a jagged metal pancake.

Hannah had hoped to do more in this realm—more for these lost souls than just crushing Tagua's pathetic crown. Still, it was a kind of liberation.

Dominic hurtled toward the golden stream, his eyes shut tight. *I'm a bird,* he told himself. *I'm a bird . . . .*

He could feel Hannah's winged helmet still tight around his head. Once before, in Virgo, this same helmet had turned him into a dove. Dominic knew that if he couldn't will it to do the same now—*right* now—he would die.

On the cliff, he had actually been about to assure Surina by saying *I'll use this helmet to turn into a bird.* He repeated that same message to himself now, over and over again, willing his outstretched arms to become wings.

And then it hit him: the shock of an otherworldly pain. He must have fallen into Draco—but when he opened his eyes, Dominic didn't find himself immersed in a golden stream. Instead, he was surrounded by black rock, coming ever closer to it, so close that his face was about to slam into the cliff. Dominic faltered and changed course, turning his arms and soaring upward, and then flapping his arms wildly. He dared to look down. The golden stream still curved below him, and the high rocks gave way. To his right he now saw a wide green pasture.

Boötes, he hoped—the realm of the shepherd.

Dominic remembered his previous flight with a new sense of nostalgia. His feelings, like his path through the zodiac, had reversed. This time, he didn't hate being a bird. He reveled in it—and instead of flying in a panic away from Virgo, he soared determinedly toward it.

Not all of the wanderers in Lupus were Tagua's subjects. Most of those original souls had already dissipated. A few of those who remained were later unfortunates like Hannah: those who had wandered by accident into the stars and fallen under Tagua's power. Hannah recognized them by a slight spark in their eyes; they still had some degree of thought, some will to exist.

Those, Hannah realized later, were the last to follow her.

As she walked through the tunnel to Libra, she heard scuffling behind her. The tunnel was dark, but as she emerged into the chamber, lit through the top with skylight, she turned to discover that several of Tagua's zombie-like minions had followed behind her. They were led, no doubt, by the power of the sacred garments—or perhaps just by Hannah's spark of life.

The Libra chamber, small and essentially empty, bore a single illustration on the stone floor: a depiction of the Libra constellation, the scales of balance. Hannah had placed the riddle in the center of it. She didn't stop to pick it up, but she paused to view the image of the scales.

Her task here, she knew, was only partially complete. Lupus had been destroyed, and its captors freed from its walls, though her own willingness to create a long-delayed balance. Now, they only needed to be freed from the stars.

She led the wanderers onward, into the Hydra tunnel

that led to Virgo.

11: Virgo

Dominic tore the crown from his head and dropped it into his lap. Despite his joy at becoming a bird, he was relieved to be a man again, with grass under his feet and the frightening golden stream a few yards at his back. The pasture was cool and bright, the grass soft and inviting beneath him. Dominic noticed another dove fluttering nearby and wondered, for a moment, if he had somehow split in two, and the bird part of him had become its own entity.

But the dove stopped mid-air and mutated, expanding its legs and wings to an impossible height and breadth. A woman suddenly stood in its place. She wore a simple white garment; her dark hair was gathered behind her head, and her dark eyes conveyed a peaceful strength. No crown adorned her head, but Dominic recognized her as Virgo, the queen of the underworld.

Her presence both frightened and reassured him. Dominic opened his mouth to greet her, but not a single word came to his mind.

"Welcome to Boötes," the queen said. "It is fitting that you're passing here alone on the way to my realm."

"Is it?" he asked.

"You should hurry. Hannah is waiting for you, and you have a long walk ahead."

"How long?"

"Boötes is the thirteenth largest constellation in the night sky," she replied crisply, as if reading from a textbook.

Dominic struggled to his feet. He picked up the helmet, contemplating another attempt at being a dove.

"It's better to walk," the queen suggested. "You will arrive at Virgo at exactly the right time." She looked him up and down, frowning contemplatively. "It seems you have lost some of your ram garments. I suppose it's appropriate that you will walk across Boötes in the celestial booties, but do you think you have enough? Remember, the shepherd Boötes is followed by *Canes Venatici*: a pair of hounds. Are you not afraid that these boots won't be enough?"

Dominic hesitated, remembering his narrow escape from the terrifying hounds at Aries. "Actually, the thing about the hunting dogs in Boötes was a translation mistake," he replied. "The Arabic word for a shepherd's hook was mistaken for the word 'dog.'"

"Perhaps," the queen replied, "but the dogs were placed in the adjacent constellation, and many people now see the hounds Asterion and Chara in the stars. I'm sure you have seen them, too."

"Yes—like you said, in the adjacent constellation, where they can stay." Dominic reached into his pants pocket. "Please stop trying to convince me that I'm going to get chased by dogs. I'm tired. And I don't just have the boots. I have this," he said, pulling the flask out and lifting it for the queen to see.

A tiny smile played on her face. "Now you look like a true shepherd. After you get home, when you look at the stars and see Boötes raising his flask in one hand and grasping the seven-starred helm in the other, I hope you will remember that you and I shared a joke about it."

Dominic forced himself to smile back at her, but he shook his head. "Was there a joke? I didn't get it."

"You'll get it later. Do you know the myth about Boötes and Virgo?"

"Um . . . Maybe. I did read something about Boötes being Virgo's lover."

"It's a myth. There are stories about Virgo being eternally about to give birth, and Boötes being the progenitor of that impending birth. The star Arcturus is supposed to represent his seed. And here you are, in the role of Boötes—and here I am."

Dominic hesitated. Virgo's stare, and her suppressed grin, gave the impression that she was hinting at some mystery that he knew little of, and of which she knew everything. A multitude of questions raced through his mind, but he asked none of them. "I'm really not into cultish mating rituals," he said, "and you're . . . too old for me."

"That's funny," she said. "I seem to remember you telling the housekeeper at Aries that I'm too young to be your girlfriend."

Dominic thought back, puzzled. "What?"

"You're right: Virgo and Boötes aren't lovers," she said. "They're just very good friends." A sudden sentimentality flashed in the queen's brown eyes. "And maybe Arcturus shines so brightly at Boötes' waist because that's where he carries a dram of blazing light from Draco's tail."

166

"If you say so," Dominic replied.

Virgo approached him with a sly look. She leaned forward, speaking as if in confidentiality. "Those boots, and that helm, have kept you safe. That flask can also do you a world of good."

"How so?"

"It would be in both of our best interests," the queen said, "for Greg Yazzie to *not* remember his journey through the stars. Remembering it would prove . . . disruptive. He is on a very good course now, and he shouldn't divert from it."

"Okay. Well, can't you just tell him that?"

"Greg is easily frightened," the queen said, "but he is also stubborn and driven. He should keep driving in the right direction. You're good at helping to drive people. In fact, Boötes is known as the one who helps drive the plough Ursa Major—and also Ursa Minor, the *wagon of heaven*. When you meet Hannah at Virgo, the two of you will help to drive a herd into that cosmic plough." Virgo plucked the flask from Dominic's grasp. She knelt by the golden stream, dipping the mouth of flask into the ethereal flow.

"Um," he said.

"Your fall toward Draco," Virgo interrupted. "I did that."

"What?"

"And your transformation to a dove. I did that, too, to bring you here."

"Darn," Dominic replied, trying to sound lighthearted. "I was really hoping my own willpower did that."

Virgo stood and faced him. She smiled—a thin, amused smile—and handed him the flask. "Hang onto that," she said. "You'll know when to use it. Bathing in Draco washes away one's memory, so that one can be born anew—but swallowing a few drops doesn't erase a lifetime. It can erase a dream, a day, a singular event." She paused, adding with emphasis: "It might erase the memory of a trip through the zodiac."

"You want me to give this to Greg," Dominic said.

"Offer it when he is thirsty," she replied. "You and your friends have traveled a long way without refreshments."

Dominic lowered the flask at his side. Slowly, he shook his head. "I can't do that. Greg can't forget what happened here; it means too much to him. When we were leaving Aquarius, he had this beautiful revelation about changing himself, and finding courage, and . . . I can't make him forget that. I'm sure you see everything that happens here, and you must have seen that."

"I did see him," Virgo replied, "well enough to create challenges for him. His revelation comes from the starry realm, and it will remain with him like a powerful dream. You need not feel any guilt over his forgetting. Just as I gave him the riddles of the zodiac, I will give him signs and obstacles in his waking life, and I will compel him to transform. Greg Yazzie is a child of the stars; I will not abandon him, just as you have not abandoned Hannah Hale."

Dominic looked into Virgo's warm gaze, less reluctant, but still not convinced.

"You can trust me, as you always have," the queen

continued. Her smile, this time, was warm and affectionate. "You have always believed in me. When I was human, your faith saved me. Likewise, I will save Greg Yazzie. I know that you will make the right choice."

The queen flitted away into a compact spark of white light. A dove flapped its pale wings in her place, and then it circled and sailed away toward Virgo.

Dominic watched the departure in confusion. Solemn and deep in thought, he started the long walk across Boötes.

Hannah walked with the lapis lazuli staff held out in front of her, listening to the drone of its weight against the smooth stone floor. Her eyes were open wide but saw nothing, and the only other sounds she heard were the quiet shufflings of Tagua's ghouls as they trailed after her through Hydra.

Aside from Cetus, Hydra was the darkest of the realms that Hannah knew. The section that stretched between Lupus and Virgo was an enclosed, unlit tunnel connecting the two—and as Hannah tread blindly through it, she recalled its nauseating effect. It started again now, first as a general queasiness; a series of dull pains moved through her body, seeming to converge, collecting into a hard little ball in her belly. The walls closed in at her sides, smooth and soft—not inflexible like hard stone, but fleshy and elastic. The tunnel constricted close around her, and for some time, Hannah heard nothing but her own ragged breath as she struggled to inhale and exhale.

The tunnel eased away; its walls once again felt like solid stone. Though the idea of returning to the underworld usually filled her with dread, Hannah was relieved to see the light of Virgo's chamber ahead. She stopped near the doorway and leaned against the wall; her heart had begun to pound, and she waited another minute before reading the next labor.

A pair of stone fangs protruded from the top of the doorway—Hydra's fangs—and onto one of the tips a scrap of papyrus was pierced. Hannah reached for the paper and read its contents in a whisper: "Labor number ten: Face the Lernaean Hydra, whose heads see places feared and sought; from its clutches, liberate the souls that time has long forgot."

She let out a slow sigh and entered the chamber, leaving Tagua's former minions to linger in Hydra's shadows.

Hannah had already caught a glimpse of those who waited inside: the seven "judges," the ill-mannered group she had met on her previous visit. Their sparkling style of dress contrasted with their sour demeanors: one judge, a human-like creature that resembled Hannah, donned a velvet robe in a bold shade of red, with matching jewels and ribbons in its hair; another wore all green, with a fringed velvet dress and emeralds shining on its wrists and throat, and even in the toes of its fine shoes. The chamber, too, struck Hannah with its beauty. The deep blue walls, streaked with gold dusting and illustrated with symbols of the constellations, made her feel as though she was standing in the center of the universe—yet its halls swarmed with ghastly figures, half-decomposed corpses of the tormented undead.

Near the queen's throne, and looking rather out of place, stood a tall creature with a bird-like head and turquoise eyes. In one hand it held a thick length of papyrus, and as Hannah stepped into the room, the creature began to write with its long, metal-tipped pen. It paused to look up at her as the lapis lazuli staff clattered to the floor. Hannah hadn't meant to drop it; it seemed to have crumbled in her grasp, and as she watched, the staff and the other garments of the underworld disintegrated into dust, some of it swirling away in a stream of gray specks, the rest settling onto Hannah's skin in piles of ash.

As she tried to brush it away, the red-clad judge looked at her in startled astonishment. "Hubris!" it spat. "How dare you enter this court, wearing royal garments?"

"I was trying to return them," Hannah replied.

"Indeed," said the one in orange, "she should be charged with hubris."

"I'm guilty," Hannah said, "but I'm not here to listen to your judgments. Those things belonged to Virgo. I thought that she would want them back, or that I could give them to Neti, the gatekeeper, in exchange for the opening of the gates."

The red-clad judge narrowed its eyes. "Your vanity is loud and obnoxious; it pollutes our ears. Do you think you've learned all the ways of the underworld, just because you solved a riddle or two?"

"No," Hannah said. "I read about it in *Inanna's Descent* when I was at the library."

The judge balked. It stammered, and then it said: "One doesn't open the gates that way. Neti only accepts these things during the descent, so that the initiate is purified for the underworld rites."

"Yes, but I'm doing everything in reverse," Hannah replied. "Besides, Inanna didn't give anything when she ascended from the underworld. The gates just opened for her."

"They opened for Inanna, princess of the Earth plane. Do you think you are also a princess?"

"I am," Hannah replied dryly. "I'm Griffin Princess. Virgo named me right here in this chamber. And, technically, even though I descended and transformed, I never went back up through the underworld gates. I think it's about time."

"But Inanna *did* give something." Now the one in orange stepped forward, its eyes lit with a sudden wiliness. "The princess sacrificed a person. No one ascends from the underworld unmarked. If you wish to return from the underworld, you must provide someone to take your place."

"Yes, I know. Inanna protected the people who fasted for her, but Dumuzi was expelled because of his selfishness. I already sacrificed such a person—but Dumuzi is only supposed to be in this realm for half of a cycle, and then sent back to Earth for the other half. I brought him to Draco instead, to be washed clean and sent to Earth, and then I took those things from him."

The glint disappeared from the judge's eyes. The red one whispered to it, and then it announced: "Virgo is nearby. When the queen of the underworld arrives, you may beseech her."

The seven figures stood in a close huddle, their whispers like serpents' slitherings in the quiet chamber. The bird-like creature, the queen's scribe. stood near the platform, its pen scratching busily against the papyrus sheet. Hannah moved to stand beside it. Its strange-looking turquoise eye seemed to fix on her.

"Wibben?" she said. "It's you, right?"

"Somewhat," it replied, from somewhere at the back of its long yellow beak. Its voice rang higher and scratchier than Wibben's, yet somehow, it sounded similar.

"Tagua is gone," Hannah said. "I pushed him into Draco. So, can you tell me how to solve the sun gate?"

"You did well, Hannah," the creature said, and resumed writing. "Do you feel like you did well?"

"I don't feel like anything. I just did what I thought was best."

The pen came to a stop. The bird-thing tilted the papyrus scroll so that Hannah could see the numbers it had scrawled across the paper:

011235843718
988764156281

"It's the Fibonacci sequence, the cycle of life and growth, reduced to its most basic expression. You know the sequence already. You mentioned it after one of your trips to the library, thinking it might be a clue. Reduce the numbers with more than one digit by adding the digits together."

Hannah frowned as she examined the code. "One, one, two, three, five, eight . . . five plus eight is . . . thirteen."

"And one plus three is four," the Wibben-bird said. "Thus, thirteen equals four."

"Oh . . . I get it." Hannah frowned as the numbers faded and vanished; the paper became a blank slate. "I do get it, but, how do I use that to open the gate?"

"Each of the symbols represents a number. The symbols need to be arranged in order around the disc, first the outside, then the inside. If the number is two, two symbols representing two must be placed there. If the number is seven, seven symbols representing seven must be placed there. You will solve that part easily, Hannah. The difficulty lies in reaching the sun gate."

Hannah looked at the undead who milled in the tunnels nearby; they shuffled past the exit at the far side of the chamber, dragging their rotted feet, emitting soft groans of discomfort and despair. "I have to help them first," she said. "I'm taking them up with me, to Ursa Major. They'll cross through Draco, and then they'll finally be free from this place." She added with a note of weary hope: "You should come up with us. The dead rising through Virgo's open gates will be . . . ." She trailed off, her breath catching as the bird-thing blinked, a ghastly white membrane suddenly passing across its eye. "It will be a unique event," she finished. "The scribe of the underworld should be there to record it."

The dead, who had gathered listlessly at the far exit, suddenly cleared away—and then Virgo passed quietly into the chamber. The woman in a simple white drapery went to the throne. "Griffin Princess," she said, "Lama-Zu, you are a sight." She picked up the tiara. "I hope you don't mind if I sit. You are also weary, but you must remain standing. You still have the last leg of your journey to finish."

Even before she placed the crown on her head, the queen had a regal look; she was poised and confident, her eyes calm but penetrating. She sat, and Hannah went to stand before her. "I would like to start that last leg now," Hannah said.

"You must have been tired of carrying those heavy things," the queen said. "I, too, tired of carrying them. They belonged to me once, in one of my human forms."

"I'm sorry," Hannah said. "I didn't know they would turn to dust."

Virgo smiled. "That is all right. I don't need them anymore. It was Tagua, and not I, who clung to them." She nodded toward the dead, who had nudged their way farther into the chamber. "The underworld dead are drawn to you. What do you think that means?"

"They will follow me," Hannah replied.

"Perhaps," the queen said, "but how far will you lead them? These souls were headed for rebirth, but they have resisted it. Some yearn for their old lives. Others hated their lives so much that they don't want to be human again. They are afraid of the same suffering, or worse. Yet, if the movement of one's soul is toward rebirth, there is no avoiding it; there is only the delaying of it. Such souls need a compassionate and courageous hand to comfort and guide them."

Hannah looked at the few dead who hovered outside

the chamber. One, a tall figure that could have been woman or man, made a soft, pitiful sound, a faded note of despair. Its clothes were mere shreds, its flesh sunken and leathery and clinging to its bones, long past any semblance of life.

"I manage the realm of life and death," Virgo continued. "My role is to serve the dead—and, sometimes, to guide the living who wander into this realm. The living, and the dead who return to Earth, are not obliged to heed my advice, or even to remember me. Humans ultimately decide their own actions." She paused. "Do you think that you could manage such a role, and patiently help the countless dead while having no control over them?"

"I don't want to," Hannah said.

"Nor did I, at first—yet here I am. The underworld is a place to show compassion and severity, leadership and humility. Its ruler must speak and listen, establish justice as well as show mercy, and encourage self-advocacy as well as advocate for others. A strong enough person can endure such an existence with love and gratitude."

Virgo lifted the tiara from her lap. She placed it on her head. For a moment, the softly shining lights of the twelve-starred crown cast a healthy glow across Virgo's face, but her cheeks suddenly became sallow, her flesh leathery and aged—an effect that looked much like the pallor of death. Hannah watched as the queen's dark locks of hair came loose. They clumped together into sections, curling and writhing like dark green eels—and then Hannah could see their small heads, their fangs, and the tiny pink throats exposed when they hissed. Virgo,

176

like Medusa, bore a head of snakes.

"The last time you saw me in this form," Virgo said, "I asked how you would have confronted a hero like Perseus, who caused death and destruction in his endeavors—but as you know, I was really asking about Tagua. In this form I also had a lock of hair whose head had been lopped off by a frightened traveler. As you can see, its head has regenerated. My serpents, in a more ethereal form, can peer into the other constellations; they can see into the other entrances and exits of the starry realms. Rather than panic and destroy them, or control and usurp them, I ask that people strive to understand them."

Hannah started to say "I understand," but thought it better to keep quiet. Perhaps she didn't understand as much as she thought.

"The same rule applies elsewhere," Virgo continued. "Courage must always be backed by wisdom; bravery might compel you to cut off the head of a problem, but cutting off the head does not address the root. Often, it only causes more heads to grow in the same place. The next time you see evil, will you call its name and demand transformation? Or will you allow it to fester because of pity and passivity?"

"I hope," Hannah said, "that I will call it out."

"The griffin has the powers of the vulture, the lion, and more. Like the crab, it has the power of regeneration, of letting go and creating itself anew. It uses the power of transformation to learn the secrets of the cosmos, starting with the simplest secret: the sublime power of balance." The queen reached up, her fingers moving between a mass of gently slithering snakes. She removed the crown and held it aloft. The serpents ducked toward her neck; their tiny eyes shut, and their mouths sealed; they mutated into dark locks of hair, neatly clasped behind Virgo's head.

"The twelve stars on Virgo's crown represent the acquired wisdom of the zodiac," the queen said. "I have worn this crown only after many tribulations and changes. You, too, through long and thoughtful study, will acquire that wisdom."

Hannah hesitated, but she told the truth: "I'm not sure that I want to."

"Yet, such knowledge is the fate of all humans—if not in one lifetime, then eventually, in another. All are bound for the underworld, and all must strip themselves of everything that made them human—not just a handful of items that happen to be in their pockets, but *everything*—and face the dark slate of creation with only what is in their hearts and minds. They must stand against the seven judges, against fear and helplessness and outrage and despair. Only then can they hope to earn this crown."

Virgo lifted the tiara from her head. She extended it to Hannah, and for a moment it seemed to blaze like a star—and then it burst into a cloud of silver dust, the specks floating gently toward the floor. "That crown, too, is merely a symbol," Virgo said. "Its stars, as you know, must shine inside of you." She lowered her hand and regarded Hannah with gentle scrutiny. "Your eyes show your anxiety; you say you may not want such knowledge, but you want it enough that you are willing to turn these realms on their heads. You would even flip the underworld and eject its dead to the surface." Virgo looked coolly down at Hannah, a hint of a challenge in her tone. "Do you not regret learning the secret of Ophiuchus? If you could go back, and find a way to change Tagua's mind, would you change the outcome?"

"No," Hannah replied.

"You have seen that time in this place isn't always linear, and that it's possible to be in the same realm with two versions of yourself: a present version and a past version, or perhaps even a future version." The queen leaned forward, regarding Hannah with intense scrutiny. "Soon, you will also know the secret of the sun gate. You can alter the course of events by telling your past self how to open it. You can ensure your survival and Tagua's."

Hannah looked back at the queen with weary suspicion. "That sounds like a trick," she said, "and I don't want Tagua to go through that gate. He would have used his powers to control people."

"But, couldn't you persuade him to do good?"

"I couldn't," Hannah replied flatly. "You know how hard I tried. Can I go now?"

Virgo leaned back in the throne, smiling—a strange, somber smile. "You can. I have said before that it is your fate to rise from the underworld, and to release the dead before you—but there will always be more dead, and even if you leave now, your endeavors have bound you to this realm. You will return and remain here for an immeasurable age. Mortal lives will pass through generation after generation, but you will still be here with the dead, hearing their cries and listening to their useless pleas."

Hannah took time to contemplate the queen's words. She repeated them silently, over and over again, examining them for any veiled message of hope, but found none. "What?"

Virgo simply looked at Hannah in silence. Hannah stared back at her, also mute, though she wanted to scream: *That's not fair!*

The scribe's voice murmured quietly in the chamber: "The queen speaks often in riddles. Do not be afraid."

"*I* am not afraid," Virgo said, "and the fate I just described is one I have experienced myself. It is the fate of a queen: to serve one's people with compassion and severity, with wisdom and curiosity. Like you, I encounter past and future versions of myself, and I must hold my tongue even when my past self is suffering."

Hannah's anger dissipated. An idea began to form in her mind, and she looked at the queen with a new sense of dread and wonder. "Who are you?" she asked.

"I think the question you should consider is: Who are *you*?"

Hannah shook her head, not wanting to believe the notion that had crept into her thoughts.

"The fate of Lupus is to be slain by Centaurus," Virgo said, "and you have played that role well. Centaurus stands on Crux, the point of final decision, the center of the celestial labyrinth and the end of the journey. Centaurus is the realm of Chiron: a healer who saved others, but who was felled by Hydra's venom. You sacrificed yourself to save Dominic, and you are determined to do the same for these wretched souls—but this realm has exhausted you. You could have resisted Tagua, but you allow him to deplete you. You will collapse before reaching the sun gate."

Before Hannah could respond, Virgo added: "That is why you must go now. You have a chance to make it home because you chose community over ego; you are no longer trying to finish this journey alone. You can go, but will come back."

"Doesn't everyone?" Hannah asked wearily.

The queen's mouth curved in a vague smile. "Everyone does. But remember: the next time you descend to the land of the dead, you won't become human again. You will stay here for generations, even for millennia."

The suggestion filled Hannah with a sense of foreboding, but she shook it off and tried to face Virgo bravely. "I know," she replied. "It's okay. I think I get it now."

Virgo's eyes seemed to brighten. "Don't think about it too much. Go and live your life. And remember, no one can ascend from this place as the person they were."

"I'm not the person I was," Hannah said.

"Before you return home, you will shed this griffin form and be a girl again." The queen lifted a hand, waving Hannah away with a playful gesture. "Go back to being a child. Your new task is to enjoy life with the people you love—and even with those you struggle to love. Grow and learn and have fun with others, and help them find reasons to smile and laugh. Your new name, when you pass through that gate, will be The Little One

Who Laughs."

Hannah started away, toward the doorway that she knew led to the realm of Leo—but the dead did not follow, and Tagua's minions remained in the shadows of Hydra. "Aren't they coming with me?" she asked.

"They will join you at Cancer, the gate to the upper world," Virgo said, "but you have not yet reached that gate. You have one more realm to pass through first. Finish your journey as Lama-Zu there. The dead will follow Hannah Hale."

12: Leo

Labor #11: Slay the Nemean lion; its final task is here assigned. Retain its steadfast strength, but leave its carcass far behind.

The paper was wedged between two stones at the right-hand-side of a cobbled court—a small realm just outside of the deep blue lapis lazuli dome that encompassed Virgo's realm. Hannah had read the riddle before, and at last she understood part of its meaning. She looked down at her golden fur, at the hand that was more like a lion's paw, and recalled Virgo's words: *Before you return home, you will shed this griffin form and be a girl again.*

"Its final task is here assigned," she whispered, reading the riddle again. "Its final task . . . ."

She replaced the riddle where she had found it and looked out across the court. It hadn't changed in any way since Hannah's first visit, when she had walked to Virgo's realm hand-in-paw with a griffin. It had only one other exit: the gated, labyrinthine path that led to the next realm. The silver gate stood tall, its bars thin but immovable; its center was decorated with the image of a crab, massive and shining like a shield, the symbol of the realm of Cancer.

Beside the gate stood Neti, a creature that looked human, but with knobby limbs, a wide head, and large, gnarled ears that lent it a goblin-like appearance. The flesh of its gaunt face stretched tight over a prominent nose and cheekbones, and its eyes looked half-blind, with clouded irises and blue-stained whites. The skin had a purplish hue, and the head was mostly bald, with a few long strands of hair hanging from the flaking scalp. The creature reminded Hannah of death, and of the sights of the underworld—of the listless, decaying dead that wandered there, unwilling to accept death, but unable to return to the lives for which they yearned. She felt a sudden anxiety that Neti was a reflection of herself, that she was one of those who had died and hadn't accepted it. Wibben had died here without knowing. How could she be sure that the same hadn't happened to her?

Neti stood like a statue, gazing at Hannah with its milky eyes.

"Hey," she greeted it, and Neti gave her a slight nod in reply.

Hannah thought over the queen's hints and divinations, striving to think of something that matched the riddle. As she stood, pondering, a voice reached her ears—a child's voice, strangely familiar, somewhere beyond the gate that led to Cancer. Hannah looked up in surprise. She hadn't made out what the voice said, but then a response came. The gatekeeper at the next gate spoke up, its voice ringing clear through the passage.

It said: "Be satisfied, Hannah Hale; a divine power of the underworld has been fulfilled."

Hannah remembered those words. The gatekeepers had spoken them to her on her first descent into the underworld. She looked questioningly at Neti, but the creature remained impassive, its eyes half-closed. "Is . . . are they talking to me?" she asked.

The gatekeeper's eyes opened, looked at her, but Neti did not respond. Hannah heard footsteps approaching in the stone passage—and then she remembered Virgo's words: *You can alter the course of events by telling your past self how to open it. . . . Like you, I encounter past and future versions of myself, and I must hold my tongue.*

Hannah sucked in a sharp breath. She backed away from the gate. For a moment she was incapable of decision, overcome by panic, but she closed her eyes and whispered words of calm. She sat in a half-crouch on the cobbled floor and folded her wings close against her back, waiting—and at length, a girl approached the opposite side of the gate, a girl who Hannah knew all too well. In her palm she held a tiny, shining star.

Neti reached through the bars, and the light disappeared into its gnarled hand. "Be satisfied, Hannah Hale," it said as it opened the gate. "A divine power of the underworld has been fulfilled."

Hannah had half-expected to see her past self, yet she stared in covetous astonishment. This younger version of herself wore a brown nightgown, with a red vest over it, and a silver helmet with wings. Her eyes were full of life, with deep brown irises and a keen expression, and her flesh was a healthy brown—not the sickly gray-blue she'd become accustomed to. It was as though she had traveled back in time and stood facing the old Hannah, the one she thought was lost to time and captivity.

The girl looked at her expectantly.

"Hello, Hannah," Hannah greeted her.

"Are you Leo?"

"No. I'm just a woman, like you. My name is . . . ."
She hesitated, and a memory came to her. *Lama-Zu, the anzu.* "Lama-Zu," she finished.

The girl seemed disconcerted. She looked Hannah's griffin-body over with something like suspicion and asked: "Do you have a riddle?"

"No . . . there's no riddle. All you have to do is walk with me to Virgo's chamber." Hannah gestured to the blue dome. "But there's a condition: we have to walk hand in hand."

The girl looked hesitantly at Hannah's paw—or perhaps at the tips of her claws, extending sharply between the digits.

"Don't be afraid of my claws," Hannah said gently. "They won't hurt you."

The girl carefully slid her hand into the paw. They started across the plaza.

Hannah was unsure of what to say. She wished the queen had given her more direction. As she walked, though, the pains of all she had experienced began to gnaw at her. She looked down at the young girl so full of innocent life; she thought about how this place would drain the youth and happiness and vitality from her— and she understood that this task, walking hand in hand across the court, had not been a test or riddle for the old Hannah, but for the new one.

Finally, the girl spoke up: "If you're a woman, how

come you have a lion's body?"

"This isn't really what I look like." Hannah paused, thinking again of the queen's words. "The lion is a symbol of strength. You see me like that because . . . because I've learned something about strength, I suppose."

They had already reached the doorway. Hannah looked down at her old self with sympathy, still remembering the pains she'd endured—the failed attempts, the humiliation, the frustration and jealousy and loneliness. She wished she had been stronger against those things—that she'd made better use of her claws and spent less time as Tagua's fool. Yet she remembered, too, her moments of strength and learning. "I wish I could tell you the answers to all of the riddles and enigmas," she said, "but I can't. I can only give you this." She gripped the girl's hand more firmly. "I've known what it's like to be alone, and to be afraid. Whenever you feel that way, like you don't have the courage and you need someone to hold your hand, remember how I held your hand like this. Remember that my grip was strong, and that my voice was strong, and that I knew the ways of this realm—and that my sharp claws never hurt you." She squeezed the small hand and released it, and then she took both of the girl's hands and pressed them together. "I'm giving you my grip. When you need help, hold your own hand; hold it firm, and know that you're not alone, that my strength is with you."

The girl nodded, but said nothing. Hannah released her and gazed through the doorway of the queen's chambers. "Go inside," she said softly.

She watched as her former self disappeared into the blue dome, and her vision blurred with tears.

Hannah wiped her eyes with the back of her furred hand and started toward the gate. Neti was unmoved by her display of emotion; it stared at her expressionlessly.

"Can you open the gate?" Hannah asked.

In a wily tone, it replied: "I *can*."

Hannah waited, but Neti did not move.

"*Will* you open the gate?" she asked. "I need to go up."

"Events in the underworld must proceed in order," Neti wheezed. "Have you slain the Nemean lion?"

She paused. "No."

"It is a fearsome beast with piercing claws and impenetrable flesh, fortified by the underworld; no mortal's weapon can remove its skin. How, then, will you slay it?"

Hannah thought back, trying to remember what she knew of the Nemean lion.

"You are thinking of the myth," Neti said. "The Nemean lion's skin could only be shed by a divinely fortified tool. Thus, its skin was pierced and removed with its own claw."

"So . . . my griffin skin has to be removed," she mused. "It won't just come off?" She paused, and then added: "Wait—*I* have to do it?"

Neti gestured toward the entrance to Virgo's dome, where two of the dead lingered in the shadows; they listened to the exchange with rotted ears, watched though they had no eyes. "If you fear transformation, and refuse to shed your skin," Neti said, "why should the dead follow you? They, too, will cling to their old selves."

Hesitantly, Hannah lifted her paw to her chest. She placed the point of one claw just below her throat. "Will it hurt?"

"Yes," Neti replied.

Hannah pierced her flesh with the claw. Immediately, her hand jerked back. The pain was deep and stinging; thinking of it as necessary, or as "not real," did not help.

"This doesn't seem fair," she said. "When animals shed their skins, they don't have to stab themselves. Their old skin just comes off." She lifted the claw again, braced herself for another sting. "I don't even know how deep to cut."

She tried again, and again, but her hand kept jerking back at every stab of the claw. *It's not fair*, she thought; *it hurts too much*. "Neti," she said, "can you do it for me?"

"It is not within my role."

"But I can't do it like this," Hannah said. "I need help." She blinked away tears; she tried to steady her voice. "The dead also need to know that it's okay to ask for help," she said stubbornly, "and that they don't have to do everything alone. I need help, Neti. Please help me."

Something seemed to shift in the creature's gaze— not emotion, for it likely had none, but some other acknowledgement, as if Hannah had just spoken the words it was waiting for. Neti stepped away from the

189

gate. "There is another creature here who possesses divinely fortified claws, and whose task is to help you shed your skin."

Hannah's gaze moved to the gate. The symbol of the crab, smooth and gleaming, covered the lower half; it seemed to stand on its two back legs, its claws reaching up toward the silver disc that adorned the top.

"The role of the gate of Cancer is this: to strip you of unneeded possessions and purify you for the next realm," Neti said, and nodded at Hannah. "Stand before the gate."

Hannah lowered her paw. Relief washed over her. She stepped forward, knowing that the task would still hurt, but confident that it would be easier this way. All she had to do was stand there.

She closed her eyes and waited.

The crab must have moved. Metal scraped against metal; behind her, one of the dead gasped. She felt it, then: a sharpness plunging into her chest, into her belly and legs and arms, and even up the middle of her face. Her breath stopped; then she cried out, certain that the crab would dig its claws beneath her open flesh and tear her from the inside. Instead, a sudden shock filled her whole body; she seemed suspended in space, unable to open her eyes, and all that remained was the lingering sensation of her face being split in two. *My face!* she thought, certain that her human face had also been cut open; the crab had surely plunged too deep. *The crab took my actual face! It ripped away my whole body!*

"Such is the task of this realm," Neti's voice said. "When you return it will, indeed, take that face from

190

you—but the land of the dead can never take your true face. What is your true face, Hannah?"

She became aware of her breath, then—and of her feet, still standing on the stone floor. She tried to flex her fingers, and feeling returned there, too. Hannah tried to move her wings next, but the attempt confirmed what she already knew: There were no wings. She was no longer Lama-Zu, the griffin. She was just Hannah Hale.

Shakily, looked down. A sheath of dirty skin and feathers lay at her feet. The queasy little ball in her belly seemed to have gone with it; it had purged itself with the discarded layer of flesh, like some old burden that she had quietly stomached until then.

A dead man, his clothes soiled and torn, ventured into Leo. His one remaining eye stared at Hannah with gleaming fascination. It looked at her feet, where the pile of fur and feathers and golden-brown skin began to crumble; at the threshold of the realm of the dead, it collapsed into grains of dust.

"Are you alive?" the dead man asked.

Other walking corpses began to filter from Virgo's dome, roused by Hannah's humanness. They fixed their rotting gazes on her and listened with new intensity.

"Yes," Hannah said weakly. "I'm alive . . . and if you follow me, I can show you how to live again." She turned to Neti. "Open the gate."

13: Cancer

"No," Neti said.

Hannah stared at the creature. "What do you mean, no? The queen said you would open it."

"Passage through the underworld gates is no leisurely stroll," Neti said in a wheedling voice.

As the gatekeeper spoke, several strange figures emerged from Virgo's dome—each one human-like except for the head, which more closely resembled a rat. The eyes were large and round, the nose pointed, the ears oversized and protruding. The creatures looked at Hannah with eyes that gleamed and yet held no emotion; their voices, when they spoke, conveyed no warmth. The tunics that draped their figures were old and stiff, scraping softly against the thin bodies as they moved.

They gathered close around Hannah. The two at her sides gripped her arms, holding her fast. She felt the sharpness of their hard, thin fingers sinking into her flesh, inhaled the musty scent of that which belonged to the underworld.

One of the figures stood tall before her. In its fist it clutched a long scepter, undecorated except for the twelve silver stars that adorned the crown. When it opened its mouth to speak, Hannah caught sight of its sharp teeth—and she recoiled a bit, then, imagining that this was a creature who would gnaw on the dead.

"You may ascend, Hannah," the underworld being said. "We will take Surina Leib in your place."

Hannah hesitated.

"The customs of the underworld must not be questioned," Neti wheezed. "Just as you sacrificed the shepherd to save yourself, you may trade your freedom for someone else's."

"I didn't sacrifice Tagua just to save myself," Hannah countered.

The mouse-like creature spoke again: "The underworld must remain balanced. Choose one to take your place, or stay and do not ascend."

Hannah pressed her lips together, restraining further protest. She considered the situation carefully, recalling stories of the underworld, of what was negotiable and what was not.

No," she said at last. "You can't have Surina. She has been my constant support. She gave me wise advice when I abused myself with poor choices. She fought by my side through the challenges of Eridanus. She didn't abandon me even after I abandoned her; she spent time and effort and took extraordinary risks to save me. She traveled all the way to the mountain temples for me, and she returned to the zodiac realm even though she was afraid. Because of her, my life was saved. I would never banish Surina in my place."

The chrome-like sheen of the creature's eyes expressed no opinion, but it said: "You may walk on. We will accompany you to the next gate."

The gate opened. Hannah turned to the roving dead and called: "If you want to live again, come this way."

They shuffled toward her, a few at first, then a few dozen—and more were still coming as Hannah passed through the gate. The Wibben-bird-scribe-thing followed as well, still scratching notes onto the empty papyrus.

The walled path sloped up and curved around to another gate, where another figure waited, a goblin-like Neti figure identical to the first.

As Hannah came near, the scepter-bearing creature stopped in front of her. It tilted its bare head to look down at her face. "You may ascend, Hannah," it said. "We will take Dominic Douglass in your place."

"No," she said, "you can't have Dominic. He encourages people when they lose hope, and he refused to give up on me. He tried to come here three times to save me, and I owe him three times as much. I would never give Dominic to you."

"You may walk on," the creature conceded. "We will accompany you to the next gate."

Hannah and the dead proceeded upward.

At the third gate, Neti waited, and the scepter-bearing figure once again challenged Hannah: "Walk on, Hannah. We will take Greg Yazzie in your place."

"No, not Greg," Hannah said. "He carried the boat of heaven for me when I was weak; he even carried it over lava and risked death for me. He is growing into a leader, and he will be a knowledgeable teacher in the Earth plane—and if I turn him over to you, he won't grow into that person. I will never give Greg to you."

The creature once again conceded, and Hannah and the dead moved upward toward the gate of Cancer. At the fourth gate, the underworld being demanded one of

Tagua's minions, and at the fifth it demanded one of the undead, but Hannah argued: those who suffered under Tagua, and in the underworld through their own stubbornness and confusion, had been confined long enough; the time for their transformation had come.

At the sixth gate, Hannah was surprised when the creature demanded that she trade herself for the bird-like scribe: "He belongs to the suffering plane of the netherworld; he was bound to wander the zodiac for eternity. We shall take him in your place and strip him of his scribe's robe."

"No," Hannah said, "you can't take Wibben. He has been bound to the zodiac long enough, and it was his fate to be freed when the celestial lyre was played. His task is to grow into a whole person—a person who rose up from cruelty and apathy, and who helps others learn how to grow. I will never give Wibben to you."

At the seventh and final gate, the creature once again stood between Hannah and the gate. "Where is the man who trapped you here?" it asked. "Give us Tagua, and you may walk on."

"I have already given you Tagua," Hannah replied. "While other people suffered, he sat on his throne in shining garments. While others wept, he sneered and gloated. He sought eternal life, but now he is in the belly of Draco, the serpent who has eternal life, and who grants life to others—but there, Tagua has no power. Surina, Dominic, and the others have suffered for a greater cause, and should be rewarded with mercy, but Tagua has earned severity. If someone must take my place, fetch Tagua from the belly of the serpent."

The mouse-like creatures released their grip. Neti opened the gate.

The underworld dead poured out ahead of Hannah, still wandering and confused, but with a new energy and curiosity—and at the rear of the crowd were Tagua's former minions, trailing behind with listless obedience. As they rose up from their long captivity, Hannah stood and held the door until every last one had passed through.

Boötes was, indeed, a large realm. Perhaps, when looking across its length and thinking of the long walk ahead, Dominic had subconsciously decided to cut across the shortest way, even though he knew where it led. It led to an archway marked *Canes Venatici*: the Hunting Dogs.

Dominic stood beneath the arch. He looked at the path ahead: a walkway, seemingly of bamboo, that disappeared into a forest of tall canes. "Canes Venatici is based on a mistranslation," he muttered to himself. "No dogs here. Just a shepherd's crook, for tending the flock. Or a club. No dogs. . . ."

The archway was also crafted from bamboo, tied together in places with thick fibers. A small signpost stood beside it, the words *Canes Venatici* painted at the top, and in smaller letters below: *Follow thus the shepherd's canes from Chara to Asterion. Meet the herd that you'll help steer, unless in fright you turn and run.*

"Shepherd's canes," Dominic whispered aloud. "Take that, Gerard of Cremona." He took a step forward, but he paused to take another cautious peek into the forest.

He saw nothing, yet he stopped in sudden fear. Some sound had reached his ears—the sound of a large creature running nearby, its feet pounding against the soft earth, the grasses brushing against its racing step.

Dominic swore under his breath. The sound, he realized, was coming from behind him. He made ready to run and glanced over his shoulder.

"Dominic!" Surina shouted.

She was hurrying down a grassy slope toward him, Greg following close behind.

"Hey," Dominic greeted her as she reached the archway. He started to say more, but could only let out a small *oof* as Surina hugged him and squeezed the air from his lungs.

She released him, but kept her hands on his shoulders. "What happened? Are you all right?"

"Fine," he said, pausing to catch his breath. "I ended up in Boötes."

"How?"

He lifted the helmet. "I flew. Virgo helped me."

"Virgo? Did you see her?"

"Yeah. We talked about old times. It was very chill; she told jokes and everything." Dominic gestured to the signpost. "We're at Canes Venatici, but according to this, it's *canes*—the English meaning, not Latin."

"Dominic!" she shouted. "I don't need a Latin lesson right now. I thought you were dead."

"I'm not," he assured her. "So, everything's fine. And like I said, there are just canes here, not dogs. If we cross through, we'll end up at Ursa Major, but we should eventually end up in Cancer. That's our last stop on the zodiac, and if it's possible to skip Virgo and Leo, I'm all for it. I already had my Virgo moment."

Greg gave him a light slap on the shoulder. "Hey, man. Glad you're all right."

"Thanks. Well, let's cut the small talk and start walking." Dominic looked hesitantly down the shaded path. "Who wants to go first?"

Greg took the lead, his shoes plunking loudly against the bamboo walkway.

"Canes Venatici is a really small constellation," Dominic said to Surina as they crossed. "It's tiny. We should reach the end of it in, like, ten seconds."

"It is a small constellation," Surina said. "But, how do you know there aren't any dogs? Just because—"

"There aren't any. Just canes. Okay? Let's just accept the fact that this place has nothing but canes and only takes ten seconds to cross. Look—there's the end of it."

Just ahead, the cane forest fell away into a sandy clearing. The trio stepped out into a barren realm, a flat dirt landscape featuring a sole focal point: an ornate wooden box atop a golden platform. It stood at a strange angle, tilting upwards from the ground rather than resting on its surface.

"We're in Ursa Major," Surina said. "Let's walk around it. If we go off to the right somewhere, we should end up at Leo."

Greg pointed to the wooden box. "What's that?"

"It's a coffin."

"Oh. Okay. That's a bad sign, right?"

"It's good," Dominic replied. "It means we're almost at the last place at the Zodiac. Like Surina said, we can just walk around it."

"So, if we make it to the last place," Greg began.

"I hope it means that we can go home," Dominic said. "Hannah will meet us soon, and Surina can open the damned gate, and we can all get out of here."

Greg nodded. He resumed walking beside Dominic. "Listen, I'm sorry about Draco—you know, the ground splitting open and all of that. I feel like it was kind of my fault, because . . . well, because I talked about it."

"No worries. I don't think you're the one who did that. Anyway, we're almost out."

"I hope so. I'm beat. I'm tired, I'm thirsty . . . ."

"Ah," Dominic said. "Right." He began to pull the flask from his pocket, hesitating only for a moment before the memory of Virgo's warm eyes vanquished his pang of guilt. "Really, this journey could have been a lot worse. You and Surina talked about plenty of terrible things; you must have mentioned your zombie run a dozen times, but we made it through the zodiac without being attacked by zombies, or getting hepatitis, or falling into a—"

The flask was knocked from Dominic's hand as Greg took off in a sudden mad dash. He slammed into Surina as he rushed past her, knocking her to the ground.

"What the hell," Dominic muttered. He extended a hand to help Surina to her feet, and then he stooped to pick up the flask. "What spooked him this time?"

Surina froze for a moment. She pointed past Dominic. "Zombies," she breathed.

Amassed at the opposite edge of Ursa Major, and headed their way, was a horde of the living dead:

limping, shuffling, groaning figures, their thin limbs just leathery bundles of sinew and bone. Below the rotting faces, the bulging eyeballs and gaping sockets, jutting ribs and exposed bone peeked from shreds of soiled cloth—and mixed in with those figures were the blue-hued forms of Tagua's minions.

"Okay, this one is definitely my fault," Dominic said. "Should we run?"

"Look!" Surina pointed again. "There's a girl. Isn't that Hannah?"

Between Lynx and Leo was the comparatively small realm of Leo Minor. It provided the quickest route from Cancer to Ursa Major, and Hannah expected it to reflect the implications of its name and history: a barely remarkable realm in which some minor event might occur.

Its features were little more than a stone floor painted with the realm's title and the stars of Leo Minor surrounding it. Two walls ensured its narrow width. Hannah went ahead of the crowd, urging them to follow her through the small domain—and as she called to them, an image caught her eye: a small lion cub painted on the wall, with the words "The Little One" painted beneath.

Hannah chuckled and moved on.

The realm widened as it approached Ursa Major, so that the trickle of wanderers once again became a crowd. Together they crossed the sandy plain toward the only notable feature of the realm: a slightly inclined casket, the doorway to the passage of rebirth.

Hannah didn't see Dominic and Surina until they had called her name several times. A slow awareness of their voices, and of their movements as they hurried toward her, compelled her to look up. A sudden burst of energy hit her, and she rushed forward, nearly catching Dominic in a hug—but her energy waned, and she leaned forward with her hands on her knees, trying to steady herself.

"We're almost there, Hannah," Dominic said. "Hang in there." He stepped aside as one of the undead reached a curious hand toward him. "Wow, look at you with all of your friends. Can you tell them to back off?"

Hannah straightened up. She took a breath and tried to raise her voice. "Everyone wait, please," she said. "We're almost there. I just need a minute." She gestured to the casket. "We need to go there."

The wooden casket was supported by a gold platform. Winged figures comprised the legs, each with blank eyes, serene faces, and cat-like paws that reached up to support the base. Hannah stood beside it. She unfolded the scrap of papyrus in her hand. "It's the last labor," she said, "from the gate at Cancer." Her voice trembled as she read aloud: "Free Cerberus from the underworld; he needs no longer guard. The Eleusinian Mysteries redeemed and served as ward, and now all souls must rise to fall, to cycle through again. Be the head that bravely leads to heaven's caravan."

She looked at Dominic. "Cerberus is a three-headed beast with a serpent's tail. It's . . . the constellations that surround the Gate of Cancer. The heads are Canis Minor, Lynx, and Leo, and the tail is Hydra."

Dominic raised his eyebrows questioningly. "So, how

do we free a bunch of constellations?"

"By freeing *them*." Hannah gestured to the wandering undead. "If they leave, Cerberus doesn't need to guard them anymore. I have to take them through Ursa Major. Ursa Major is . . . ."

"It's a coffin," Surina said. "Right? That's what I found when I went there. In Arab mythology, Ursa Major is a casket, and the stars that include Miza and Alcor are the funeral procession." She glanced uneasily at the listless crowd. "Is that why they're going? Maybe I'm wrong, but I think they're already dead."

"So was I," said a high, scratchy voice. The bird-thing stood nearby, still taking notes as it spoke. "I was dead when I first came here, but I didn't know it. Ursa Major is a realm for those who have yet to accept their deaths. Stepping into the casket is an act of acceptance. The passage brings them to the waters of Draco; they wade through, and the memories of their past lives are washed away, though some of the residue remains. Then they proceed to Ursa Minor, the chariot of the heavens, to be reborn."

Dominic looked at Hannah for affirmation, and she nodded. Tears stood in her eyes.

"What's the matter?" he asked. "Are you worried about them?"

"I . . . can't come home with you," Hannah said.

"What do you mean?"

She gestured to the vacant-eyed dead. "I have to lead them into Ursa Minor. If I don't, they'll stay trapped here. They need someone to help them move on."

"So . . . let them move on. You can take them and

come back. We'll go with you."

"I need to lead them *in*." Hannah's voice cracked; her face bore a sad serenity. "I need to go through the doorway first, and through Draco, to show them it's okay. If I don't lead them, they won't go."

"No. Hannah . . . ."

"Hannah," Surina said, "You don't have to go that far."

"I do," Hannah replied. "Virgo told me I wouldn't make it to the sun gate. It's okay. I've accepted it." She cleared her throat, tried to steady her voice. "Thanks for everything you did. It really means a lot to me." She gave Dominic a firm but weary hug. "I'll miss you guys. Especially you."

Dominic was about to protest again, but the bird-like scribe gently pushed Hannah away from him.

"Let me take this task," it said. "You have done enough."

She stared up at it, uncomprehending.

The creature spoke again: "This is a community effort, remember? You don't have to fix everything by yourself—and you don't have to reach the sun gate by yourself. The queen didn't say you wouldn't reach the gate; she said you would collapse before it, but here you have friends to help carry you." The scratchy voice took on a quiet, gentle tone. "Any transgressions you committed here have been very small, and you have already redeemed yourself—but I still need to be redeemed. I shall help others redeem themselves."

"Are you sure?" Tears streamed down Hannah's cheeks as she gazed up at the creature.

"I am. Virgo didn't make me a scribe so that I could keep records; she kept me safe in the underworld so that I could tell you how to open the gate. Go back to Lupus. I will take them from here."

Hannah looked uncertainly at the doorway. "But . . . they won't follow you. You're not alive."

"They went ahead of you through the gates of the underworld. Perhaps they will go ahead of you now. If they refuse, then we will resort to your plan, but let us try mine first."

"Wait," Hannah said. "Tell them how to open the sun gate, just in case . . . ."

"Ah—yes." The scribe stepped away from the platform. Its tall figure crouched down until it was on its knees. The creature set its paper and pen aside and extended one scrawny finger, using the clawed tip to draw numbers in the sand:

1 1 2 3 5 8 13 21 34 55 89

"Do you know this pattern?" it asked.

"It's the Fibonacci sequence," Surina said. "You add one plus one to get two, and then you add the two plus the one before it to get three, and then three plus the two to get five, and five plus three to get—"

"Yes, that's it. The golden ratio."

Surina frowned. "But . . . ."

"That *is* it, but you have to reduce each number in the sequence to a single digit," the scribe explained. "You can do that by adding the digits of each number together until you're left with one digit. So, when you get thirteen, it reduces to four. Twenty-one reduces to three. If you keep doing that, you end up with a repeating sequence of twenty-four numbers." Wibben scrawled more figures into the sand, arranging a set of numbers in two lines:

011235843718
988764156281

"You need to add zero at the beginning," the scribe continued. "Zero is a reflection of nine; zero is emptiness, and nine is fullness. If you arrange these numbers in a circle within a circle, like a number dial, you can see how each is a reflection of another number; they are opposites and complements. Eight reflects one, seven reflects two, six reflects three, and five reflects four." He drew a large circle, and another slightly smaller circle within it, and filled the inner borders with the two lines of numbers. "If you add each number with its reflection, they balance and equal nine, fullness. The sequence shows you the foundations of the starry dimension. Each of its realms teaches a principle of balance; you learned such a balance at Ophiuchus. On the sun gate, each symbol represents a number. I figured them out by counting the amount of each symbol, but you won't have to do that. I will write the key here—but you must take care to remember it."

"Can't you write it on that paper?" Surina asked. "We could take it with us."

"As you can see," the scribe replied, "the writings quickly fade. My observations are etched into the fabric of this place; they are not mere scribblings on paper."

The rough hand drew another set of numbers into the sand, along with the symbol each represented: "1=tower," "2= two pillars," and so on.

"That doesn't seem so hard to remember," Dominic mused. "The tower looks like the number one, the two pillars equal two, the triangle is three. We'll be able to figure it out."

"Arrange the symbols according to their number," the scribe continued. "Nine discs with the jug symbol should be placed in the number nine slot; eight discs with the infinity symbol in each number eight slot. Understand?"

"I think so," Hannah said.

"You can make the dial like I drew it here, with the zero and nine at the top—but even if you start the numbers somewhere else, as long as they are all in order, they will unlock the gate." The scribe stood, leaving the papyrus and pen on the ground. "You and your friends can go home, but if you come across any wanderers on the way, don't take them with you, no matter how much they might plead. It will only make it harder for them to find their way."

The creature reached down to open the casket, and Dominic helped it heft the lid onto the ground. A narrow stone stairway led down into the dark unknown; Hannah looked into it and felt a pang of fear.

Dominic had much the same reaction. "They could have made it more inviting," he said. "No wonder so many people don't want to go in."

"Well, that's death for you," Surina murmured.

The scribe held out a long, thin hand to Hannah. "Help me into the casket and tell them to follow me."

She started to comply, but she hesitated. "Are you ready?"

"I am here; therefore I am ready," it replied quietly.

Hannah took its downy hand and looked out at the crowd. "Everyone come this way," she said. "We have to keep going through the portal here."

The Wibben-bird-thing gazed at Hannah as the first of the undead began to approach. Quietly, it said: "I will not remember this place. The impressions will still be there, but I am afraid that any wisdom I've gained in the stars will be overpowered by the circumstances of my new life. I'm afraid of . . . becoming who I used to be."

"You'll be all right," Hannah assured it. "I know that you will do well this time." She squeezed the creature's hand. "Goodbye."

The scribe descended the stairs. A half-decomposed woman, with a vaguely curious look in her eye, lingered at the threshold.

Hannah grasped what was left of the woman's ruined hand. "It's all right," she said. "Pretty soon, you'll be free."

She and Dominic stood on either side of the coffin and helped the dead descend into the unseen domain. Dominic found himself flinching at their decay, and he watched in quiet awe as Hannah grasped the rotten hands and bare bones with warmth and encouragement.

When the dead had all gone, Dominic placed a gentle hand on Hannah's shoulder. "Who was Big Bird?" he asked. "Friend of yours?"

"That was Wibben," Hannah replied.

"What? Bernhard Wibben? That Wibben?"

"What?" Surina echoed. "How is he a bird? He died!" She raised her hands to her cheeks. "Oh . . . he died in Phoenix. He must have been reborn." Slowly, she lowered her hands. The surprise faded from her face, and her eyes seemed to darken. "Why does *he* get to be a person again? He was one of the worst humans."

"He has to make up for it," Hannah replied.

"How? He'll need a thousand lifetimes to make up for that."

"He has to start with this one."

"Let's discuss it later," Dominic interrupted. "We still have a long walk ahead."

Before they left, they replaced the lid of the coffin—just in case. Dominic and Surina had hardly finished positioning it when they heard a cry in the distance—a human cry, a sound of grief-laden protest. Dominic looked to the outskirts of the realm, fearing that something had happened to Greg, but a most unexpected sight met his eyes: Tagua, thin and pale and dressed only in a rag around his waist, was being dragged into Ursa Major. Strange creatures gathered close around him, beings that resembled humans, but with skeleton-thin bodies and rodent-like heads. The one in the foreground carried a long scepter; the one at the back held a mace.

"We have a problem," Dominic said. "Somehow, Tagua is back."

"Oh," Hannah said, "that's not a problem. They're forcing him to go to the underworld. They must have picked him out of Draco before he reached Ursa Minor."

She looked across the plain. Perhaps out of weariness, she seemed unfazed by the sight of Tagua struggling to escape his captors. Two creatures stood on either side, clutching his arms, rendering him helpless; his feet dragged across the plain in useless resistance.

"My journey up from the Gate of Cancer was kind of like what I read about in *Inanna's Descent*—the Sumerian story," Hannah continued. "I didn't know how to get through the gates, so I just followed the story; I kind of plagiarized it." She laughed softly. "At the end of that story, a selfish shepherd is supposed to take Inanna's place in the underworld, but when the underworld servants come for him, he develops serpent qualities that help him escape for a little while—kind of like Tagua almost escaping through Draco. He gets caught at the edge of the realms and dragged to the underworld, and he has to stay there for half a cycle." She paused to watch the group proceed toward Leo Minor. As Tagua came closer, a frantic resistance was visible in his eyes, but he seemed not to see Hannah and the others—or perhaps he simply didn't recognize them. "He doesn't remember us," Hannah said. "And he has no power. It's kind of satisfying to see him like that. Who knows . . . maybe someday, he'll even change." She smiled at Dominic and added: "But that's none of my business. It's out of my hands, and always has been."

They found Greg hiding among the tall canes at Canes Venatici. He came out slowly, with a look of embarrassment rather than caution, his head bowed in a gesture of shame. "Sorry," he began, and then he saw

Hannah. He gaped, and Hannah lifted a hand in a weary greeting.

"Isn't that Hannah?" he asked.

"In the flesh," she replied weakly.

"What happened to the bird thing? See, I *knew* that thing wasn't Hannah!"

"It was me," she said. "I was a griffin."

"Oh, wow." Greg fidgeted, shifted his weight from side to side. "Maybe I'm hallucinating all this, but it's cool. I really didn't think we'd find you alive. No offense."

"That's okay," Hannah replied.

"So, um, what next? Can we go home now?"

"We can get out through Lupus," Dominic said. "It's that way."

Greg, seeing Hannah's weak disposition, offered to carry her piggy-back, and she bashfully accepted. The group followed a narrow passage between Canes Venatici and Virgo, and as they went, Dominic noted Surina's distant, troubled expression. "You okay?" he asked.

"I'm thinking about Bernhard Wibben," she said. "About the conversations I had with him. He was part of this heinous, evil thing back on Earth. He was looking for artifacts to help the Nazis, but the only thing he really remembered was some woman who rejected him."

"Well, that's fitting. Do you know how many guys blame their angst and aggression on that same thing? He was a 1940s incel."

"Back then," Surina said, "when I talked to him, I kind of forgave him . . . but after I went home, I watched

The Pianist, about the Jewish pianist who survived the holocaust in Warsaw. And I was seeing all of these ordinary people going around and slaughtering other innocent people—kids, adults, babies. It just filled me with despair, and I thought, 'How could anyone with a shred of humanity support such a thing? How can someone do that, and then claim to be a decent person? How dare they ask for forgiveness?' Even if Wibben served his sentence, I don't forgive him. There's no sentence long enough for that."

"He didn't claim to be a decent person back *then*," Dominic said. "I mean, based on what you told me, it sounded like he would agree with you—but back then, when he was alive, he had his excuses. Like, he was just running around and looking for cult artifacts for the Nazis, and he didn't actually partake in any—"

"No, Dominic, don't even go there. He partook because he *knew*," she said. "People always made excuses and said, 'Oh, I didn't know how bad it really was,' but you know that's B.S. It was wrong from the beginning—stripping people of their dignity, of their rights. People should have stopped it immediately. That's always how it starts: Some nefarious group commits a small atrocity, people make excuses and accept it, it becomes the norm, and then the actors make an even more heinous move—and eventually it's a bloodbath, and everyone's like, 'How did this happen?'"

"You don't have to convince me," Dominic said. "People do monstrous things—things I can't even wrap my head around. But I think Wibben will be a decent person this time around."

"I don't know. . . ."

"What's the alternative? Stay a monster, and hurt more people? It sounds like he wants to help other people learn how to change for the better. And, honestly, I don't know if this whole 'get reincarnated through Ursa Minor' thing is real or not, but you know how scientists say that energy doesn't die; it just changes into something else. If that's the case, then maybe we do just get recycled in some way, and then we *have* to change—and if there's a therapy program that can make people face themselves, and change for the better, it's this one." Dominic made a sweeping gesture in the direction of the Virgo realm.

Surina glanced up, still with a brooding expression. "Yes, but . . . ." She came to a sudden halt. Her face seemed to blanch.

"What is it?" Dominic asked.

She took Dominic's arm with surprising strength and pulled him forward. "Nothing. Let's keep going."

"Ow. Okay, I'll go. No need to torture me."

She waited until they had walked some distance, and then she confided in a low tone: "I swear I just saw myself. Or, someone who looked a lot like me." She glanced back again, as if afraid of being followed. "Remember what Aquarius said about how I would have a chance to change my past? I think I just had that chance. God, how I wanted to run up to myself and . . . ."

"It was a challenge, was it?"

"It's *still* a challenge," she said, her voice strained with anxiety. "I so want to keep myself from marrying my prick ex-husband. He lied about every damn thing. He put me through hell, and he stole my entire life's savings."

"Yes, I know."

Surina came to an abrupt halt. "I could at least warn myself not to open a shared bank account with him."

"No, Surina. You can't change anything," Dominic cautioned her.

"I could just give myself a hint, like, 'Just because some mystical queen told you to hang with Victor, it doesn't mean you should trust him completely. Protect your money.'"

"Surina, don't. You can make more money."

"How? I want to be a music teacher! Teachers don't make money. It's a lifetime of being overworked and underpaid."

Dominic gripped Surina's arm as she took a step toward Virgo. "You'll figure things out. We're about to go home, and if you change one little thing, everything will be different. We could die in here."

"That whole thing was her fault. Victor had all of these red flags, but I married him because Virgo told me . . . ." Surina trailed off.

"She didn't tell you to marry him," Dominic reminded her. "She said he would help balance you. It's the same way Tagua helped Hannah."

Surina's gaze shifted to Greg and Hannah, who were gaining ground ahead of them.

"I think it's good that you went through that experience," Dominic said. "It made you fierce. Do you really want to go back to being the person who allows yourself to get stepped on?"

Surina stared down at him. Her eyes narrowed. "You sound like Virgo," she said.

"She's right about this one."

Surina gave another hard glance at the Virgo realm and resolutely turned away. "Let's keep going. I have to get out of here, or I'll just be tempted."

She quickened her pace, passing Greg, who was cheerfully educating Hannah about the wonders of calcium: "So, the sandstone at Wupatki is in the upper layer, and that's full of quartz, and below that is the Kaibab limestone. Now, *that's* full of calcium. As conditions change, it's becoming dolomitic, which means that it's slowly absorbing more magnesium. So, the ground at Wupatki is naturally composing itself in the same way that a lot of these ancient temples are structured. A lot of them are purposely made with granite and dolomitic limestone alongside each other, but no one knows why."

"Isn't it because calcium and magnesium have opposite energies?" Hannah asked. "My foster mom had to take magnesium and calcium supplements, and her doctor always said that they're both important for human life, but that she shouldn't take them together because they compete with each other—and magnesium usually loses because it's less aggressive. Calcium is the high-energy one, and magnesium creates calmness. Calcium helps muscles contract, but magnesium helps them relax. Calcium clots the blood, but magnesium increases its flow. Calcium lives in the bones, but magnesium likes the soft tissues. When you put two opposites together, an energy is created between them, and it helps create transformation and balance." Hannah paused, and added: "Well, the calcium stuff I learned from Carmina's doctor, but that last part I learned here."

Dominic glanced back at the duo as he hurried after Surina. Hannah rested with her chin tucked snugly onto Greg's shoulder, tired but still with a spark of interest in her eyes.

"So, if more magnesium keeps building up in a stone that's full of calcium," Hannah continued, "doesn't it just create a stronger energy? And if the sandstone is full of quartz crystals and water—well, then that's just going to amplify the energy even more. . . ."

Dominic chuckled as he and Surina moved well ahead of the other two. "Hannah is solving all the mysteries of the universe."

"That's our Hannah," Surina murmured.

"So, tell me what happened back in Ophiuchus. I mean, I kind of know what happened: Hannah opened a portal to Draco. How did she open it?"

"Oh . . . ." Surina sighed. "I had to play the lyre at Lyra, using the circle of fifths. It's a Western music thing that shows the harmonic relationship between the twelve notes, so I guess it's appropriate that I used it in the zodiac realm, where there's a circle of twelve realms. It actually looks a lot like the Fibonacci circle that Wibben made, with twelve notes on the outer circle, and twelve on the inner circle." She paused. "It's interesting, because before we came here, I was reading about how music that uses the circle of fifths is supposed to sound beautiful, and people have used the Fibonacci sequence

215

and the golden ratio to make all kinds of pretty songs—but it depends on how you use it. Music that uses Fibonacci ratios can also be unsettling and discordant. I was listening to this golden mean-based composition by John Chowning called *Stria*, and it gave me this feeling of . . . uneasy alertness. I realized that it's the same feeling I get when I enter this dimension. Don't you feel strange when you're in here? Like . . . there's this slight, general uneasiness, almost like nausea, but . . . it's not nausea."

"Yes, I know what you mean."

"Anyway," Surina continued, "the Fibonacci sequence is like a mathematical expression of life on Earth. If you don't reduce it, it just keeps progressing—but if you reduce it to its basic parts, it's actually just goes through the same twelve steps, and then through an opposite set of twelve steps."

"Like how we're going the opposite way on the zodiac," Dominic said.

"Yes, except that it happens over and over again. And it's a perfect expression of balance and imbalance: It expresses a perfect ratio that allows for life, but it has to follow a path of imbalance, because life needs opposing forces to create movement. So, I think that's also appropriate—that we're using that sequence to return to our own world. It seems like the Ophiuchus realm is about confronting our imbalances and growing through them; we need imbalance to move, but we also have to keep moving toward balance. In our world, once we finally achieve balance, maybe we won't belong there anymore. No more being shuttled back to Earth by

Draco. We're just done being human, and who knows what comes next?"

"Well, I'm glad we get to be human for a little longer," Dominic said. He glanced back and added: "We're passing out of Virgo. Feeling better?"

"No, I don't feel better," she replied, and sighed again. "I admit that I have learned things here, but I hate this place."

"Oh, it's not so bad. Really, this place has grown on me. We had adventures, met interesting people, learned a new game . . . I got to watch Greg make an ass of himself in front of you . . . ."

"Dominic!" Surina gave him a hard nudge. "Greg helped us a lot."

"I don't disagree. He helped *me* a lot."

"Dominic, knock it off. You guys aren't competing, okay?"

He laughed. "Well, *I* was competing. I had fun competing with him. He made me look good."

Surina narrowed her eyes at Dominic. "Was that fun for you? This place is horrible. You said yourself that the first time you were here, it was awful."

"It was."

"I thought this was such an amazing experience when I first came here, even though it only lasted a minute. I thought I was dreaming or hallucinating or whatever, but I took it seriously. I was like, 'Wow, I'm in this magical world, receiving a message from a divine being. I'm so special.'"

"Well . . . I don't let it go to my head, but we *are* lucky to have been here," Dominic replied. "I mean, this isn't a common experience. There are other people who could benefit from it, and who may need it more, but it's us. I don't know why."

"I don't know why I'm here either," Surina said. "I guess it did help me become a stronger person, but I'm still pissed at Virgo, or whatever she is."

"I like her," Dominic replied. "I feel like the queen of the underworld is my BFF."

Surina gave him an astonished look. "What's there to like? She's a conniving, emotionless . . . ."

"She's not. She's generous. And she's wise."

"A wise-*ass*, and a cold-hearted one. I'm mad. I'm always going to be pissed off at her and this whole place." Surina stopped and turned aside. "DO YOU HEAR THAT?" she shouted. "THIS PLACE SUCKS!"

Dominic laid a hand on her arm. "Knock it off; you'll jinx it. Wait until we get home before you start spewing curses."

"Maybe you should wait 'til we get home before you call the queen your BFF," Surina retorted. "She might have some last-minute surprise in store for you."

"If she does, I'm sure it will be a good surprise."

As they reached the outskirts of Lupus, Greg stopped and eased Hannah from his back. "Hey," he said to Dominic, "do you still have that flask? You were about to give it to me when I got freaked out by the zombies."

"Ah, yes." Dominic retrieved the flask and extended it to Greg.

"Thanks, man." Greg opened it and drank deeply, but suddenly he stopped and turned the flask upright. "Oh—sorry. I suppose other people are thirsty, too." He offered it to Surina.

Dominic's hand snapped out. He knocked the flask from Greg's hand before Surina could touch it. "Oops," he said. He stooped to pick it up, holding it upside-down so that the last remaining drops sprinkled into the dirt. "Looks like it's empty."

Surina gave him a look of suspicious disbelief. He smiled and kept walking.

In the ruins of Lupus, Dominic stood with his hands on his hips, gazing upward in consternation.

"The sun gate is up there," he said, pointing to an upper floor of the partially collapsed building. "How the hell do we get up? There's no moving platform, no winged helmet, no flying griffin—"

"I made a rope," Hannah said. "It's probably not very strong, but it was all I could think of."

She led them to the length of knotted tunics. It didn't quite reach the ground, but the group boosted themselves up by stacking rubble beneath it.

"I'll test it out first," Dominic said, yanking on the makeshift rope. "It seems likely to . . . ." He trailed off, staring at the off-white fabric in his hand. "Hannah, what did you make this out of?"

"Clothes."

"Whose clothes?"

"You know who," she said softly. "The kids who were here. The ones who disappeared. Toward the end, there were a lot of them."

Dominic let out a long sigh. "Well . . . here I go."

The silence of the place seemed louder as Dominic

climbed. He heard only the sounds of his own breathing and measured grunts as he hoisted himself to the column where Hannah had tied the rope. He reached the upper floor without incident, and Surina followed. A debate ensued, then, about whether Hannah and Greg would be too heavy together; Hannah was too weak to climb alone.

"It's not real, remember?" Greg called at last. "We're not really climbing the rope, so we can't be too heavy for it. Let me just give it a try."

Greg, too, ascended the rope without incident, with Hannah's arms and legs clasped around him.

"One last challenge to go," Dominic, helping Hannah down from Greg's back.

Hannah led the way down the now-familiar path to the sun disc room, through a labyrinth of small, empty spaces divided by pale walls and into a much larger square arena. The near-empty space seemed to loom ominously around the group; their voices echoed as they murmured to one another in low tones. A pair of chairs still sat empty in the center of the black-and-white tiled floor, facing each other, as if inviting two occupants to sit together in debate or collaboration. The room was otherwise featureless except for the far wall, where the sun disc gleamed in the haze of light from the ruined ceiling. Twisted shards of metal radiated from behind the disc, pointed at the tips like stylized sun rays.

The group gathered close to the disc. In its center, a few verses were etched:

Living creatures show the map by which they grow and thrive,
patterned on the bud and limb, seen by the learned eye.
Form and color may abate as all reduce to basic state.
Dextral mapping leads halfway to loosening the beast;
young relative steps widdershins, and he shall be released.
A map within a map unlocks the door and marks an end,
and starts the world where this will happen time and time again.

A collection of small round magnets lay scattered around the surface, close to the outer edge, leaving the center empty. Hannah pointed out the lightly etched diving lines on the disc: One was in the shape of a circle, creating a smaller disc within the larger disc, and the others ran straight from the center to the circumference, dividing each disc into twelve segments.

"A map within a map," she recited. "Wibben said that we have to put the symbol for each number in the right space. We're supposed to start with the number zero at the top, so . . . I think we don't put anything in the top space. The symbol for the number one must go here." She pointed to a space just to the right of the top slot. "But . . . I don't remember if we start with the outside spaces, or the inside spaces."

"I'm lost," Dominic said. "I know I said it should be

easy, but I don't know where to start. What's the symbol for one?"

Hannah surveyed the collection of magnets. The pieces were small, only an inch in diameter. After a moment she moved close and collected a handful of them.

"The tower represents one," she said. "Let's try filling the outside circle first. It goes zero, one, one, two, three, five, eight . . . ."

"We need to figure out which symbols represent the rest of the numbers," Surina said. "Whatever the number is, that's how many magnets we put in that space."

"The triangle symbol was three," Dominic said. He pointed to a disc bearing a pair of capped pillars, one black and one white. "The pillars are two. A lot of these are geometric; the throne looks like a rectangle, and I think that was four."

Together they worked to figure out the images, halting at times until someone spotted a clue: "The mask has a figure-eight symbol for its eyes, the infinity symbol. That must be number eight." "This figure has a five-pointed crown, so it could be five."

Eventually, they came up with a possible solution. The image of a six-pointed star in a rayed disc was six, the pyramid with a rectangular throne at its base was seven, and so on. The last number to solve was nine, so the group assigned it to the remaining image, a reddish-brown jug on a yellow background. The outer circle filled up as they worked, first with one image of a tower, then another image of a tower, then with two magnets featuring a pair of capped pillars, then three magnets bearing triangles. In this way, a code began to appear in the twelve segments: one, one, two, three, five, eight, and so on. Greg volunteered to do the required math, finishing with another number eight near the top of the dial.

"Now we have to start filling the inside circle, with the number nine at the top," Hannah explained. She and Greg shifted the jug-themed magnets into the top slot, and then Hannah lowered her arms wearily. She turned to Surina and Dominic, who sat close together on the floor. "What are you doing?" she asked.

"Writing the code," Surina replied, holding up a shard of debris. "If you just write the numbers' complements beneath them, you don't have to do the math." She moved back so that Hannah could see the series of numbers she had scratched into one of the white tiles:

0 11235843718
9 88764156281

"You're a genius." Hannah turned again to the dial, reaching for a magnet with an open-mouthed mask on its surface. "Eight eights here, and in the next one, too." She paused, letting her arms fall once again to her sides. "Can you guys finish it?" she asked. "I know how to do it, but . . . I need to sit down for a while. I'm so dizzy."

"Yeah, we got it." Dominic helped Hannah to sit, and then he turned his attention back to the disc, counting as he worked.

He stopped to check on Hannah just as she began to slump toward the floor; he swore under his breath and caught her head before it hit the hard tiles. "Hurry, guys. Look at her face! She's turning completely blue."

"We're almost there," Surina said. "Where's the last tower?"

"I got it," Greg said. He placed the tower disc in the final slot and stepped back. "Okay, so, I'm counting, and everything looks right. How come nothing's . . . ."

He trailed off as the disc swung noiselessly away from the wall. Dominic held his breath and braced himself, expecting to be blasted by a stream of glorious and fearsome light, but behind the gate was just an ordinary-looking tunnel of smooth gray stone, leading into darkness.

"Greg, help," he said, urgency straining his voice. "Can you carry Hannah again? She's totally out."

"Yeah. Help me get her over my shoulder; I think that's the easiest way to get her through the tunnel."

Surina and Dominic helped to hoist her up. Dominic went into the tunnel first, to act as a guide through the darkness, with Greg following close behind. Surina hurried after them, but she stopped a few paces from the gate. She looked back into Lupus, into the near-empty room with the checkered floor—and then she reached out and closed the gate behind her.

14: Flagstaff

Dominic walked briskly, with one hand trailing along the stone wall and the other held out in front of him.

"Dominic," Greg said, "Can you talk, or sing, or something, so I know where you are?"

"Sing?"

"Or whatever. Just make noise."

"Ah . . . my mind is blank."

"Okay. Then, talk about how your mind is blank, or just start counting. And let me know if there are any curves or obstacles."

The tunnel was smooth and straight, and thus it was easy to navigate even as it descended into blackness—but Dominic's anxiety increased as the minutes went by and the tunnel narrowed.

"Come on," he whispered. "Come on, Wupatki."

"I think we're getting there," Greg called. "Do you feel that?"

"What?" Dominic asked—but then he felt it.

"Wind," Greg said.

Dominic had forgotten about the dynamics of Wupatki: the need of the caves and tunnels to maintain and relieve pressure, the flow of cool air in and out of the site's blowholes. As he walked, the flow strengthened, pulling at his clothes and hair.

"It's pushing us forward," Greg said. "That's a good sign, right?"

"Only good signs from now on," Dominic replied. "Surina, are you still behind us?"

She replied in the affirmative.

"I see something up ahead; looks like a light." Dominic moved closer, closer, and hope stirred inside of him. "It's an opening. It looks like—aghh!"

Fear sounded in Greg's voice. "What is it?"

"I just banged my leg against the rock. Be careful up here. I think . . . we won't be able to walk anymore. There's kind of a step, and . . . okay, it's . . . it's a small passageway. Greg, why don't you go in first? You're going to have to pull Hannah behind you, and we'll try to push her. Do you see the light? I'm hoping that's Wupatki."

They eased Hannah to the ground while Greg fumbled his way into the tunnel. "Look out," he said. "I have to go in backwards, so I need some space."

Dominic listened to the sound of his struggling, and after a minute, Greg said: "Okay. Put her in feet first. I don't want to drag her by her shoulders; if I pull on her vest, I'm worried I'll choke her."

"What about her head?" Dominic asked. "I don't want her head bumping against the rock while you drag her."

"You'll have to try to hold her head from behind."

They eased Hannah into the passage, and Dominic tried to keep one hand under her head as they made a slow journey through the tunnel. "Just a moment; just a moment. Her damn braids are getting pinned under my arm," Dominic said. "I'm going to try tying them under her chin."

Sharp rocks scratched his flesh as the trek resumed, and as the tunnel became smaller and the movements slower, he silently assured himself: *Easy, Dominic. Don't panic. It's just a moment of compression and darkness, and then light. Think of it as being reborn. We're almost there.*

"Stop for a minute," Greg said.

"Everything okay?"

"Yeah."

Dominic listened to the sound of Greg's movements and quiet grunts. Suddenly, the noises stopped; silence ensued, and just as Dominic was about to call out again, Greg cried: "It's our chamber!"

"What?"

"We're back at Wupatki! My climbing gear is here!"

Dominic breathed a sigh of relief. He heard Surina's grateful murmurs behind him. "Can you pull Hannah out?" he asked. "Slowly, though, so I can keep my hand under her head."

They worked her out of the tunnel, and then Dominic could see it: the faint stream of sunlight flowing down into the chamber, and the thin black outlines of the climbing ropes. Dawn had arrived; darkness had passed, and the earth at Wupatki breathed night's essence back into the upper world. Greg laid Hannah on the ground and helped Dominic out, and then Surina.

"She's alive," Dominic said in a trembling voice, his fingers pressed against Hannah's neck. "Greg, you can carry her up, can't you? Where's the harness?"

"We won't fit together," Greg replied. "I'll have to go first, and then you'll have to harness her, and I'll try to pull her up." He switched on one of the headlamps and set it on the ground. "Put your helmet on her."

"Who has a phone?" Dominic asked.

"I lost mine—in there, somewhere," Greg said.

"Mine's in your car. It's in the door compartment in the back. Greg, before you pull Hannah up, run to the car and call an ambulance."

While Greg secured his gear and climbed back to the surface, Surina and Dominic worked together to fit Hannah into the harness and helmet. Then they waited with her sleeping figure held between them. Dominic listened to the haggard sound of his own breath in the sudden stillness. Surina smiled at him, her eyes shining in the stream of dawn light. "We did it," she said softly. "*You* did it."

"Me? That was definitely a team effort."

"I suppose so. But you . . . ."

Dominic raised his eyebrows and waited, but Surina didn't finish the thought.

Hannah was above ground when paramedics finally arrived. Surina asked to ride with her in the ambulance, but was refused, and Greg graciously offered to drop his passengers off at Flagstaff Medical Center. The trio didn't talk during the drive; Greg blasted his stereo, using the noise to help him stay awake.

Likewise, Dominic and Surina yearned for sleep. They fell asleep on the couches in the hospital lounge, waking sometime later to commotion. Hannah's foster parents had arrived; they had seen Hannah, though she was still unconscious. The police also showed up, and Dominic and Surina gave them a sluggish account of what had happened: Determined to find Hannah, they went back into the tunnels. They found her huddled in a crevice and brought her to safety. End of story.

The police didn't quite buy it, but no other explanation made sense—and then Hannah woke up, groggy and weak, asking for Dominic and Surina and Greg, quietly crowing about how they had saved her.

"The press will come, too," Dominic said, when the officers had departed. "My plan is to avoid them. Refuse interviews."

"Good plan," Surina murmured.

A nurse in blue scrubs approached. He smiled down at the two scruffy visitors. "Hannah is ready to see you," he said.

Dominic experienced a surreal moment as he stood in the doorway of the hospital room. Hannah lay in the bed, looking small and emaciated in an oversized hospital gown and thick bedding—but *alive*. Dominic realized how impossible it had seemed that he would see her again in this world, despite all of his determination and hope; the odds had simply been far out of his favor.

Her eyes met Dominic's, and she smiled—a smile of love, gratitude, and a shared secret whose magnitude could not be put into words. Dominic stood there, overcome by emotion, until Hannah's voice rasped: "Come here and hug me."

Dominic moved to the bed, carefully avoiding Hannah's IV as he wrapped his arms around her. He embraced her carefully, as though she was a piece of paper that might crumple, but she squeezed him back with surprising fierceness.

"Thank you," she whispered.

Surina came in for a hug, beaming at Hannah with that same look of requited gratitude.

"Don't just leave me," Hannah whispered to her. "I have to talk to you again. No one else will understand."

"We won't leave," Surina replied quietly. "We'll be here."

"We're not going anywhere," Dominic assured her. "I mean, we'll go home and shower, but we'll come back."

Hannah chuckled.

The nurse spoke up: "How about some rest, Hannah? You look like you're ready to doze off again."

Hannah murmured her agreement, and the group stepped outside. Hannah's foster parents expressed another round of profuse thanks, their eyes shining with gratitude and the tearful remnants of their fear and grief. They seemed like decent people, Dominic thought—committed to supporting their foster daughter, yet to discover how much Hannah had changed during her time spent buried deep in the earth.

The police were coming back for another round of

questioning, so Dominic and Surina lingered in the lounge, waiting for their return.

"We'll have to watch the Draconids in October," Surina said. She curled up in a chair, facing Dominic and drawing her knees up to her chest. "With all of those extra souls coming from the underworld, it should be quite a show. We might even see Tagua's people falling back to Earth. Maybe they'll be born in better circumstances this time."

Dominic stared at her in puzzlement.

"Remember, we read somewhere that the shooting stars are supposed to represent souls coming to Earth to be born," she said. "If we can see them from Earth, they're headed for the Earth plane. And if they look like they're coming from Draco, well . . . ."

"I don't remember reading that."

"The Ursids are in December. Ursa Minor is supposed to be the carousel, or the 'wagon,' that spews all of the souls back down to Earth. I'm not sure why some of them appear to come from Draco. Maybe there are two ways to come back."

"Do you really believe that—that the stars are souls coming to Earth to be born?"

"Are you really asking me that? I don't know what I believe anymore."

"Well . . . I don't, either."

Surina closed her eyes. Dominic thought she might have fallen asleep, but suddenly she said, "Dominic."

"What?"

"Remember when you punched Tagua in the balls?"

They burst out laughing. Surina's eyes squeezed shut and her smile stretched wide with the force of her amusement, and she covered her face with her hands.

"That was so bad," she murmured.

"Um, no, it was well deserved. If anyone deserved it, that guy did."

Surina snuggled more securely into the chair, still laughing. "I can't wait to go home and take a nap. And a shower."

"You're still tired? You slept a lot already."

"I'm exhausted."

"I feel fine now," Dominic said. "I don't even have, whatever you might call in—interdimensional jet lag. I was awake most of the time that you were sleeping." He paused. "Actually, while you were asleep, I was looking out the window at those flag poles and thinking about how Flagstaff got its name. It was the centennial of the Declaration of Independence, and some dudes from Boston decided to honor the event by choosing a good pine tree, cutting off its branches, erecting it, hoisting their flag at the top, and having a ceremony around it. And then they named the town Flagstaff in honor of this sacred tree. And then, of course, to help celebrate their independence, they continued stripping indigenous people of *their* independence.

"Then in 1974, the Relocation Act was passed, and it kicked a lot of Navajo out of their homelands. A group of Navajo went to Washington to protest, and there was a group of Lakota elders there, and apparently they shared the Sun Dance ceremony with the Navajo as a way of helping them cope with being uprooted. So some of the Navajo talked about it, and they made plans and gathered resources, and there was a Sun Dance held in 1976—again, on the centennial. It was controversial because Navajo already have their own ceremonies, and then some fake spiritual leaders showed up and tried to hold a Sun Dance, but here's what stands out to me: At the beginning of the Sun Dance, a group goes out, and, I don't know all of the details, but basically, they select a good pine tree, they cut off the limbs, they erect it in the middle of the Sun Dance circle, they tie their prayer flags to it, and they have a ceremony around it. The staff is at the center of this most sacred ceremony of healing and commitment and . . . all things sacred. So, to some of my Hopi relatives—the open-minded ones—Flagstaff doesn't represent the centennial of invaders and colonization. It represents the united cause of indigenous people in overcoming oppression and maintaining our spiritual ways—of flipping colonization on its head. We're all dancing our way to that sacred center. No colonist can pervert that; subconsciously, they're seeking the same thing.

"Phoenix got its name in an interesting way, too. When the town was founded, someone wanted to name it after a Confederate general, and some other names were thrown around, but 'Phoenix' was the only one that sounded right. It makes sense, because underneath us, probably stretching across miles and miles of land, there's this realm of transformation and rebirth, living in the water and rocks, and reflecting the heavens." Dominic paused. "Hannah's dad is in Phoenix. Maybe . . . ." He trailed off. "Surina?"

Surina's eyes were closed, and her head had fallen forward, so that her throat rumbled with a light snore.

"Did you seriously just fall asleep? That was an amazing, inspiring speech that you just missed."

A familiar voice called out: "Hey!"

Greg was coming down the hall, a grin spread across his face. The bright hospital lights reflected on his glasses and obscured his eyes. "Hey, how's it going? How is Hannah?"

Surina, roused by the volume of his voice, sat up. "Hi, Greg," she said. "Hannah's good. We just talked to her, but she's sleeping now."

"Aw. I was hoping I could see her for a minute."

"She wants to see you, too," Surina said. "She's grateful to you."

"Oh, did you tell her about me?"

Surina gave him a puzzled look.

"I mean, she was unconscious when we found her, right?" Greg asked.

"Um," Surina said.

"I think the lack of oxygen got to me. I can't really remember finding Hannah. I remember going down to find you guys—and, seriously, I don't know why I did that, and I'm sorry I put you in danger. I'm usually a chicken; I never do things that are that dangerous, or that dumb. I know I was looking for you guys, and I thought I fell into some water, but the next thing I remember is helping to pull Hannah through that tiny tunnel."

Surina looked at Dominic, but he tried not to look back at her. "There's not much to remember," he claimed. "We found her and pulled her out."

"Yeah. Well . . . congratulations," Greg said. "I mean, I don't really know what else to say. I'm glad you found her, and that I agreed to help." He laughed awkwardly. "You know, it's funny—we didn't spend that much time together, but the circumstances . . . I guess the extreme circumstances just made me feel like I've known you guys for a while. Or maybe it's just gratitude. You know? It's good to know that there are people out there who never give up on the people they care about—or on a stranger, I guess, in this case. I feel like . . . even though I barely know you, you're, like, the kind of people I would move mountains for."

Dominic smiled. Surina pretended to rest her head on her hand, but Greg didn't fail to notice that she was doing a face palm. He smiled sheepishly and asked: "Too corny?"

"No," Dominic replied. "Not at all. I agree with you one hundred percent. You take risks for the people you care about. You help them through challenges, push them when they need a push, jump into flaming rivers for them . . . ."

"Yeah, yeah." Greg chuckled. "Exactly. Well, I'm actually on my way to a meeting, so I'll get going."

"Is it a meeting about your unapproved venture into Wupatki?" Dominic asked.

"No, I have yet to hear from anyone about that. I'm nervous, but . . . ." Greg shrugged. "Whatever happens, I'll figure out how to deal with it. Keep in touch, okay? Seriously." He waved and started away.

Dominic called after him: "Greg."

Greg half-turned, and Dominic continued: "Thanks for helping save Hannah's life. You may not remember, but you did a lot for her; you carried her practically all the way out. We couldn't have saved her without you, so thank you for risking arrest, and risking your career, and for the equipment, and . . . for everything else. It really means the world to me."

Greg nodded. "Any time, man." He waved at Surina and left.

Dominic leaned close to Surina. He spoke in a low voice. "You know the real reason he's leaving, right?"

She looked at him blankly. Dominic put two fingers to his lips, mimicking smoking a cigarette, but she still didn't respond. "He has to smoke," Dominic explained. "He's gone without his fix for several hours—two or three days if you count in zodiac time. He has to catch up."

A look of realization crossed Surina's face. She shook her head. "You don't quit, do you?"

He grinned. "I haven't used that joke in a while. I had to pull it out again. It *is* a joke, but that doesn't mean it's not true," he added quickly. "You can tell by looking at his eyes. He doesn't wear anti-glare glasses on purpose, because he doesn't want people to notice."

"He doesn't remember anything. Don't you think that's strange? Chad didn't remember anything either."

"Well, I think Chad chose a certain route that made

234

him forget," Dominic replied. "And Greg . . . ." He hesitated. "Greg may have taken a sip of water from the Lethe."

"What? The river Lethe? When?"

"When we were crossing into Lupus at the end. He was thirsty, so I handed him my flask."

"When . . . wait a minute." Surina's eyes narrowed. "You had water from the Lethe in your flask?"

"Um . . . maybe. Yes. Well, it was from Draco, but you know that Draco is the Lethe."

"Why would you do that?"

"It was Virgo's idea," Dominic said. "Greg kept going on about how he was going to tell the world about our adventures, and she didn't seem to appreciate his lack of discretion. She suggested that I could stow away some water from the river and slip it to him later."

"Are you serious?" Surina looked at him in disbelief. "She *suggested* that you could do it?"

"It was more than a suggestion."

"That wasn't kosher, Dominic. It was a test."

"No, I had her full approval. She's the one who filled the flask."

Surina slowly raised her eyebrows. "You little liar. You didn't want Greg to remember anything because you don't like him."

"I swear, the queen of the underworld told me to do it. She even promised—wait, did you just call me 'little'?"

"You didn't want him to become friends with us."

"I think his babbling mouth would be a bigger problem than his friendship," Dominic insisted. "It's too late, anyway; he already thinks we're friends. And I'm pretty sure Aquarius told us to stick together, and . . . I have things I need to talk to him about. We should all get together sometime. He can send you tumbling down a cliff—"

"That was an accident."

"—or knock you into a thicket and leave you to get kidnapped, or throw you onto the ground in front of a bunch of zombies, and so forth."

"Right. Well, that wasn't an accident, but I don't hold it against him."

"Neither do I. I like Greg, really. He makes me look like a better man." Dominic sat there for a while with a satisfied grin, but suddenly his tone became serious. "Do me a favor, will you?"

"What?"

"Come with me when I visit Hannah. It'll look weird if I'm trying to hang out with a little girl by myself."

Surina smiled vaguely. "Right. We'll go together."

"Thanks."

They sat quietly, and then Surina said, "You know what else we should do? We're good at solving puzzles together. Have you ever done an escape room? It's where you have to solve a bunch of—"

"Absolutely not," Dominic interrupted. "No more puzzles. I'm sick of them."

"Okay, but I really want you to go on my next mud run," she insisted. "They're kind of expensive, but if—"

"Um, do you know what else is expensive? Hepatitis. How many hundreds of dollars did you say it cost you to find out that your mud run gave you liver disease?"

"You won't get hepatitis. That's really rare."

"No! No more mud runs. I'm not good at them anyway, and if I ever have to climb another knotted rope . . . just no. If you want an adventure, you know what we could do? We could go to the beach. We could lay on the sand, or go swimming, or kayaking, and do things that have absolutely nothing to do with riddles or obstacles or filth."

Surina contemplated that. "Dominic, if you really want to go somewhere with me," she said, "let's go to

Brazil, or somewhere else. There are so many amazing places to see, and if we save our money for a while, we can go somewhere more exciting than the beach. I know you don't want another adventure *now*, but after a while . . . ."

"We're broke, remember? How about California? We can go kayaking at La Jolla, stop at Joshua Tree and the Painted Canyons . . . ."

"Yes!"

"I have a friend who lives in San Diego. He's been asking me to come visit; I bet he would let us stay a night at his place. If you want to make it a longer trip, we can head up the coast and see Pfieffer Beach, and Natural Bridges, and a dozen other places on the way."

"Okay, but now that you've said that, you can't take it back. We're going to California, right?"

"Sure. I need to save some money first. The trip to Peru wiped out my savings."

"Mine too. I'll work hard and save up."

"Should we invite Greg? He could probably introduce you to some new adventures, too. If you want to start smoking, he can hook you up."

Surina narrowed her eyes at Dominic, but there was a wily quality in her gaze rather than annoyance. "You know I want to go with *you*," she said. "What about in the meantime? I'll see you, right?"

He smiled—warmly, but perhaps a little nervously. "Yes, you'll see me. Make a point of seeing me soon."

Surina must have sensed the sudden hint of nervousness in him; she seemed amused by it, or perhaps she was simply pleased with Dominic's response, because she smiled at him in that way that made her whole being seem to light up.

He figured it was a good sign.

Appendix: Dominic's Notes & "Maps"

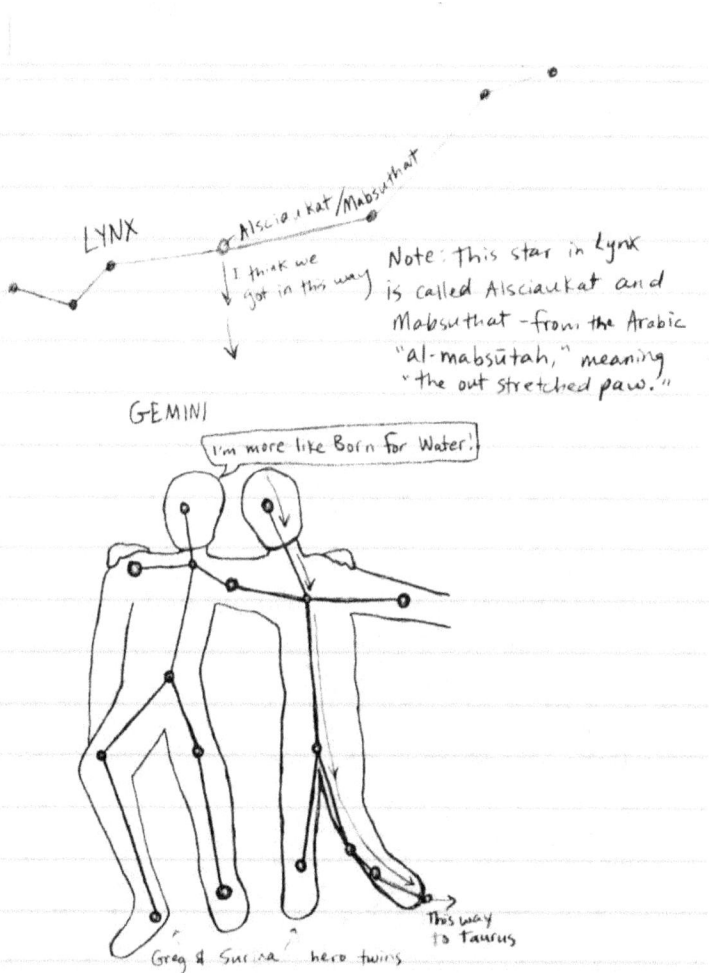

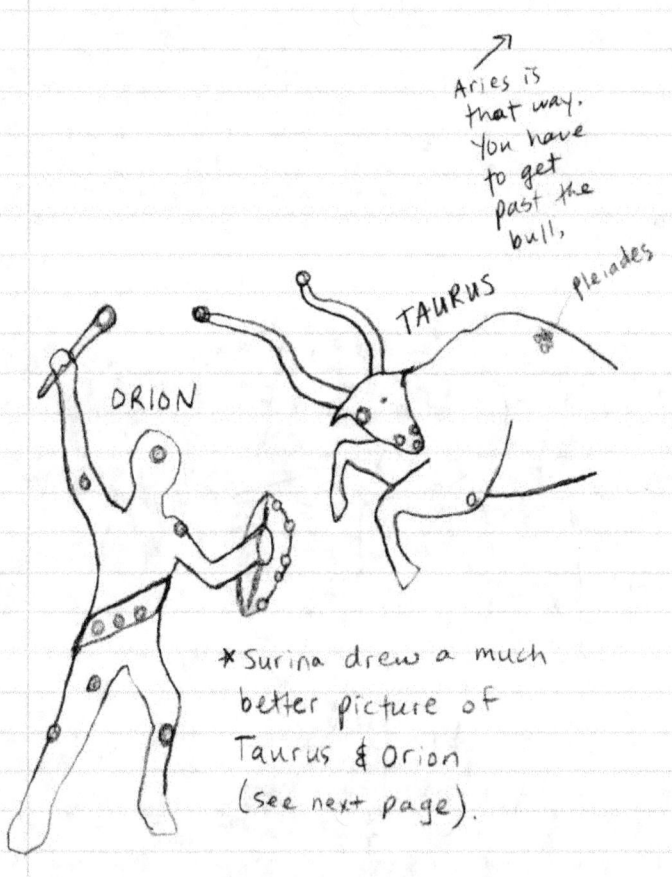

Aries is
that way.
You have
to get
past the
bull.

ORION

TAURUS

pleiades

*Surina drew a much
better picture of
Taurus & Orion
(see next page).

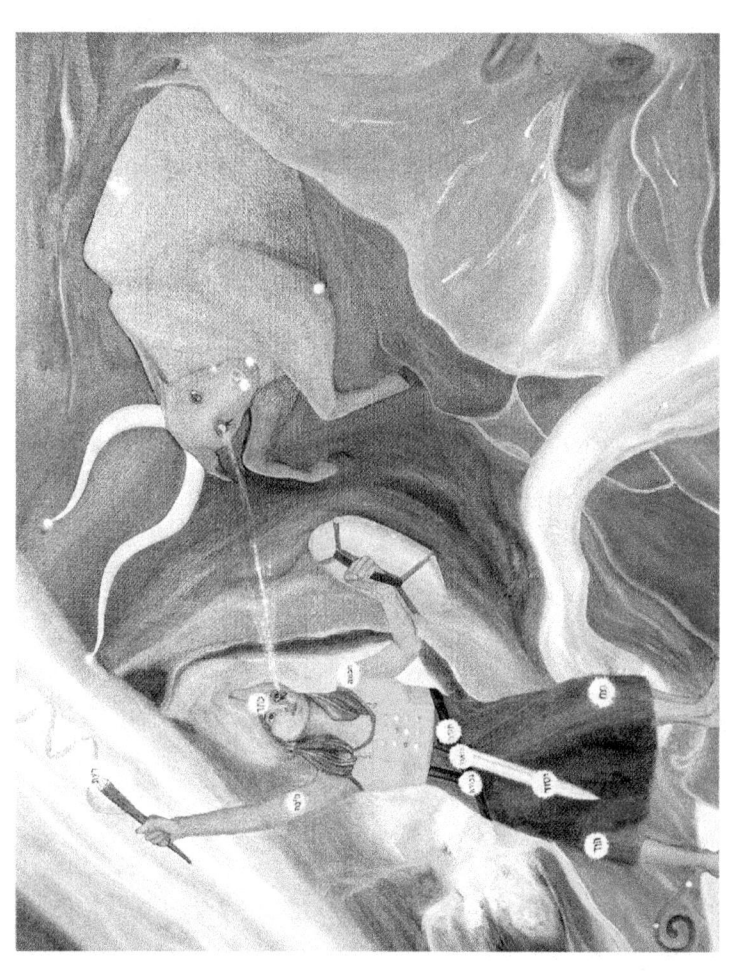

ARIES

Aasha (The Royal Game of Ur)

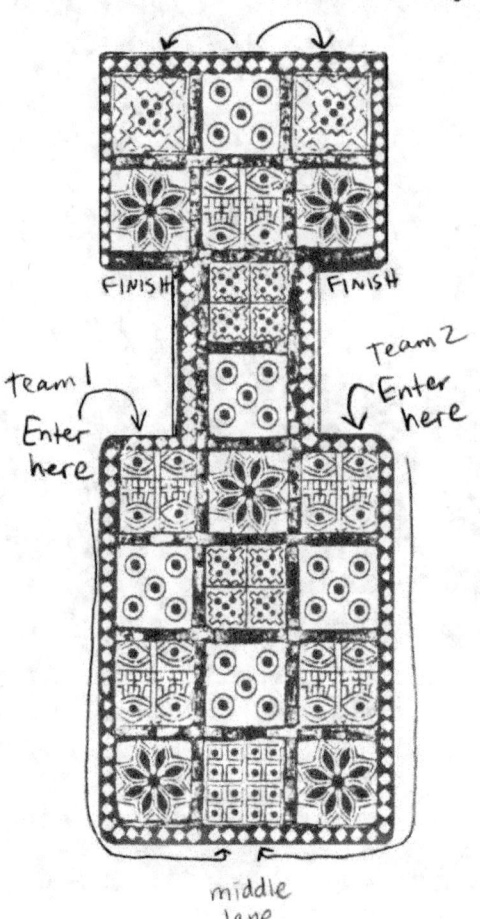

FINISH

FINISH

team 1 Enter here

Team 2 Enter here

middle lane

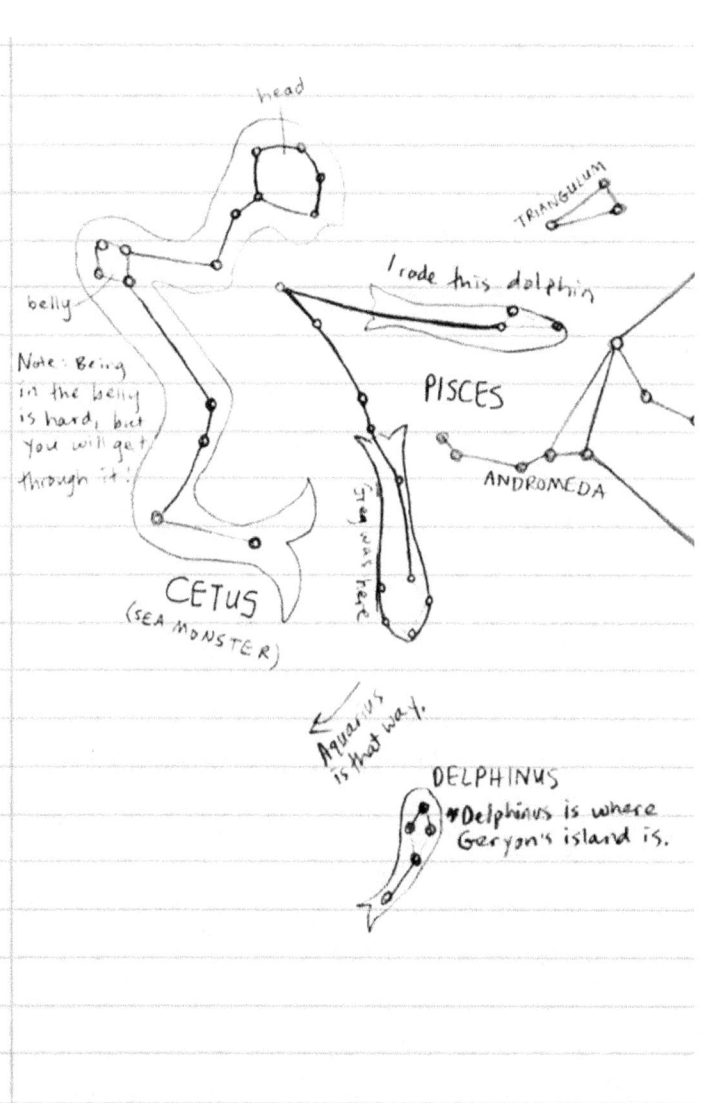

243

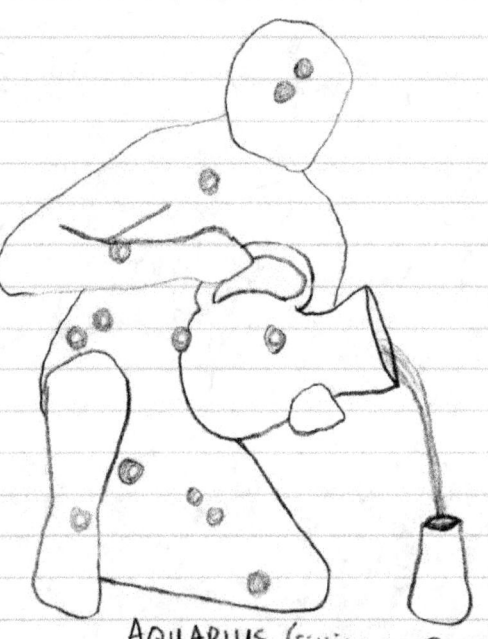

AQUARIUS (filling my flask)

Note: Aquarius filled this flask
with the water of life.
Virgo filled it with the water
of Draco, the river that leads
to death.

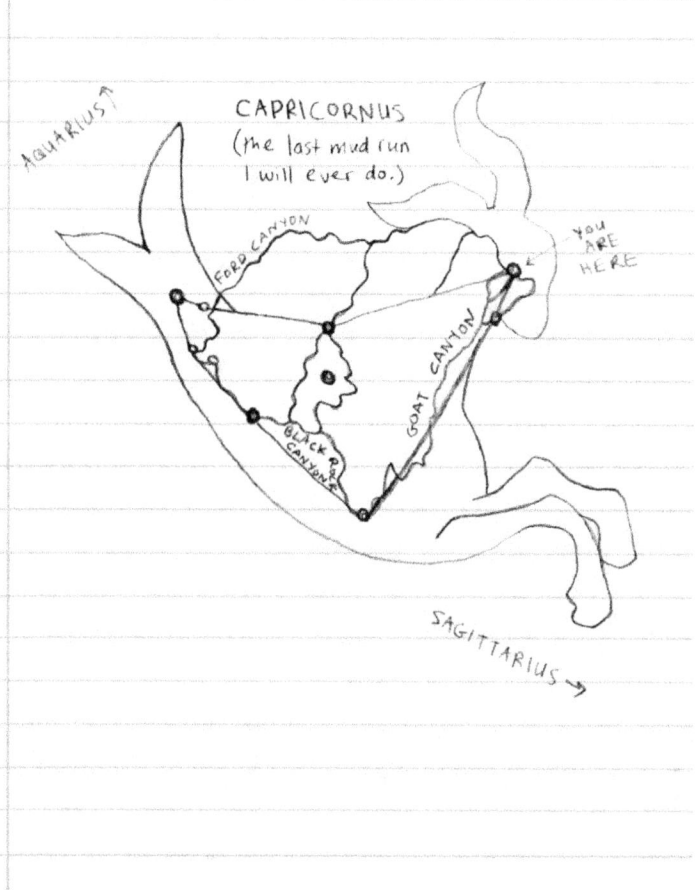

CAPRICORNUS
(the last mud run
I will ever do.)

AQUARIUS?

FORD CANYON

YOU
ARE
HERE

GOAT CANYON

BLACK R
CANYON?

SAGITTARIUS →

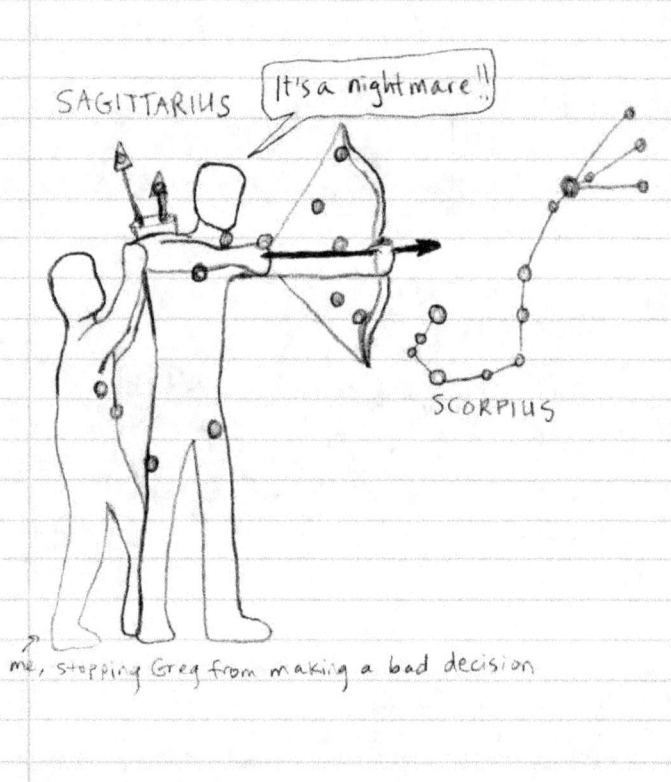

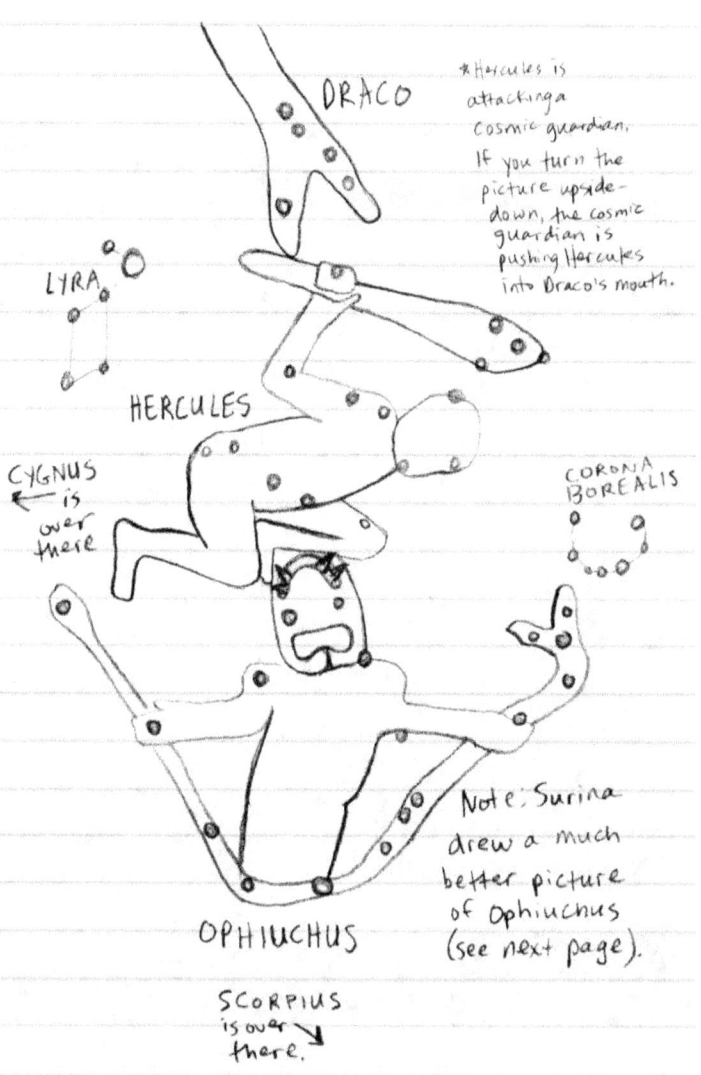

DRACO

LYRA

HERCULES

CYGNUS
← is
over
there

CORONA
BOREALIS

OPHIUCHUS

SCORPIUS
is over ↘
there.

*Hercules is
attacking a
cosmic guardian.
If you turn the
picture upside-
down, the cosmic
guardian is
pushing Hercules
into Draco's mouth.

Note: Surina
drew a much
better picture
of Ophiuchus
(see next page).

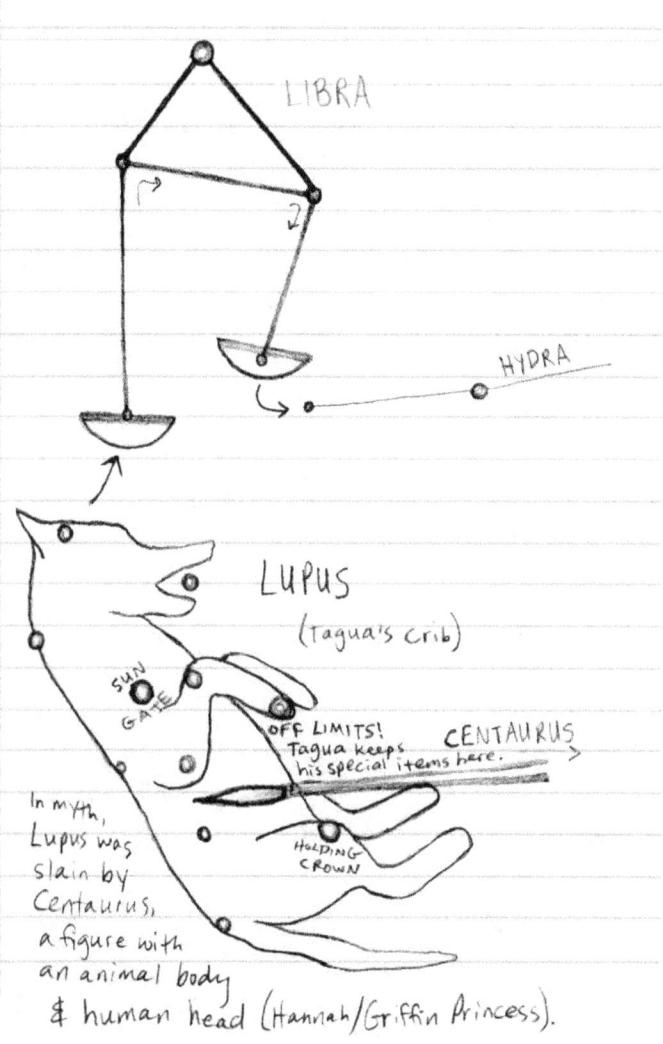

LIBRA

HYDRA

LUPUS

(Tagua's crib)

SUN GATE

OFF LIMITS!
Tagua keeps
his special items here.

CENTAURUS

HOLDING CROWN

In myth,
Lupus was
slain by
Centaurus,
a figure with
an animal body
& human head (Hannah/Griffin Princess).

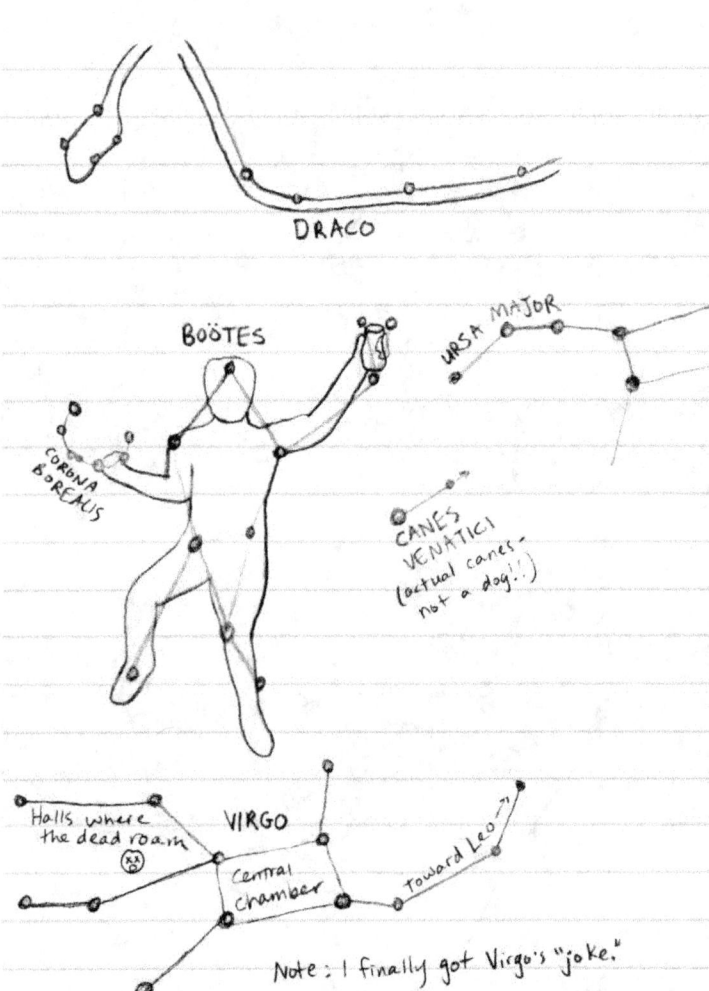

DRACO

BOÖTES

URSA MAJOR

CORONA
BOREALIS

CANES
VENATICI
(actual canes -
not a dog!!)

VIRGO

Halls where
the dead roam

Central
Chamber

Toward Leo →

Note: I finally got Virgo's "joke."

Entrance
from Hydra

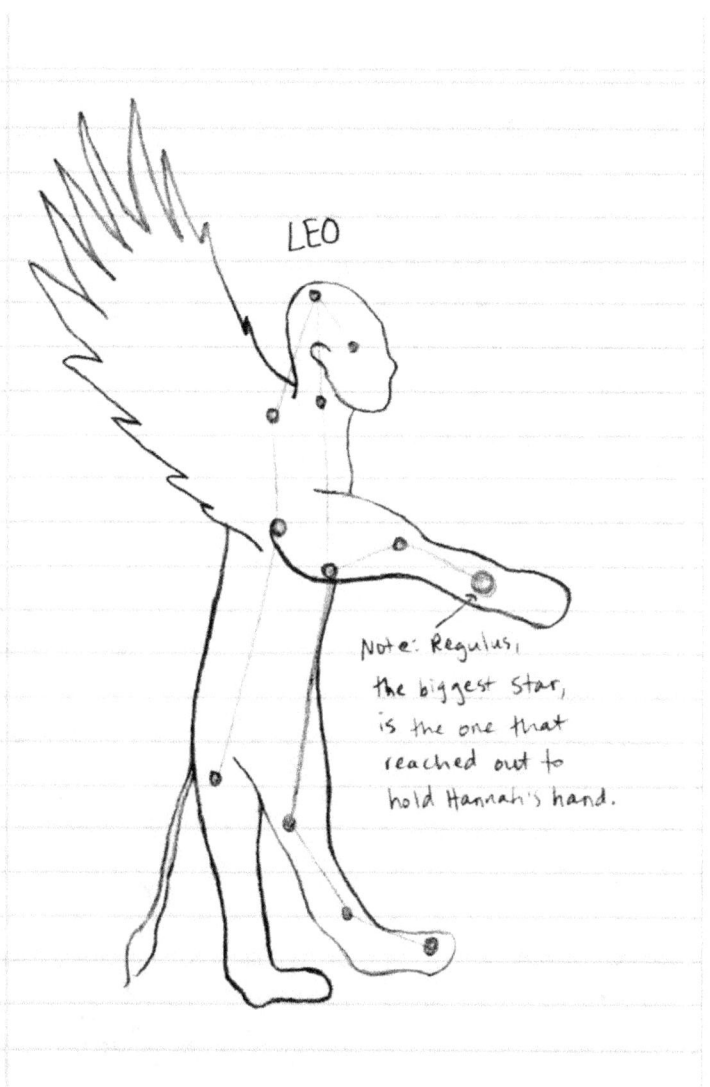

LEO

Note: Regulus, the biggest star, is the one that reached out to hold Hannah's hand.

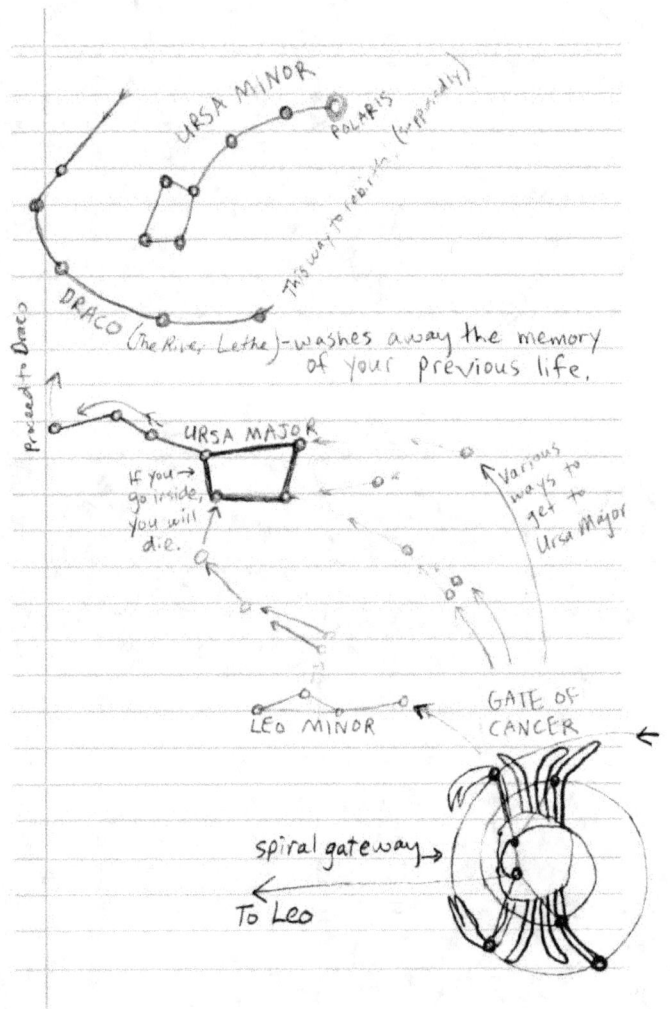

URSA MINOR

POLARIS (supposedly)

This way to rebirth.

Proceed to Draco

DRACO (The River Lethe)—washes away the memory of your previous life.

URSA MAJOR

If you go inside, you will die.

Various ways to get to Ursa Major

LEO MINOR

GATE OF CANCER

spiral gateway →

← To Leo

Author's Note

I started writing the *Enigma* trilogy after a visit to the Chavín temple in Peru. After I left, I happened to see a depiction of Ophiuchus and was struck by the similarity of Chavín's "Raimondi Stele" and the Ophiuchus constellation. As I examined the constellations and associated myths, a story began to fall into place.

While much of *Enigma* refers to Greek mythology, it also borrows heavily from ancient Sumerian stories. In the first book, Dominic's fall into the underworld is based on Enkidu's fall into the realm of the dead, where he observes the suffering souls trapped there. Chad and Dominic's trek through Leo is a retelling of *The Epic of Gilgamesh*. *Eridanus* is a retelling of how Inanna obtained the sacred *me*s from the water deity Enki, and the characters' trek through Fornax is a retelling of Inanna and the ḫalub tree. The gate of Cancer is the Sumerian gate of Ganzer, the entrance to the netherworld. Hannah's descent into (and ascent from) Virgo is a retelling of Inanna's descent.

Of particular interest to me was the similarity between Inanna's descent and the Eleusinian Mysteries of ancient Greece, and the rites of the descent into the netherworld that are still carried out by modern societies. For example, the Order of Skull and Bones, a Yale secret society that produces many powerful alumni, practices such rites. According to observers, initiates are placed in a coffin and transported to a central "tomb" adorned with a skull and thigh bones to represent the realm of the dead; they wrestle in mud while being taunted by others in skeleton costumes, and ultimately they receive a new symbolic name; the initiate's name is written on a thigh bone, and they are "reborn" into the order. This recalls both Sumerian tales and Jacob's encounter in the Book of Genesis: Jacob spends a full night wrestling with a divine being, who strikes his thigh and gives him a new name (Israel, etymologized as "Contends with God"). In the Sumerian tale of Inanna's descent, Inanna descends with the "seven divine powers," and she is stripped of all Earthly things on her way into the underworld. There, the judges of the underworld direct wrath, guilt, and death at her; she is hung on a hook, and there she stays for three days and nights before she is resurrected with the bread and water of life. Similarly, the Gospel of Matthew says that Jonah was in the belly of a sea monster (usually interpreted as a whale) for three days and nights, while Christ was in the heart of the Earth for the same duration before being resurrected. Hannah's venture into Cetus is, of course, a retelling of the story of Jonah and the whale.

Enigma often addresses perspective in storytelling and reminds the reader that stories are told from a particular point of view. The conquering colonists will portray themselves as heroes and the oppressed as wayward villains. The Sumerian king Gilgamesh is lauded as a hero, though he was also described as a heartless aggressor who harmed his subjects through his selfish exploits. His extreme egocentrism was slightly reduced by the influence of his gentler friend, Enkidu, who represented his opposite—yet Gilgamesh maintained a conquer-and-colonize attitude that laid an entire ecosystem to waste, while his killing of the Bull of Heaven (and the tearing off of its thigh) resulted in Enkidu's death. The Greco-Roman Hercules is typically portrayed as a hero, but in *The Secret of Ophiuchus*, the characters must restore the damage done when he attacked the cosmic guardians. The image on the back cover shows Hercules about to club Ophiuchus over the head while Draco waits in the background, ready to swallow the victim. If you turn the image upside-down, the image changes: Ophiuchus' headdress is actually a grinning jaguar head with very sharp teeth. Ophiuchus becomes the aggressive jaguar deity, using its staffs and its teeth to push Hercules into Draco's mouth, where Hercules will be shuttled through Draco's tail and reborn through the cosmic carousel. This depiction is based not just on the arrangement of the constellations, but on the Raimondi Stele at Chavín.

As far as acknowledgements go, I have far too many people to thank for the research and notes that helped form the basis for this book, but I want to give a special mention to the University of Oxford for its translations of Sumerian literature, and the American Association of Variable Star Observers (AAVSO) for some of the harder-to-find star info—and all of the people who make accessible records of their research and share it with others.

I'll close with a couple of fun facts: Each book in this series is dedicated to one of the three children of one of my best and oldest friends. In books two and three, Dominic tries to make Surina laugh by joking about how Greg looks like a stoner who constantly smokes weed. This is something I got from the kids' father, who used this same routine to tease me about my boyfriends.

I started the *Enigma* series by taking notes and writing riddles, but I didn't have any scenes in mind until one day when I was listening to the Muse song "Exogenesis: Symphony, Pt. 1 (Overture)." The first scene I imagined was the part where Hannah puts on the holding crown, and I worked out the story from there.

I hope you enjoyed the tale. May your own journey be filled with insight, courage, and good signs.